M LE NGST

Vol. II

SMOKIN' THUY'D
(Part 1)

Written by
Bobby Cenoura

MALE ANGST Vol II: *Smokin' Thuy'd (Part 1)*

First paperback edition January 2023

ISBN 978-1-0880-8846-3 (paperback)
ISBN 978-1-0880-8847-0 (eBook)

Cover design/Artwork: Anduanet Campos Andersson
Layout design/Text Illustrations: Lazar Kackarovski
Editor: T.D.

www.sliceofpain.com

SLICE OF PAIN

PUBLISHING AND MEDIA

Published by Slice of Pain Publishing and Media, all rights reserved. Other works published by Slice of Pain include, but are not limited to: *Seoul Revelations; Male Angst Vol. I: FML: I Always Get Those Chicks, Black Names Matter: The Black Names Book.*
All of the aforementioned titles can be found on multiple platforms such as Amazon, Apple Books, Nook and others.

TABLE OF **CONTENTS**

SPECIAL THANKS:

My illustrious illustrator, Aduanet Campos Andersson,
my excellent editrix T.D.,
my top-of-the-line layout editor Lazar Kackarovski,
and to the following:
BFR, RAR, ABC, ARH, VCR, B. Furmong, KYL, FW/WF, T "A.J." L

FOREWORD

I t has been said that if you want to hear God laugh, tell Him your plans; and it has also been said that everybody has a plan until they get punched in the mouth. If both of those statements are true, then it must follow that God laughs every time someone gets punched in the mouth. Isn't that a fitting statement to apply to the ups and downs of life—and the interplay of relationships akin to characters in a book or a screenplay? The ebb and flow and yin and yang of the natural order of things suggest that those who burn the brightest burn the shortest. I dedicate this book to a childhood friend who lived his life fast, hard, and fun. He was a supernova, and all of the light that he shone reached people from many different walks of life. Alas, like the McDonald's McRib sandwich, he was only here for a limited time.

PROLOGUE

Ode to Reggie Jenkins: The "Classic Man"

I t has been said that there are at the most, five Black Americas. If this is the case, it could be that the "Classic Black Man" (derogatively called the "Educated Lame" and considered an oddity) inhabits one of them. The Classic Man in each of these Americas has his own uniqueness, separating him from the rest of the pack.

Socially, there appears to be a continuum regarding examples of Classic Men, from Steve Urkel to Stringer Bell, and all the gradients in between. Steve Urkel represents those with extreme intelligence, but no street smarts and social mores. Meanwhile, Stringer Bell represents the extreme street-smart thug who's intelligent but loves the inner city's acceptance so much that he risks life and limb to remain in company below his level of intelligence. The average Classic Man exhibits traits of both eclectic curiosity and intelligence, but also has street knowledge that renders him a multidimensional archetype of sorts.

It is erroneous to infer Black men's "classic" behavior by comparing to mainstream stereotypes of the White nerd/beta male and the White jock/alpha male. Socioeconomically, alpha traits in the mainstream Black Amalgam (a term coined by YouTuber Lets_B_Frank to describe the Black American collective, since there is no physical Black community in the economic sense), which are exemplified in Black ghettos, are more in line with White "trailer-park toughness". This is due to socioeconomic similarities between both poor Whites and Blacks in the aforementioned locations.

The error in comparing Black men to White men lies in cultural values. Whites tend to look down on "trailer park" behaviors, while thuggish behavior is often celebrated by Blacks, especially in mainstream hip-hop. Whether the elevation of thug culture is the intention or direct creation of Black Americans themselves, or a social experiment by "the man" to suppress Black success, is irrelevant. What matters is that these phenomena exist, and the Classic Man must navigate through these perceptions.

Therefore, the existences of Classic Men are a social adaptation to realization of the following:

1. The "trap game", or earning through illegal and violent behaviors, produces no long-term benefits.
2. Mating choices and markets are intersectional.

In other words, when you remove the luster of clothing, shoes, cars, and other material possessions, what you have is man in his natural habitat, competing with other men for scarce resources—the most important possibly being the right to mate and procreate.

To paraphrase comedian Katt Williams: *"I don't buy shiny things because I like shiny things. I buy shiny things because bitches like shiny things."* His competitive behavior is dependent on the preferences of women that he is competing to attract. Because he has children, Katt Williams has successfully accomplished this.

Not everybody has the gritty street image/credibility that Katt Williams has though. A lot of Classic Men realize the costs of playing the trap game outweigh the long-term benefits. Without going into a diatribe about the Black community, its ills, and whether it exists, I want to revert to the behaviors of Classic Men.

In the 2016 presidential election, 8% of voters who identified as Black voted for Donald Trump, and twice as many Black men than women approved of Trump (*http://www.chicagotribune.com/news/nationworld/politics/ct-trump-approval-men-20180120-story.html*). This could be extrapolated to saying 66% of Black voters who voted for Trump were men. I could go out a limb and assume that these Black men have a more traditionally conservative slant, but in all actuality, they would likely be classical liberal, or Libertarian.

They are Libertarian in the sense that most Black men don't give a hoot about suppressing gay rights and see abortion and birth controls not as religious hindrances, but tools to halt the decay of Black society (i.e preventing struggling women from raising babies who may later become potential criminals). On the same note, they favor economic policies that would prevent said mothers' abilities to extract resources from a social net that would levy taxes on people who had no say in their decision to get pregnant and/or have their babies to term.

Two general attitudes regarding whether the Black community can be saved appear to divide Classic Men. The minority of liberal Classic Men seem to believe that it can, meaning it is possible to have intact, two-parent families that identify as Black in America.

The conservative majority of Classic Men believe the Black community cannot be saved. In fact, they believe there is no Black community in the first place—at least not in the economic sense. And if there was, this segment of Classic Men feel it wouldn't be sustainable. Hence, trying to create it would be an exercise in futility at the cost of the people who had nothing to do with the conditions causing Black neighborhoods to run awry. This conservative majority believe Black Americans should assimilate into greater American culture and let go of separatist notions of a Black ethno-state.

The reason for this is simple: contemporary mainstream Black media does not laud Black male roles as successful law-abiding people in a plethora of fields (e.g. doctors, mechanics, engineers and even garbage men) as it did in the past (i.e., The Cosby Show, Roc, etc.) In other words, there aren't enough examples of Black men playing "the long game" rather than "the trap game" anymore. Therefore, conservative Classic Men cannot justify bringing long term benefits back to a place and people who bullied them, called them "lame" and/or "nerd", and picked them last in the dating pool. Instead, they prefer to live in broader American society, irrespective of racial makeup, with people who share common socioeconomic mindsets.

A lot of Classic Men tend to have average attractiveness and play on the strengths they build over time—professionalism, industriousness, conscientiousness, etc. This is the "long game" belief. In this long game, they usually seek female partners who are quality in terms of building an economically stable future.

The challenge here is that American women have surpassed men in education and are now on par with men when it comes to average earnings. As a result, they don't often have an incentive to give up short-term guaranteed pleasures (i.e. the bad boys who gives them the chills) in lieu of future long-term family stability.

For "tradcons" (traditional conservatives), who seemingly derive their value from husband and father roles, this is especially daunting. More libertarian Classic Men, however, have no problem with this; they tend to be more of the ""go-your-own-way" and "do-your-own-thing" types. Classic Men build in areas such as education, entrepreneurship, and tradesmanship.

While the classic Black man may be more socially mobile amongst non-blacks, to his chagrin, he is often compared against the Black American male massive archetypes which may or may not assist in what he is trying to accomplish. For example, if he is in a place where nonblacks only associate Black culture with hip hop, he may be asked if he knows the latest dance fad, which he may or more than likely, may not. He is too busy trying to move up economically to follow what rappers are doing in the clubs and in videos. However, he is aware that hip-hop is a ubiquitous portrayal of Blacks to non-blacks of good socioeconomic standing, who view the dances as a fun pastime after the toils of work.

The conservative Classic Man sees the obsession with hip-hop culture as a lollygagging that prevents intellectual progress. The liberal Classic Man, on the contrary, may embrace thug culture to the degree that it could get him what he wants (i.e., social acceptance, attraction from the opposite sex). To look cool, he will don the façade of a life he doesn't lead despite it failing to debunk the belief that "hip-hop thug" is the primary Black male narrative.

Often, classic Black "liberal ambassadors" use the fact that they're Black American when they're not "about that life", just to gain credibility. For non-blacks, this behavior is a welcome introduction, or a little taste of blackness. But to the Black massive, especially thug-cultured Blacks, the liberal Classical Man appears silly and is a target in his own community.

In the Classic Man camp, there is a "Professor X versus Magneto" approach to dealing with the Black massive. Conservatives see liberals as perpetuating the Black plight through lack of personal responsibility. Liberals see conservatives as vectors of White supremacy, out-of-touch with the true needs of Black people, and selfish. The battle wages because the overwhelming question is: Can the Black community be saved?

To some, the answer is yes. To others, the answer is no. Yet, the real question, which both liberal and conservative Classic Men attest to, is whether or not the Black community exists in earnest at all. And such is the dichotomy that our 35- to 45-year-old protagonist, Reggie Jenkins, navigates throughout his dating experiences in this book.

TETELESTAI

The Chinese character for both "doomed" and "destined" is "zhu4 ding4". In Chinese culture, a future event will surely occur regardless of one's perception of it. Hence, whether one is "doomed" or "destined" depends on the observer.

Paralleling outcome and perception, it is also believed by some that the biochemical pathways of excitement and anxiety are often the same; both feelings are dependent on one's vantage point. For example, on Christmas Eve, middle-class neighborhood kids all across the western world lie in bed with their eyes wide open in anticipatory anxiety about what gifts they may receive the next day.

In contrast, Reggie lied awake staring at the ceiling, anticipating how things would go down with Thuy, the abandonment of his principles, and the result thereafter. The fear of being alone again ravaged his thoughts. After what seemed an eternity, time crept forward to what the American public considered a reasonable hour to start the workday.

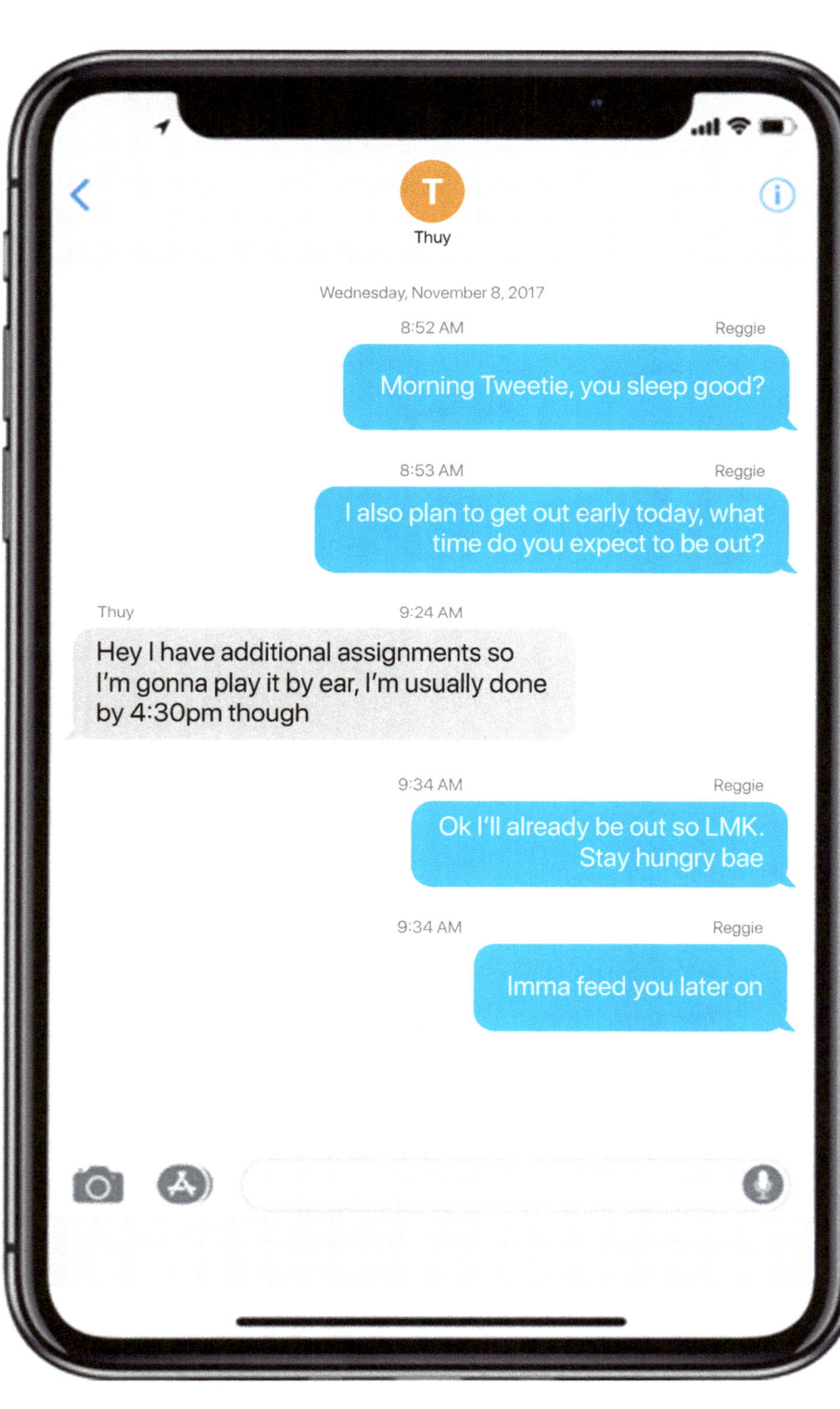

Since Thuy let Reggie in on her whereabouts, he presumed he was gaining headway. He pictured them sitting across from each other, speaking in such a way to let bygones be bygones. He hoped Thuy wouldn't eat anything before they met up; he was hoping to treat her to a good meal. And who knows, if things were agreeable, maybe they'd sip on some wine, share a little humor, and possibly rekindle things. His phone dinged, and he instantly grew excited about what Thuy would say next.

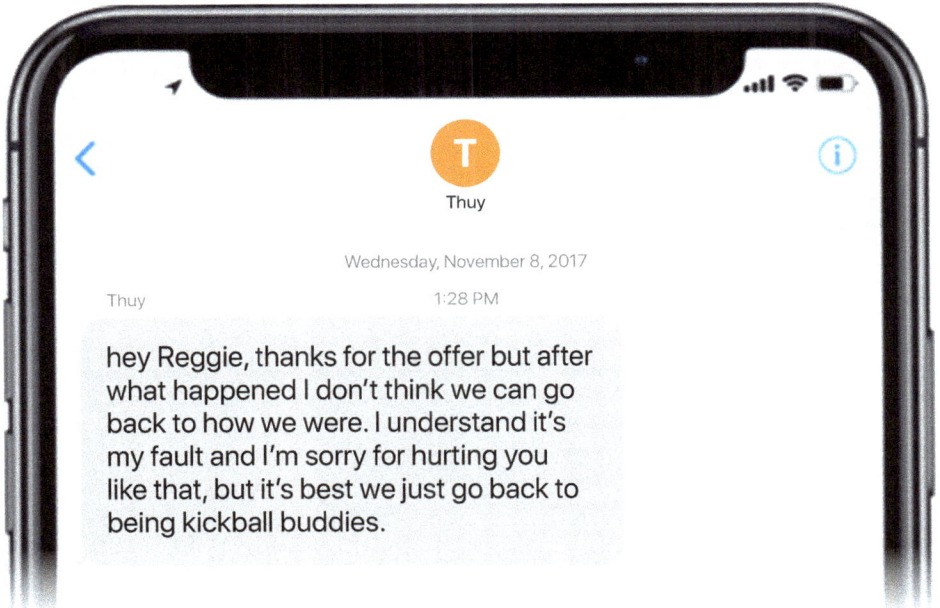

Reggie stared at Thuy's response, the corners of his mouth involuntarily sagging downward in dismay. Like a horrible Monopoly board game innuendo, Reggie just got punched in his community chest by chance and there was no passing go. Everything that happened a couple weeks ago had sealed the deal. He and Thuy were done. Finished. Like Jesus giving up the ghost, *tetelestai*. The only thing he could do was accept it. Resigned, he decided he might as well let Thuy off the hook regarding their meet up.

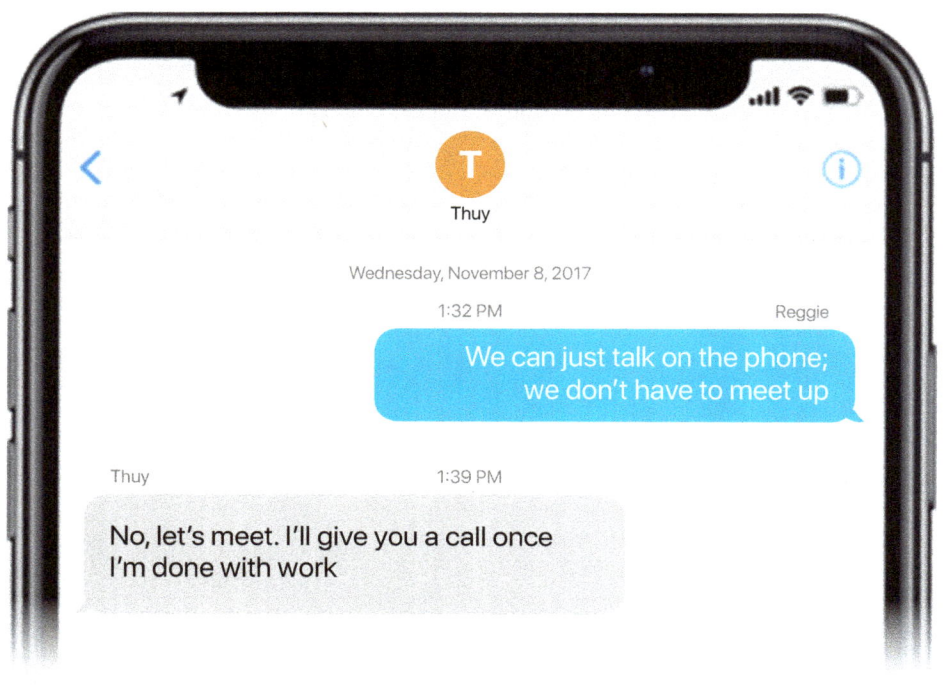

* * *

Reggie knew it was definitely over when he got to the restaurant and discovered Thuy had already eaten. Although they decided to meet at *MyThai*, it turned out she had been there all along. From the looks of it, she purposely hadn't wanted to commune with Reggie.

Nevertheless, Reggie took a seat across from her. Just then, the waiter approached, hovering around Reggie like a yellowjacket around a soda bottle, so he ordered something small to avoid being an asshole. "I'll just have a bowl of Tom Yum soup please. Thanks."

The waiter nodded and shuffled off, his feet dragging the ground.

Reggie turned his attention back to Thuy. "So, how you been lately?"

"I been well. How about you?"

"I've been hanging in there. You kickballing Sunday?"

"Probably not. I missed a deadline for one of my assignments, so I'm going to use the weekend to catch up."

Reggie's soup came, and he slurped a spoonful here and there. An awkward silence persisted until Reggie set down his spoon and decided to release the floodgates of emotions he'd been holding in.

"You know, it's been about a week and a half since I last seen you, and to be honest, it seemed like an eternity to me. The last few texts we exchanged seemed mundane, and I figure you're trying to keep your distance and that's cool. I totally dig it. But I have to tell you that I lied last time when you asked me if I was doing good. I wasn't. I've been working through getting over the situation and restructuring my life to get back to normal, whatever that is." Reggie took another slurp of soup, then continued. "The reason why I wanted to meet up with you was to share my true feelings. It's been the most exhilarating four weeks of my life, from meeting to mating. I joined kickball not expecting to hook up with anybody. But then I met you and I had a lot of fun and I felt that we connected on more than just physical levels. I really *vibed* with your personality, including the corniness which we both accused each other of. The sex was great, but what really hooked me was all of your little affections, like listening to music out of the same earbuds, walking with you under my arm, your PDA... Walking you home after hanging out. I felt you were more like a high school sweetheart than us being two grownups in our 30s. So I want to thank you for that."

Reggie paused for a moment and then placed another spoonful of soup into his mouth.

"The last thing I'll confess," Reggie continued, "is that I was able to be open with you, which is something I've been reluctant to do with people for a long time." He took a deep breath. "I wish you well, and hope that you had more good experiences with me than bad. I always considered you very intelligent, and the only time I ever looked down on you was to give you a kiss."

An awkward silence followed Reggie's last sentence. Although Thuy had stared directly at him during most of his diatribe, there had been moments when she'd glanced behind him, to the side of him, up at the ceiling, and down at the table between them. All the while, she tried to formulate how to respond, knowing the ball was now in her court.

Thuy took a sip of water.

"I have never had anyone express themselves to me the way you just did," she said slowly. "I had a lot of fun and learned a lot from you. I'm more aware of my posture now and stand tall rather than look at the ground when I walk. I also eat more veggies. I hope you understand that I kept my distance because I didn't want to hurt you any further, and I—"

"And I thank you for that. I really do—looking out for my feelings. Just understand that I'm not salty. I was just shocked by the way shit went down. It seemed like a freak occurrence, like something out of a movie or a novel. It felt like a part of a weird social experiment. That's what set me off. The loss of control. When we first started, we always had an open-door policy—I just hope you know that. I don't need you to feel guilty or sorry for me. I just want you to be honest, that's all. Sorry for interrupting."

"I understand. But I just felt like you had certain expectations of me, and took things personally when I didn't meet those expectations... If that makes sense. Not to say your expectations are bad or anything. I'm just saying, I'm selfish and reckless right now, and I might do or say things that might hurt or upset you."

"The only thing I expected was for you to be honest with me about what you wanted to do. If you felt like you wanted to make changes, I thought you'd tell me, not to out me in public."

"I know, Reggie. And I was totally wrong for that. I wasn't myself then."

"Then what is it about? Was this about when I told you that you could come by my mom's place to help me walk the dogs? You thought I expected you to be a family woman or something? That's the reason I asked if you wanted to stay in the car—so you didn't feel like I had an expectation. But you came anyway. Why?"

"Can I be completely honest with you?" Thuy said after a brief pause.

"Yes."

"Okay. Here goes. The relationship between you and I was getting too close, and I'm not ready for that kind of commitment."

"I understand, but we've always had an open-door policy. If you felt that way, why didn't you say something?"

"Because my feelings and emotions were mixed about what we were doing and where we were going. And I let myself lose control at the party, and I'm really sorry I did that to you."

"So basically, I'm too clingy. Is that it?"

"It's not that."

"It can't be that, because of the way we communicated. We saw each other based on our terms. So what is it?"

Thuy didn't know how to explain. Her feelings were subconscious and innate. Reggie had failed her shit test. And although she didn't consciously know why she wanted to betray Reggie, she knew this was her "out", like Megan had told her.

As the long pause stretched on, Reggie decided there was no point in waiting for her to answer.

"I guess you're past the point where you're afraid to meet people, now that you got your feet wet. I guess you can say you're back to achieving the original objective you were looking to achieve when we first hooked up."

Thuy tilted her head. "I forgot. What was it?"

"To get back out there and explore."

* * *

Thuy and Reggie left the restaurant together until they reached the juncture whereby Reggie would go upstairs, and Thuy would go to her car. They paused and looked at each other for a moment.

"Welp, looks like this is it," Thuy said.

"Yeah, I guess so." Reggie extended his hand to her.

Thuy looked down at Reggie's hand, then up at him. Bypassing a handshake, she gave him a full-on hug. The hug had the same strength of the one she'd given him the day they'd met at the crosswalk, when she'd ran across the street and practically jumped into his arms.

Reggie patted Thuy on the back, signaling her to release him.

Thuy stepped back and released Reggie from her hold. Noticing the way his eyes were starting to water, Thuy used her thumb to catch a teardrop before it ran down his cheek. She then realized it was time for her to go. "Bye, Reggie," she whispered.

"Bye," Reggie said, his bottom lip quivering slightly. He watched Thuy walk off to her car.

Right before she disappeared from his view, she turned around and shouted, "You're a good dude, Reggie Jenkins!"

Reggie turned toward the elevator and pressed the 'up' button, knowing that into the foreseeable future, he would be going up this way alone.

Yeah, but not good enough, Reggie thought to himself, reflecting on Thuy's parting words.

EPHEMERAL

The late, great comedian George Carlin, in one of his standup routines, made a point that the president of the United States reflects the values of the general society. As a result, if people want to have a better president, then each individual should become a better person, yielding a better society and in turn, better pickings among presidential candidates. That moment of comedy was probably one of the most esoteric, "woo-woo" things that Carlin said, even though he didn't believe in metaphysics. The lesson: *As above, so below.*

The post-modern culture in the late 2010s, especially in regards to dating and relationships, had become largely non-committal, with people choosing to exit rather than put up with another person's shit for extended periods. No marriage, houses, or careers—only friends with benefits, luxury apartment buildings, and gig-economies. And such as the general society, governmental hiring practices followed suit.

The new trend was a top-heavy government agency shuffling around employees making lateral moves. They're not interested in cultivating new talent to replace retirees. Hell, the only way they'll hire someone without prior government agency experience is if there is a specific program promoting such a hiring effort. Instead, they hire contracting companies to perform the work at higher overall prices. But since a contract's termination is known for certain, the ease of non-commitment causes the overall prices to inflate year after year, as contract companies with asshole names that play off human resource jargon proliferate the market.

Vectorplex, the company Reggie works for, is one such contracting company that provides accounting services to the government. He's been there for over five years—he started there a year after his relationship with Linh ended.

Information Systems Firmware, Information Security Software Development, and Info-matic Server Technology won't all fit on the divider tabs. But their acronyms, ISF, ISSD, and IMST will, Reggie thought to himself while formatting the Avery divider tab label names in Microsoft

Word. His goal was to get all the divider tabs containing the financial projections in the correct order and ready for his *Big Boss* to present to government senior leadership.

If spelled out in alphabetical order, it would go ISF, ISSD and IMST because of the hyphen. But in acronym order, it would go: IMST, ISF, ISSD...

To the average person, putting labels on a divider was easy work. But the task wasn't simple for Reggie. He needed to align the dividers perfectly to avoid the wrath of his "Big Bawss" Ishmael—a Mexican Jew who was super neurotic, often cutting off his nose to spite his face.. Ishmael was known for his skittishness and waiting to the last minute to request work out of employees, often resulting in them staying late or coming in early. This usually caused a lot of anxiety for nothing, as projects with the government typically got finished when they were good and ready.

Knowing how skittish Ishmael was, Reggie sent him a message:

TO: *Hernandez.Ishmael@vectorplex.com*

FROM: *Jenkins.Reginald@vectorplex.com*

Hello Ishmael,

I know how important it is to have the presentation contents in the proper order. Would you like them in the order of acronym or actual division name?

Thanks,
Reggie

---

* * *

Khalil Sesay, the son of Sierra Leonian immigrants, worked for GuideTech, Vectorplex's sister company. He was raised in the U.S. and under the tutelage of his uncles, acquired business acumen at young age.

To an onlooker, Khalil appeared as one of those Neo-Soul brothas who listened to late '90s R&B in his brand-spanking new Tesla. He pretty much bought out Zara and had every one of their diagonal checkered (or diamond shaped, depending on the perspective) sweaters that he wore under a leather jacket, with a pair of café-crème Cole Hans.

He also had a new cornrow pattern every week, as if ancient aliens were trying to send messages through his scalp.

"Hey, Reggie. Feeling better today?" Khalil said as Reggie came around the corner.

Reggie sighed. "What's going on, K? I got to get these presentation books done by COB today, man, and—I'm just trying to keep shit together."

Khalil put his hand on Reggie's shoulder. "And shorty?"

Reggie turned and gave Khalil a forlorn look. "Let's get some air."

Outside of Vectorplex's box-shaped building was a circular, man-made pond that was frequented by geese. The pathway around the pond was a haven for the multiple IT folks, often of East Asian and/or Indian persuasion, either strolling about with their hands behind their backs as if surveying the place or taking power-walks.
Reggie and Khalil made their way toward the pond—their go-to spot for confiding in each other about work and personal issues.

"I just got taken by surprise. I-I just never knew," Reggie stammered.

"Knew what, Reggie? That you'd fall for her that fast?" Khalil asked.

"Not just that fast, but that hard. You know what, man? I was walking back from Hushui after getting some food the other day, and I saw her and Megan and one of her other girlfriends walking on the other side of the street. She was in the middle, and she happened to look over and see me. Then she said something to her girlfriends, and they all turned and looked in my direction, then turned back to each other and started giggling."

"It sucks that you guys live in the same general area. You're likely to bump into each other from time to time—"

"Yeah, but to add insult to injury, I feel like the laughingstock. Plus, Megan was still on the kickball team after the whole ordeal. And she probably knows about the burnt Trump mask."

"Look, my dude, you're reading too much into the situation. She was probably just telling her friends, *'That's the guy'.*"

"That's the guy? That's the guy—what?"

"'That's the guy that I was dating, and things didn't work out'."

Reggie looked at the ground, staring at blades of grass saturated with water droplets from the nearby pond. "Or more like, *'That's the loser'.*"

"You're being way too hard on yourself. Remember, you weren't in the wrong. Yeah, you could've handled things different, but the fact of the matter is that shorty disrespected you."

"Then why do I feel this way?" Reggie said, regretting the way his eyes had started to tear up against his will.

"Listen, my man, you just need time," Khalil said, sensing Reggie's emotional state and not wanting to turn this into an 'I-told-you-so' moment. He'd been giving Reggie advice all along, though some seemed to go in through one ear and out the other. "Maybe go on another one of those vacations with Kayla?"

"Ha. Kayla got a new relationship situation, and it has moved us apart as far as hanging out. But you were right about that 'Three Musketeers' thing. It's not likely to last."

"Then you can always throw yourself into your work. What's happening with the presentation schedule?"

"Oh shit! I'm waiting on Ishmael to reply to my email. You know how he can be." Reggie dapped up Khalil. "Hey, Khalil, I appreciate you, bro."

Khalil nodded, and Reggie jogged down to the entrance of the building.

* * *

TO: *Jenkins.Reginald@vectorplex.com*

FROM: *Hernandez.Ishmael@vectorplex.com*

Reginald,

When you accepted this job, you listed that you were a "self-starter" and because of your position rank, you are supposed to require minimal supervision. I am tied up with setting up mission critical meetings and little details like the order in which things are set, I leave up to my staff, which you are part of. Please, take note and execute accordingly.

Thanks,
Ishmael

Muthafucka! Reggie slammed his fist down on his desk. Fuming, he decided to just organize the tabs in order of acronym, since the acronyms were easier to fit on the labels.

Fuck 'em. I'll put it in this order and give his ass something to chew on. Regardless of whether it's right or wrong, at least I'll have something turned in. Fucking asshole, I'm trying to help him. Big-Bird-sounding motherfucker.

* * *

Setting his irritation aside, Reggie contacted the department's data guru, Felipe, for access to the files he needed to complete the project. As he waited for those files, he busied himself by laying out multiple, empty, three-ring binder notebooks on the conference room's table. With the dividers arranged in the order he'd settled on earlier that day, he spent his last hour before quitting time adding the finishing touches to all Ishmael's presentation notebooks.

The whole process—from using the guillotine paper cutter for fashioning major section dividers, to typesetting the divider stickies, formatting the spreadsheet data, and hole punching the sheets—took hours. Reggie's process resembled an assembly line. Yet, the whole time, he took care to craft a finished presentation notebook, complete with Vectorplex's logo on the front plastic insert. Finally done, he placed the finished product in the mounted mailbox outside Ishmael's closed door.

Motherfucking Ishmael. Antsy motherfucker. I'll just drop this off here and finish the rest of my books. That way, I'll give his bitch ass something to chew on so he can't blame me for shit, Reggie thought as he returned to the conference room.

Within the next half hour, he completed inserting all the printed financial presentation data. Then, leaving the notebooks open, he took a moment to look for Felipe's email regarding when the ISSD data would be ready for download.

In the meantime, Reggie put on his virtual board shorts as he prepared to peruse the world wide web.

I wonder if Oshay Duke Jackson got another video out? That nigga's always got the fire when it comes to commentary and comedy! Chuckling to himself, Reggie put in the earbuds connected to his laptop. He found his favorite YouTuber's channel, the title reading: STRUGGLE BONNET WEARERS GET BANNED FROM ENTERING A DALLAS APARTMENT COMPLEX AND GUESS WHO'S MAD?!

The thumbnail included a picture of an overweight, African American woman wearing a bonnet that made her look like she was fresh out of the shower.

This is gonna be a good one. Reggie chuckled to himself again. He double-clicked on the video, leaned back in his chair, and watched the show begin. His viewing was interrupted, however, when he received an email in the middle of the video.

As expected, it was from Felipe in regards to the location of the files he needed to insert in the presentation books. This was the final blow, as far as Reggie was concerned. There were now about thirty minutes left in the day; he figured Ishmael's door would be closed and that he'd be at a meeting that would extend beyond Reggie's log-off time.

Reggie formatted the documents and sent them to the printer. Since the printer room was adjacent to the conference room, all he had to do was grab the printouts, punch holes in them, insert them, and head out. With all of the shenanigans of the day, plus trying to stay calm after what happened with Thuy last week, he just wanted to go home, have a beer, and watch another episode of *Animal Kingdom*. He was anticipating Smurf doing some *Naughty America* shit.

She's not a Russian MILF, but she'll do. Reggie laughed in his head.

Reggie began inserting the files into the folder until a shallow knock on the door stopped him in his tracks. The door to the conference room was already open, and the door opened inward. Reggie couldn't fathom why the hell anyone would feel the need to go inside the room and knock on a door that was currently flushed against the wall. He furrowed his eyebrows at the blurry outline of a pudgy figure in his periphery.

Sure enough, it was Ishmael.

Mutha—

Ishmael was so annoying that he interrupted Reggie's thoughts before he could even finish cussing him in his mind. Reggie was pretty sure Ishmael did this on purpose—that he spied on people's conversations right in their own heads just so that he could intervene and dish out a new task.

"What-what is this?" Ishmael held up the finished notebook Reggie had left in his mailbox. With his nose turned upward, he flipped the notebook over in his hand, examining it from every angle.

"That's the finished presentation data organized in order of—" Reggie started.

"In order of acronym?" Ishmael tossed the binder down on the table, causing a bang.

Reggie's shoulders went up, and his eyebrows went down. "You're angry, aren't you?"

Ishmael slowly drew closer to Reggie, whose stomach had started to tighten. Reggie could feel his blood simmering. He clinched his fists.

All the while, Ishmael continued to advance on him. "I knew guys like you. Growing up in LA, I've seen them all the time. They're ephemeral. Do you know what that means—ephemeral?"

Now, Reggie moved closer to Ishmael, who is a head shorter than him but had a Napoleon complex to rival Jacob Vargas' Joker character from *Friday After Next*. One more step, and they would either be kissing or grappling. "It means, Ishmael, that you can be here one day, and gone the next."

They stared at each other for a second or two before Ishmael spoke. "Get this to me tomorrow by ten AM with the dividers reorganized by the *department name,* not their acronym." He backed up and grabbed the finished binder he'd slammed on the table and proceeded to examine it again, rubbing his fingers along its sides. He nodded then in approval. "Good work on the cover and spine though."

Ishmael noisily dropped the book back onto the table and made his exit.

Having been gaslit into a rage, Reggie ripped the dividers out of the books and threw them about the room. In this period of vulnerability, he'd let Ishmael get in his head; it was like Ishmael could sense that Reggie was having a hard time just like sharks could smell blood in water.

* * *

Todd's weight caused the refrigerator door to lean. At 6'2" and 260 lbs with muscle left over from his high school wrestling days, Todd's visceral fat made his rock-gut belly appear like Garbage Pail Kids' "Les Vegas". Todd was the Son of Sam—Sarasota Sam, that is. His huge forearms cramped the refrigerator's style like the shiny suit on a hook-nosed blaxploitation pimp.

This guy—dude eats like a fuckin' rabbit. No wonder why that little Asian girl bounced on him, Todd said to himself as he looked at the vegetables Reggie had stored in the bottom of the refrigerator. *I gotta get myself some real food. Somethin' with some substance.*

Todd turned his attention to the cheese and meat-based leftovers in the plastic Tupperware containers with black bottoms and clear tops that his parents stockpiled in their pantries. After his mom prepared a hearty dish, Todd often made off like a bandit with the leftovers.

He grabbed leftovers that looked like vomit on top of corned-beef hash. Then, after taking another second or two to scoff at the health food, like a dumbass, he put the whole plastic to-go container in the microwave for three minutes. Apparently, he wanted to nuke the shit out of his food.

After a minute and thirty seconds, Todd took his food out, stirred it with a spoon, and stuck it back in the microwave. As the food continued heating, he licked all angles of the spoon and glanced toward the closed door on the other side of the apartment.

I wonder if he's home already?

No sooner than when the thought crossed his mind, the deadbolt latch release from the door jamb and Reggie entered the apartment.

"Yohhhh…" Todd said.

"Whatup, Todd?" Reggie said, looking at the mess on the side of Todd's mouth and his gaping belly.

Todd self-consciously wiped his mouth with his hands. "So, how was work?" He looked at the kitchen clock. "You're back pretty late."

"I'm dealing, Todd. I had to get some shit done, so I stayed late. Hey, listen bro, I'm about to call it a night. See you tomorrow."

Todd extended his hand to give Reggie five, but Reggie offered his fist instead. Reggie didn't like how Todd always wiped his mouth with his hands and licked everything. Todd's large, padded knuckles touched and eclipsed Reggie's fist as they fist bumped.

"If you need anything, just let me know," Todd said as Reggie made his way to open the door Todd had been previously looking at.

"Sure thing, Todd. Sure thing," Reggie said, retreating to his room.

Reggie tossed his satchel on the foot of the bed, changed his clothes, and powered up his personal laptop. He pulled up YouTube to select some music to help him unwind. Heavy-hearted and exhausted, he figured he'd go downstairs to MyThai, an Asian fusion restaurant, to grab a light soup and head to bed early.

After exiting the elevator and walking through the multi-level parking garage walkway, he ended up in front of MyThai. Before entering, he looked up at the sign in glittery gold writing against a background of purple with accent lights underneath. Glancing up higher, he looked at the number of windows leading to his apartment. When his eyes finally reached the top, he saw his bedroom light shining through the halfway open blinds.

"I'm eating under you babe," a voice in his head said.

He lowered his gaze back down to the MyThai sign and studied it for a minute. Before going inside, he peered through the window and noticed all the couples eating and conversating. Then he looked at *that* table, and saw a man and woman sitting opposite each other— mirroring him and Thuy on *that* day. He released a deep sigh and finally entered in the restaurant.

After getting back up to his room, he opened the brown bag that was stapled together as if it concealed a top-secret document, courtesy of the annoying Thai waitstaff. He shook his head as he almost cut his hand on the staples trying to remove his Tom Yum Goon.

With his soup at his side, he checked his Facebook account. He had some notifications, one being from Coach Neil. It read: *Hey bud, just checking in on you to see if you're alright. Just want to let you know, you're good in my book. If you need to talk, I'm here for ya.*

Reggie started to reply, but stopped. Moved by the words, he clicked on some of the pictures that showed the team, with himself in the front, holding the kickball after their victory. Thuy was smiling beside him, leaning in with her hand on his shoulder. Her dimples threatened to pierce through her cheeks. Reggie zoomed in on her.

The YouTube music playlist Reggie chose before going to get soup kept playing in the background while Reggie continued clicking through team pictures featuring him and Thuy. Maxwell's "Till The Cops Come Knocking" lulled through his bedroom. *"Sex on a Thursday night and you'll be jonesin' baby…"* Maxwell sang, bringing Reggie to a halt.

How the fuck did Maxwell know his and Thuy's initial arrangement? Was this another one of God's cruel jokes? Reggie sank down—first to his knees, next, to the floor—as the music flooded him with memories.

Fuck my life. I always get 'those' chicks, he lamented.

EASE

The 2008 to 2009 recession and subsequent economic fallout and restructuring of banking systems took a toll on professionals aged 25 to 40. College grads and seasoned professionals alike faced the question of whether to purchase or rent a place. The housing market appeared to be inflated, not because of intrinsic values of the house and land, but because of the mortgage loan market. Before the mortgage bubble swelled and burst, credit was loose, and loans were given out like syphilis to uniformed servicemen.

People were playing "hot potato" with housing—using Adjustable-Rate Mortgages (ARMs) to buy somewhat decent houses, making minor cosmetic changes to them, and sticking them back on the market as fast as possible. Every Tom, Dick, and Harriet became a DIY overnight—fixing windows, mailboxes, and shutters, replacing doorknobs and locks, and white-washing picket fences like Tom Sawyer—before getting some government employee moonlighting as a real-estate agent to put the house back on the market. The name of the game was to sell the house before the term on the ARM caused the interest rate to balloon. But alas, many people got stuck holding the hot potato with houses now upside down, like an overpriced exhibit in Orlando, Florida.

From the ashes of this busted bubble arose the luxury apartment town center complex. Apartments with insides structured like hotels, complete with business centers that had PC and Apple computers sitting side-by-side singing kumbaya, incandescently lit board meeting rooms with white boards and stinky markers, and symmetrical building layouts and hallways traversed by—get this—recycling and garbage collection services! Working professionals are now too busy to carry their trash to the dumpster.

There are pools with gas grills on deck and Whole Foods bags in the vicinity, where hipsters and *buppies* can be caught grilling tofu skewers and free-range chicken, arguing over which styles of *Untuckit* brand shirts and *Margaritaville* shoes are the most appropriate for casual Friday. If the sheer size of the gentrified, "smart urban" landscape wasn't enough, consider that these huge multiplexes were built into a town center style—with upscale 24-hour grocery chain's illuminated signs causing light pollution, alongside other date-night chain restaurants that look to suck the life out a man's wallet, but leave his balls full.

Although the DC area was relatively cushioned from the economic fallout regarding employment (due to government hiring of employees and contractors), the housing market, like the dating market, appeared highly segmented. Some statisticians called it bimodal, having either very high quality (i.e. beautiful people breeding) and low quality (i.e. hate fucking) elements, but no middle-ground. The declining marriage rates, juxtaposed against increasing divorce rates, have appeared to create a new "bachelor class" of which Reggie is a part.

As a bachelor (though the question that hangs is whether he's an "eligible" bachelor), Reggie lived in such a bachelor pad. Atop the aforementioned town center, he had a spacious, two-bedroom, roommate-style apartment with caddy-cornered rooms for increased privacy. In between the rooms was the kitchen and a combined living/dining room area. The sink and dishwasher were on an island in the center of the kitchen, opposite a stainless-steel refrigerator surrounded by dark brown woodgrain cabinets with silver handles. Starting at ground level, these cabinets rose to the level of the sink and the white porcelain countertops. The cabinets then continued, rising about eight to nine feet high. There was also a gas-powered range, where Reggie stir-fried vegetables in olive oil, with his *buppy* ass.

Although Reggie made a decent salary, his frugality would prevent him from paying upward of $2,200 per month for rent, even with such amenities.

What's his motivation for living in this place then, you ask?

Todd. "Sarasota" Sam's son.

"Sarasota" Sam Wilson was a guy Reggie met three years ago at another contracting job. Their friendship budded from bathroom humor.

As their trust grew, so did their friendship. Reggie became acquainted with Sam's entire family. As an avid sportsman, he had his sons train in football and *wrastlin'*—the same sports he played year-round as a youth in the Okeechobee heat.

Sam and all of his sons stood six feet tall or more, with Todd being the oldest and biggest. He'd been a championship wrestler in his high school days, but now, at 28, his hobbies are cryptocurrency, designer drugs (including the misuse of cough syrup), and online gaming. One of Todd's issues is staying up gaming all night, and barely being able to go in to work the next day—often calling off. He's lucky that his father has good connections that provide him multiple chances. Otherwise, according to Reggie, "A nigga woulda been fired."

* * *

Reggie awakened to Todd stomping across the floor in the process of walking. While good at the grappling arts, Todd could never be a ninja or a ballerino; he was way too ungraceful with his footing and weight distribution.

The impact of Todd's feet sent such strong vibrations through the floor that Reggie could feel them on the arm he was cradling his head with. Slightly dazed, Reggie opened his eyes to see the bottom portion of his bookshelf—the wooden edges thereof—warping the carpet surrounding it.

I gotta move my furniture around a bit, thought the perfectionist-minded pragmatist as he sat up. The single top lamp light from the seven-foot stand that held three individual lights shown dimly through his room. His computer screen had blackened, but the lights behind the keys were still illuminated.

He could hear Todd sliding his monster feet across the floor, and opening and slamming (what Todd called closing) the refrigerator door.

"Hey, Todd," Reggie said, having emerged from his bed.

"Yohhhh," Todd said as they made brief eye contact. Todd was about 12 feet away in the general kitchen area, while Reggie headed for the bathroom located in front of his room.

I wish I had a master bathroom, so I don't have to see people in the living room every time I need to piss, Reggie thought as he closed the bathroom door after entering. He let the contents of his bladder flow into the toilet, and looked over at the bathtub. *But Todd's bathroom only has a stand-up shower, and I like my Mr. Bubble.*

After urinating, a move to the mirror confirmed that his formerly cried tears left what appeared to be dried-up traces of salt under his eyes and the side of his face.

My eyes are baggy as fuck. Being depressed sucks. I wonder if Todd can... Naw, I gotta stay away from Sarah.

Reggie exited the bathroom and entered the kitchen.

"Yohhh, my man." Todd extended his hand to give Reggie dap.

Reggie stared at Todd's hand, debating whether to touch his open palms. But after a moment's hesitation, he decided needed to be close to someone and gave Todd a dap-hug. They patted each other on the back.

"How you been holding up lately?" Todd asked with an audible sniff.

"Man, Todd, this shit sucks. Going through a breakup *really* sucks. I almost lost it at work. I'm thinking about seeing a therapist."

"Really? Wow." Todd sniffed again. "It must be some pretty deep stuff."

"It is. It almost feels like karma for what went down with Judy."

"Judy really had it bad for you, bro."

"Yeah, I know. But I just couldn't deal with her smothering me. And the funny thing is, she and I didn't even see each other that much. It's just like I could feel the neediness in her energy, and it just... It just repelled me."

Todd sniffed yet again before replying. "Yoh, I can dig it, man. It's probably that you let Thuy move you off your basis and you didn't stick to what you knew was right." *Sniff.* "Like when you stopped working on things that you yourself enjoyed." *Sniff.* "The things that gave you that energy. The energy that attracted Thuy in the first place. You caved to her bro." *Sniff, sniff.* Todd wiped his runny nose.

Reggie observed Todd's face and noticed that his eyes were glassier than a fishbowl. Ironically, Todd always gave the best advice when intoxicated. "Thanks, man, that was really insightful," Reggie said. "I'm just going to take this opportunity to do some deep work with the EASE program. Maybe I can gain some insights."

Todd nodded.

"What do you think?" Reggie asked.

"Well, considering the two parallels—*sniff*—between your relationship with Judy and your relationship with Thuy, I noticed three things."

"Do tell."

Reggie said, anticipating Todd's analysis.

"First, both relationships were short-term, but Judy's was three times longer, and she lived in the building. Second, the intensity of the relationships was high, but the compatibility was low," *Sniff*. "And finally, they both ended in extreme emotions. The only difference—*sniff*—amigo, is the direction of the pain. In this case, you had it more in for Thuy than she did for you."

"True. True. But also, Thuy's *SMV* was higher than Judy's."

"Yes, but most people don't think like you, Reggie. Most people don't go around thinking about whether or not their life—" *sniff* "—will conform to some theoretical analysis of how relationships work."

Reggie nodded.

Todd continued. "In the first relationship, Judy fell in love with you. In this relationship, you fell in love with Thuy. The tendency for a person to fall in love—" *Sniff, sniff* "—is related to the amount of insecurity that one has in life. Judy had it emotionally rougher, having a miscarriage and all—and all that other jacked up stuff," *sniff*, "that happened to her. So she clung to you harder. The same goes for you in the direction of Thuy."

Reggie shook his head. "Well, hot damn, Todd. Did you ever think about going into counseling?"

Todd waved his hand dismissively. "I have too many extracurriculars to qualify."

"True—true."

"Well, listen, I'm going to get back to it," Todd said.

"Okay, right on."

Reggie and Todd gave each other dap again.

Todd then returned to his room and closed the door—presumably to return to the "extracurriculars" he'd referenced, which was merely a euphemism for getting high, playing videogames, and watching internet porn.

Reggie popped a Tylenol nighttime and went back to his room.

* * *

The sun played peek-a-boo behind the pastel-colored-brick elevator townhomes opposite Reggie's window. There was a quarter of a football field of space behind the townhomes that made a gradual descent into a manmade lake. It was rumored that on one occasion, under icy conditions, a kid fell through and drowned. Sitting together on one block, the townhomes appeared as a single edifice, like a hotel. During Reggie's visualization exercises, he would imagine there was a beach behind them.

Reggie sat on the corner of his bed putting on his socks.

Fuck, I still feel groggy. Maybe if I just do the elliptical, I can get the Tylenol out of my system, he thought as he grabbed his resistance bands and his key fob before heading to the door.

The hallway was empty, though the mixed scents of cologne, perfume, and shower gel wafted through the air. The vents that kept the insides of the building warm as autumn's chilly days started to descend into winter hummed like a mechanical church choir. People getting ready for work—the smell of bacon and coffee, and the faint sounds of conversations between family members, drifted through the hall as Reggie made his way to the elevator.

I hope they're happy. I don't know what it's like to be a part of something meaningful anymore. Reggie pushed the elevator button. The shaft cables moved about behind the metallic door before it opened. Nobody was there, thank God, because Reggie didn't want to be seen.

Walking through the building's lobby to get outside, he felt the gust of cold air.

I haven't seen Big Retch lately. I wonder if she moved. Reggie briefly remembered Gretchen "Big Retch" Elmendorf, an Amazonian, slightly overweight white woman from Wisconsin. Retch lived in the eastside sister building opposite him. He and Gretchen mostly saw each other on mornings when Reggie got up early enough to take the complementary shuttle for Overture apartment denizens going to the Metrorail.

Gretchen, over six feet tall with eyebrow ridges to rival Jason Momoa, loved to eat egg salad and Limburger cheese sandwiches in the morning—with the eggs still steaming. One day, while waiting on the shuttle and chomping down on one of those sandwiches, she flirted with Reggie. Reggie, in the process of listening to her talk, smelled the horrific *budussy*-meets-Haitian-underarms sandwich. Nauseous from the aroma, Reggie politely declined, imagining what it would be like to kiss her after she'd eaten one of those things.

What stuck out at him was when she said that she *used to* be overweight.

She never stopped being overweight, he thought, chuckling to himself as he carried on with his morning routine.

* * *

Fingertips click-clacking on a keyboard, dry roast coffee percolating, papers shuffling, the HVAC unit over the vents humming—all the sounds and smells related to the post-modern office setting echoed in Reggie's head as he stared at a blank cursor on a white background.

A pen gently tapped on the outside metal edge of Reggie's cubicle enclosure. He turned around to see Denise, his supervisor and Ishmael's direct report.

Denise was a 60-something-year-old former government pencil-pusher-turned consultant and native Washingtonian. Her government contacts and deep agency knowledge allowed her to do what a lot of boomers who don't want to retire do—double-dip by accepting retirement and benefits from the government, then return as a sub-contracting business liaison. Her skin was midnight, yet her eyes still shone with the determination and compassion she used to raise her own family and provide for her grandkids. She had nary a wrinkle—black don't crack.

"Hey, I heard you had to stay late yesterday, and I was just checking—" Denise paused, noticing Reggie's eyes were puffy. "Can you come over to my office when you have a second?"

Reggie nodded.

* * *

Like a Peeping Tom, sunlight peered in through the horizontal blinds in Denise's office, lining her face with a binary sunlight-shade pattern. At times, the light would hit her in the eyes as she typed, making her squint.

Ah, the price to pay for having an office with windows.

Fuck, I forgot to pay my cable bill... Maybe they'll wave the late fee, Denise said to herself as she click-clacked on her keyboard with flared nostrils and a furrowed brow. She was stopped mid-password entry by a gentle rapping on her half-opened door. Looking up and seeing half of Reggie standing there, she motioned for him to come in. "Close the door behind you please and have a seat."

Reggie plopped down in the chair facing Denise's mahogany desk. Pictures of her family peppered the desk and credenza. In one of them, a black girl in a ballet leotard contorted her body.

"I heard you stayed late the other night..." Denise looked to-and-fro, and then continued in a lower voice. "Dealing with Ishmael's punk ass."

Reggie nodded.

"What happened?" Denise asked.

"Ishmael asked me to produce a work product, and when I asked him to be specific about what he wanted, he told me to make a creative decision. When he came back, he found something trivial—not with the data, but with the presentation—"

"Something that basically nobody would notice except for his perfectionist ass."

Reggie nodded again.

"You been sleeping okay?" Denise asked, sensing Reggie was out of sorts.

He looked down and shook his head, just barely holding it together.

"Let me know if you want to go to HR about Ishmael. If he's bullying you, that's wrong," Denise said sternly.

Still trying to hold it together, Reggie slowly bobbed his head up and down, his energy molasses-like.

"Well, that's all. I just wanted to check in on you..." Denise's voice drifted off on a note of concern as she stood from her seat.

"Thanks," Reggie said, also standing.

Denise took in the way Reggie hung his head somewhat low. "You look like you need a hug... Can I give you a hug?"

"Yeah," Reggie said softly.

Denise extended her arms in a motherly fashion and gathered Reggie into them.

As he returned the hug her, everything hit him at once—the breakup, his career, his social circle... He felt like he didn't belong anywhere. He didn't know whose life he was living. A deep sense of loss overwhelming him, he started to sob.

"I know. I know...Let it all out," Denise soothed as she patted Reggie on the back. Having raised her own sons and being a pillar in her family, she knew Reggie was going through something difficult.

The more she patted his back, the more he cried. For a while now, Reggie had been feeling that everywhere he turned to for comfort, he was met with another cold shoulder. Hence, having Denise's support felt like a brief blessing he didn't even know he'd needed.

* * *

The Employee Assistance Service Enterprise, or EASE, was the mental health and life services contractor for Vectorplex. One of their many marketing materials includes a pamphlet featuring a collage depicting images like people helping the elderly, and distraught individuals curled into the fetal position.

As Reggie ran his fingers over the pamphlet, he immediately identified with the sad-faced person on the cover. He thumbed through the pamphlet and located the phone number for counseling services.

If I call them, will they report the findings to management? he wondered.

Although the pamphlet described the program as confidential, Reggie remained aware of the stigma around participating in counseling services. Seeking counseling could create the appearance of not operating at the mental capacity to perform satisfactorily at work—or "looking crazy", as they say.

But Reggie needed enough emotional bandwidth to do his job—and the circumstances surrounding the breakup and the intensity thereof was affecting his emotional bandwidth.

Reggie looked at the pamphlet once more. *It's worth a shot,* he said to himself.

Abruptly stricken with a brilliant idea, he began to send an email:

TO: *Hernandez.Ishmael@vectorplex.com*

CC: *Hopkins.Denise@vectorplex.com*

FROM: *Jenkins.Reginald@vectorplex.com*

Hello Ishmael,

My mental health has been compromised. Emotional turmoil that I have been experiencing lately has been adversely affecting my work. I am requesting to utilize the EASE program to help me resolve these situations as to provide better service to you and all our company's stakeholders.

Thank You,
Reggie

What a brilliant strategy. Instead of going head-to-head with Ishmael, Reggie appealed to Ishmael's position as a leader and steward of his employees—thus, putting the prideful boss at a position to pat his ego and make a formal mental health request.

Reggie smiled at his own guile. But the victory was short-lived as flashbacks of his ex's smile and the feel of her wetness haunted him. It wasn't the flashbacks of physical intimacy that made him feel bad, but the perception that those moments are gone forever.

Using his resourcefulness to help combat mourning his former lover, Reggie pulled up YouTube, where there was a series of motivational talks and soothsayers with wisdom to give.

"Experiencing a breakup is a huge pulling apart of energy," said a bohemian-dressed YouTube woman. *"It's like pulling out a tooth. You feel like you lost a part of your body, and you know you won't be getting it back."*

Reggie watched intently, listening through his earphones.

"And while you may feel stuck in a time-bubble, you must understand that life will continue on, with or without your consent, whether you like it or not. The sun will still rise in the east and set in the west. The question is: How long will it take you to return to being an active participant in life?"

At these words, Reggie recalled how engrossed he'd been in the kickball experience due to of the camaraderie. But now that all that shit went down, it seemed that particular bridge had been burned.

As he thought about his next move, a "ding" hit his inbox with a reply from Ishmael.

Reggie held his breath and opened the email.

TO: *Jenkins.Reginald@vectorplex.com*

CC: *Hopkins.Denise@vectorplex.com*

FROM: *Hernandez.Ishmael@vectorplex.com*

Hello Reggie,

Please take whatever time you need, and any resources that Denise and myself can provide for you, don't be afraid to ask.

Thanks,
Ishmael.

Ishmael's response had confirmed Reggie's beliefs. Immediately, he returned to Denise's office and knocked on the already opened door to get her attention.

Busy browsing Home Depot's website for new Kohler faucets to put in her kitchen, Denise glanced toward the door.

"Hey, Denise," Reggie said, entering her office.

"Hey, Reggie. You feelin' better? I got your email."

"I'm getting there, but I'll need to take a couple days of sick leave, please."

"No problem. Just submit a request in the time-keeping tool and keep me posted on your progress. Since the budget books were the priority—and by the way, the executive management loved them—things should be quiet for a while."

"Thanks, Denise," Reggie said.

She smiled, nodded, and went back to her devices.

Reggie then hurried back to his workstation, powered down his laptop, grabbed his EASE pamphlet, and headed out of the building.

ASIAN **FLUSH**

Anvi Chen was born to a Taiwanese father and Cantonese mother during a love affair in 1970s Hong Kong. Anvi's mother spoke English and Cantonese, and initially, her father only spoke Taiwanese mandarin. Nevertheless, he won over her mother's heart by writing love letters using traditional Chinese characters, a mutually intelligible writing system. They continued using writing and body language to communicate until her father learned English and they moved to the U.S, where they gave birth to Anvi.

Anvi's mother encouraged her to take up the physical sciences, but Anvi tended to prefer the social sciences. She first studied economics to placate her parents' bias towards quantitative disciplines, but then added psychology as a second major, which she loved.

Anvi succeeded in starting a mental health contracting firm, winning corporate and government organizational contracts with her pitch on the long run profitability of treating employees' mental health. As a result, the EASE initiative was born.

Anvi glanced at the photo of her mom and dad holding the "love you forever" glyph.

She smiled, thinking about how her mother and father were a symbol of communication and patience—something she encouraged in the couples she worked with. Then she heard a knock on her office door.

"Come in," she said, delicately adjusting the picture to a pleasing direction.

The office administrator poked her head into Anvi's office. "Your 10:30's here."

Anvi looked at the clock. It was 10:21. *The sooner I get started, the sooner I can go to lunch,* she thought. "Go ahead and send him in. Thanks."

"Will do," the administrator said, leaving the door cracked.

* * *

"It's got to be part of the security itself—the structure of these buildings," Reggie said as he sat down in the chair opposite Anvi's desk. "I walked up and down the halls trying to find your location. I was like Theseus with no rope."

"Theseus?" Anvi tilted her head to the side, her eyebrows furrowed like a Rottweiler trying to understand a new command.

"The guy from the labyrinth maze in Greek mythology."

"Oh... That's his name?"

"Yeah."

"So, how can I help you?" Anvi asked after a brief pause. "It says on your intake form that you have recently experienced a loss."

"I recently went through a breakup, and the emotional fallout has caused me to underperform at work, have trouble sleeping, etcetera."

"Oh wow." With her notepad positioned in front of her, Anvi jotted down a few quick notes. "Okay. How long did this relationship last?"

"Well, it was kind of a *situationship*."

"Ah—catchy. A relationship-situation. This is my first time hearing that portmanteau."

"Porter who?" Reggie asked, being out-vocabularied.

"It's like a new word formed by joining two words together. Like 'chillax'," Anvi explained.

Reggie nodded. "Right on. Anyway, to answer your question, I think we were seeing each other for about a month."

"A month? Is it typical for you to form strong feelings in short time spans?"

"It was pretty intense," Reggie said, spotting a 5K prize on Anvi's shelf. "You're a runner, right?"

Anvi nodded the affirmative.

"Well, I see feelings in relationships as equivalent to running a certain distance. The longer you run, the farther you go. But you can also go the same distance by running faster in a short period of time."

"Interesting analogy. So your *situationship*, was more like an intense sprint rather than a cross-country run?"

"Yes."

"How did you meet this person?"

"We met playing happy hour kickball."

"Kickball. Oh, wow." Anvi smiled. "I haven't played that game since I was a kid."

"Yeah, you know all the grown *yuppies* and 80s babies love bringing back childhood games to use as an excuse to drink."

"Tell me a little bit about it."

* * *

One of the rules in coed kickball is to have an equal number of girls and guys on the team. To the extent that there are enough women on the kickball team, players line up boy-girl-boy-girl or girl-boy-girl-boy, depending on how you view the world. Then, a row of Antarean "Kickballaz" stand before you. And on their shirts, their mascot—the personified image of Antares, the blazing red giant—has resting bitch-face.

Reggie had a "don't-fuck-this-up" mentality. He didn't know which was a tougher sell—being responsible for catching a ball in the outfield or being responsible for kicking it into the outfield. His insecurities began to rise to the top like bubbles in a champagne glass. The reason for the pressure was simple—he wanted to grow a network, a social life he hadn't really been a part of since Vuth passed away.

The mere thought triggered a floodgate of memories. Reggie found himself abruptly reliving events from a few months ago, whereby Judy, raging like a *Quintesson* on meth, screamed she hated her life all because of Reggie.

To an onlooker, Reggie was simply surveying the field, deciding where to kick the ball and assessing who was the weakest link on the opposing team. But in reality, Reggie had a front row seat to the screen of his own mind—minus the sticky floors, popcorn, and horny teenagers making out.

Coach Neil looked at his kickers roster before putting his hands over his mouth, forming an inverted cup, and shouting, "Tweeeeed!" His booming voice snapped Reggie out of his personal hellhole, and back to surveying the other team's positioning on the field.

Reggie turned toward the clamor in the background, and saw her—a five-foot-four, Karen Fukuhara-esque woman with a round babyface, dimples, and cheeks likely reddened from the fall weather. She looked like an Asian Cabbage Patch Kid.

The woman ran as if she didn't have a care in the world, like she was running through a meadow of buttercups. Racing down the line towards home plate to kick, she gave their teammates high-fives, looking like a contestant on *The Price is Right*.

Standing on the other side of the backstop with his fingers interlaced in the fence like Tony Montana in the Freedomtown refugee camp, Reggie watched as she made her way towards him. *That's odd,* he marveled, *I haven't seen her on the field before...*

Passing Coach Neil, the young woman said, "There's no 'd' in 'Thuy'. She then left Coach Neil's hand high and dry before turning and spotting Reggie. She gave him a "what's up" head nod, which he returned.

What she's going to do now? Reggie wondered. Thuy was the first kicker in the inning, and the outfielders for this team were strong.

The pitcher wound up and then pitched the ball down the center.

Thuy didn't kick it.

"Strike!" called the umpire.

Reggie continued watching from behind the backstop, noticing that Thuy had angled her body slightly different. From the front, she eyed a spot on the field.

The pitcher pitched the ball again, straight down the middle.

This time, Thuy, in a cat-like stance, took a running start and smacked the ball with the inside of her foot and ankle. A grounder, the ball spun past the pitcher and towards third base.

"Yes!" Coach Neil yelled as the Antareans cheered Thuy on.

The opposing team converged towards the grounded ball, quickly passing it to first base.

Thuy sprinted towards first base as far as her little legs would take her while the ball was being thrown from hand-to-hand. The first baseman waited with his foot on the base and his arm extended. Just before he received the ball, Thuy tapped first base with her foot and ran past.

"Safe!" the umpire cried.

Now that's what's up. Reggie nodded in approval.

After a series of plays, they reached the last inning. The opposing team was up by one point, Thuy was on third base, and Reggie was up to kick.

The pitcher let the ball fly, and after squaring up with it, Reggie blasted the ball into outfield and immediately ran. Thuy looked up in the air at the ball, her hands over her brow until realizing people were converging in the outfield to catch it. She made a mad dash for home as Reggie sprinted to first plate.

Unfortunately for them, the outfielder caught the ball, and was chugging it infield to get Thuy. Once the ball hit the third baseperson, Thuy was halfway to home plate. The third baseperson threw the ball to the catcher, who ran forward to collect it. At this point Thuy was sandwiched between the third baseperson and the catcher who threatened to tag her out. Thuy ran backward, then forward again, until the catcher decided to peg her with the ball. The round rubber ball slammed her upper back, propelling the little woman forward.

"Ow!" Thuy cried.

"Out!" shouted the umpire.

"Redo!" Coach Neil yelled, approaching the female umpire. "Unsportsmanlike...er, uh... *unsportspersonlike* conduct!"

The umpire turned toward Coach Neil. "She would've been out, there's no way she could have avoided that! The ruling still holds!"

Thuy trotted back to the team, who congratulated her on a good run.

Moments later, the catcher—a six-foot plus white guy—came over. "Sorry about hitting you so hard with the ball. I got excited, and you were a little evasive."

Thuy extended her hand. "No biggie."

The two of them chuckled as Reggie looked on.

* * *

The Wagging Tail is a dive bar located among rows of upscale, drain-your-pockets, date-night restaurants. It was built earlier than the other trendy restaurants, when the area's income and image were a lot more working class. It stands now as one of the more popular places hipsters go to feel down-to-earth—a spot where they can rub elbows with the regulars who still show up for economically priced drinks, all while remaining in the backdrop of their $2,000/month studio apartments.

Since the kickball games happen in fall—mostly on late mornings until the early afternoon on Sundays—the area is generally in brunch mode now. Nevertheless, The Wagging Tail was setup for the kickball teams to compete in drinking games. Aside from the multiple stand-up bar tables littering the main area in the upstairs party-room, there are tables set up for games such as "flip cup" and "beer pong". And under a group of flat screen TVs, one could find an area set up for cornhole.

Amongst the hum of people talking, Reggie saw Thuy standing at a high table with a couple of their teammates. Theodore "Bigfoot Teddy" Giannopoulos, one of the "slug foot" kickers, stood with his girlfriend, Maria, cradled under his arm as he gulped back some suds.

"'Sup, Reggie?" Theo said as he approached the table.

"'Sup, Theo," Reggie fist-bumped him and then smiled at the small-statured woman beside him, who was just a tad taller than Thuy. "'Sup, Maria?" Last, he turned his attention to Thuy. "Those were some good runs you made out there. The name's Reggie—Reggie Jenkins." He extended his hand.

Thuy gave Reggie a "just-a-minute" hand signal as she gulped down her beer. The orange-yellow fluid drained down into her gullet, and everybody looked in awe as she destroyed the pint. She finished with the air from the beer causing her cheeks to inflate—and finally, she burped like Majin Buu.

Theo and Reggie exchanged humored looks with each other.

Thuy extended her hand. "The name's Thuy. Hey, do we have to give last names?"

Reggie shrugged. "Not if you don't want to."

"Cool. Just call me 'Thuy' then."

"Right on. I didn't know that all the pro kickballers drank Hefeweizen," Reggie said.

"Heffa-what?"

"That orange colored beer you just drank... What do *you* call it?"

"Oh, I just downed a Blue Moon, dude."

Did she just call me 'dude'? Reggie blinked, and then gathered himself. "Isn't Blue Moon a Hefeweizen?" He thought he knew his beers. Whenever he asked for a Hefeweizen, he got one that looked like what Thuy was drinking.

"It's actually a *Witbier*. Hefeweizen is a *weizenbock*. It's German and gets its flavors from natural ingredients that aren't added to the mash. Witbier, of the Blue Moon type, is Belgian and usually has a lemony finish. Blue Moon uses an orange finish instead of lemon."

Theo smirked, flashing Reggie a look that implied he'd just been schooled.

"Well, well, you know your stuff. Belgium, Germany... A brother's in the ballpark, right? Belgium borders Germany, you know," Reggie said, attempting to not seem clueless.

"That's true. But Hefeweizen is Bavarian, while Blue Moon is from a region called *Hoegaarden*," Thuy further explained.

Reggie turned to Theo. "Did she say what I just think she said?"

"I probably did, mister" Thuy interjected. "I said *Hoegaarden,* which probably sounds like 'hoe garden', like a garden for garden tools."

Reggie suppressed the urge to laugh. "You know what, Ms. Thuy? I'm going to leave that one alone. But, I'll give it a shot. Would you care for another?"

Thuy looked at Maria, who smiled and then turned to Theo. "Hey babe, let's go see what's up with cornhole," Maria suggested.

"Cornhole! Right on!" Theo exclaimed.

They walked away, leaving Thuy and Reggie at the table. When the server came, Reggie placed an order for two Blue Moons.

"Hoegaarden, Cornhole—I'm up to my ears in NSFW double-entendres," Reggie joked. "This is my first year playing on the team and I didn't see you at the beginning of the season. Where did you come from?"

"Like, what do you mean 'where'?" Thuy asked.

Reggie regrouped to rephrase his words; there were a lot of sensitive people abound and he never knew when he was running into one of them. "Like, which city?"

"Oh. I thought you were asking about my nationality."

"Well, I wasn't making any assumptions. I just thought you might not be from around here, since this kickball league comprises people from many cities in this county. I noticed people knew you, but this is my first year, so I assumed you might be from around here." Reggie finished his recovery just as the server returned to place two frosty glasses of Blue Moon on their table.

Thuy picked up her mug and raised her glass towards Reggie's. "Cheers!"

He clinked his glass with hers.

Thuy took a couple of gulps before setting her glass down and cracking an ear-to-ear grin. "I was just putting you on the spot, dude."

Reggie relaxed and smiled back at her.

"You should've seen the look on your face when I said, 'What do you mean where?'" Thuy continued teasing. "It was classic!"

"Ha-ha-ha," Reggie replied sarcastically before taking a couple of gulps of his beer.

"I've noticed it too. People in the DC area get so sensitive about stuff like nationality, ethnicity, race..."

This girl actually has a sense of humor. She totally pulled my leg! Reggie thought. "So, I take it you're not from the DC area, since you referred it in the abstract."

"Bingo. I'm actually from the West Coast." Thuy sipped some more beer, and Reggie mirrored her actions.

"That's a rather large area. There are only three states on the West Coast. Can you be more specific Miss... Miss Thuy?"

"I'm from California."

"Again, that's a large place."

"Are you familiar with southern California?"

"Try me."

"I'm from Santa Ana."

"Of course, I know Santa Ana—the best *pho* I've ever had. My Vietnamese friends say the competition is so heavy that the pho there is better than the pho in Vietnam."

"That is so true! You just won brownie points with me. What do you remember about it, besides that it's pretty much a Vietnamese town?"

"I remember that one of the guys we were hanging out with was living in what looked like a gated trailer community. It was really weird. It's not like the trailer parks you find in the southeastern US. They're like the Cadillacs of trailers, with multiple bedrooms, a large kitchen and dining area, and a deck!"

"You're full of surprises, mister!"

Reggie and Thuy clinked glasses again. Reggie eyed the mug of beer as it partially ensconced her face. He then observed the rosiness of her cheeks as she put her mug down and smiled at him.

Was she blushing? Nah, she just had *Asian Flush*.

* * *

Anvi jotted down some notes on her notepad. Although Reggie never left the room or closed his eyes, he seemed to relive the experience after telling Anvi about it and giving her some background information on Thuy.

Anvi tapped her pen on her notepad and carefully considered her next words. "Thanks for sharing that with me, Reggie. I want to check with you though—do you have any concerns about sessions with me potentially becoming triggering for you?"

"How so?" Reggie asked.

"With me having similarities to Thuy, seeing as I am also Asian and presumably in her age bracket."

"Why would I be triggered?"

"Sometimes, as a survival mechanism, trauma survivors may be triggered by people or situations that remind them of their pain."

Reggie stared at Anvi while reflecting on her words. She was cute. The corner of her mouth extended a little beyond the lip line, giving it the shape of a cupid's bow. "Umm-no," he said hesitantly. He shifted his gaze to the degree posted on her wall. "Anvi Chen."

"That's my name."

"You're of Chinese origin."

"Yep."

"Thuy is Vietnamese. No offence, but while you may share some similarities, Vietnamese people tend to be less conservative than Chinese people."

"I'm not offended at all. From my experience, that actually, seems to be accurate. If you're okay with it, I'm okay with it," Anvi said.

"Okay with what?"

"Continuing our sessions, as long as I'm not a reminder of your pain. If at any time you find it hard, we can discontinue and I'll have your case transferred to another counselor."

If I find it hard? You mean my dick? Reggie said to himself. "Uh, yeah. Yeah, sure thing. I respect that. Besides..." He paused to look at Anvi's photographs, with her tall white husband, her *hapa* baby, and an older, full-blooded Asian child, possibly from her first marriage. "I feel like speaking to you will be cathartic, since I can say things to you and express myself to you in a way that I was unable to with her."

Anvi nodded and jotted down a few more notes. "Okay. You met this girl at a bar, and had a few drinks."

"Yeah. And she was *already* ahead of me when I met her..."

Anvi titled her head. "It sounds like the fact that she'd already been drinking stood out to you. Were you seeing that as a red flag?"

See what as a red flag? Reggie thought. How being so short, she was able to take all that dick like a soldier? "I wasn't really paying attention to that."

"Okay, I see." Anvi nodded understandingly. "Now, thinking back on what you've said, she struck you as standoffish, but more open when she drank."

"But isn't that like anybody?"

"Yes. However, when I think back to the way you've described your interaction during that meeting... Please correct me if I'm wrong, but it seems like something may have bothered you a bit about the way things happened. I'm just trying to understand what and why."

"I never thought about it like that, but I guess you're right. Are you psychic? There was something a little passive aggressive about how it all went down."

Anvi chuckled. "Just my intuition, I suppose."

What a cute laugh. I bet you her moans are sexy as hell, Reggie thought, unable to keep a lid on his lower mind. Taking it as a sign that he was feeling better, he amused himself with sexual thoughts rather than feelings of being a loser.

"So, what happened after?" Anvi asked. "I'm sure things didn't end there."

"She gave me her phone number, and we talked about getting together another time to shoot the breeze."

Anvi jotted more notes, and then checked the time. "Well, that looks like all the time we've got for today," she said, extending her hand to Reggie.

"Okay," he said, shaking her hand goodbye.

"Reggie, you're going to be A-Ok," Anvi said. "Remember, you're currently mourning a loss. Grieving is a process. It's important to take baby-steps and congratulate yourself on daily progress. Focus on the little, incremental wins you experience each day."

"Thanks, Anvi. I'll focus on the little wins, and not on the little *Nguyens.*" At this, they shared a laugh. Then Reggie made his exit.

GET ME **NEXT TIME**

Reggie reflected on the advice Anvi had given him about reviewing the situation and getting a full perspective from both sides to help balance his beliefs regarding what he and Thuy were up to and why.

Maybe Anvi's right. Maybe looking at the actual texts Thuy and I sent to each other can help me rehash the situation...

With this in mind, Reggie opened his smartphone and scrolled back to when he and Thuy first started communicating.

* * *

After making good conversation at the Wagging Tail, Reggie and Thuy exchanged phone numbers and kept their communication going through text messaging.

Two days had passed since their last text exchange, with Thuy texting Reggie around 10:30 PM when he'd been ready to call it a night.

I'll get my morning started, then text her back, he'd decided before going to bed.

Now, on this morning, he went to the gym for his morning routine, returned to his apartment for a shower, got dressed, and finally replied to Thuy's text before hitting the door and heading to work.

Before officially starting his work day, Reggie took a trip to the building's bottom floor to buy a smoothie, and then made his way to his office to begin his opening duties and analysis.

Just the same as any other day, Reggie put his phone on silent during work hours. Not wanting calls and text to hinder his focus, he placed his phone inside the cabinet beside his desk, as usual. On the hour, he would lift the cabinet's horizontal door, peering inside at the relative darkness to check whether the tale-tell blue indicator light on the phone's upper right corner was blinking, indicating a missed call or message.

When anticipating a call, Reggie checked his phone more frequently. But since his social life mainly consisted of four direct family members, four friends, and sparse extended family members and long-lost friends, he rarely missed a beat. Hence, the addition of his kickball team, including Thuy, had helped step up what the post-modern age may consider a rather bland social life.

Oh, look! There goes the blinking blue light of anticipation.

Reggie recoiled at Thuy calling him "dude" in her text. Although he knew her vocabulary was Californian, he considered the usage of "dude" as a reduction to platonic circumstances. As far as he was concerned, it meant she either wasn't interested in him physically, or was putting up a wall to discourage him from escaping the friend-zone.

To Reggie, it was like using the word/name *joe* in D.C.—slang to indicate a random individual. By contrast, softer names, like "shorty", was typically a term of light endearment. When used toward a female target, it was often a test; a woman who had no negative response to the term likely understood a man's intentions of trying to warm up to her.

On the other hand, if a woman reacted negatively, she might respond with, *"I'm not your shorty"*, or state something matter-of-fact, like, *"I'm actually taller than you"* or *"I'm not short for the average girl."*

Letting the word "dude" sink in, Reggie decided to back off and give Thuy some space, limiting his contact with her to the weekends. For now, he would simply attend to his normal weekly work schedule.

* * *

With the Sunday kickball game approaching, Reggie decided to give Thuy a call because firstly, he'd put enough space between them to gather how he was going to approach the situation, and secondly, if the communication went cold, he could easily move on. The whole "dude" thing had turned him off quite a bit. Thus, texting her now was a way to test the temperature of things between them.

As Reggie went about running his errands for the day, he texted Thuy intermittently.

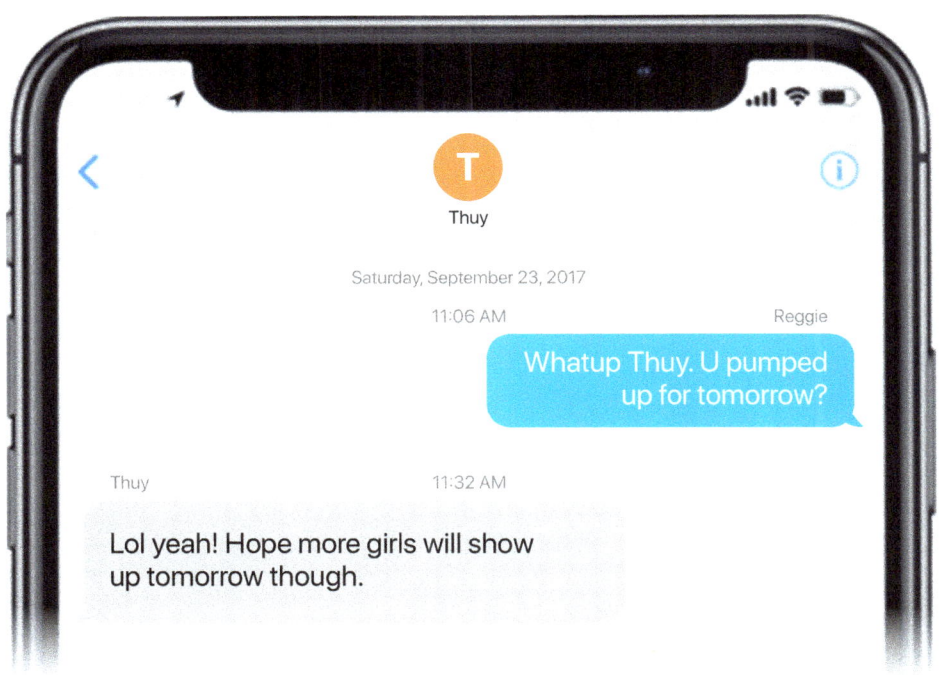

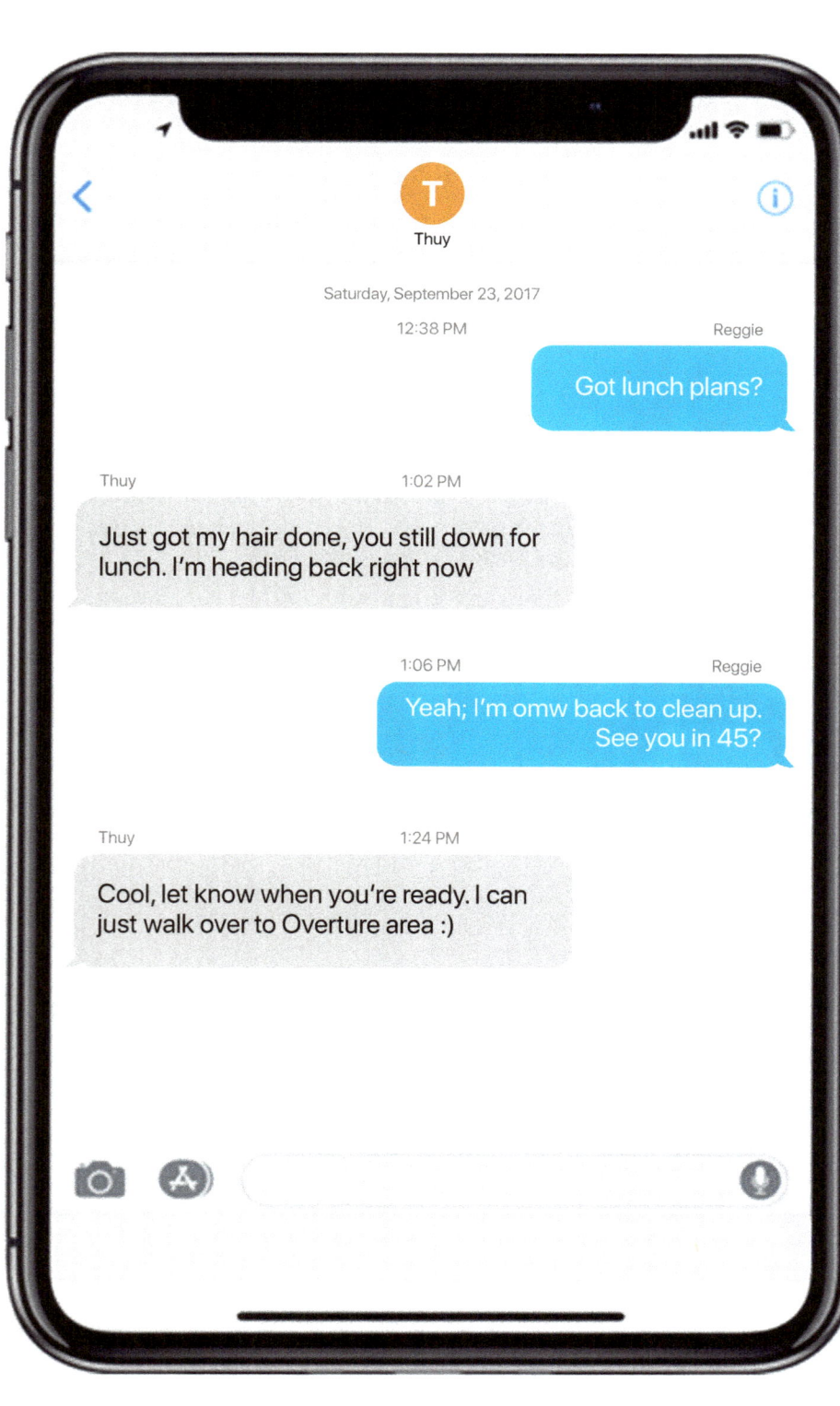

An actual date? Reggie thought. *No way! But is it really a date? Maybe she just wants to talk about kickball strategies, or hang out as friends... I hate being called 'dude' by her! I guess there's only one way to tell what she wants though, and that's going to meet her. No internet bullshit, just straight up work in the field.*

In anticipation of the outing, Reggie did a few warmup exercises and stretches before taking a cold shower. All the while, he mentally prepared himself to let things go as they would go, vowing to do more listening than talking.

Reggie entered the elevator and made his way to the bottom floor. He stared at the shiny metallic finish of the Overture's elevator four walls as it led to the parking garage area. He shifted his gaze to the floor, the sides, and the top.

How would someone escape this elevator if it was locked? he wondered. *It looks too high to get stable footing to climb up. The grill that separates the lighting from the rest of the area looks bolted tight. They probably make repairs to the elevator by locking it and either working from above or below... And they approach the shaft—"*

Reggie's wandering mind was interrupted by the doors sliding open, delivering him to the street level of the apartment complex.

As he walked out to meet Thuy, his mental torture continued until he reached the intersection of the street separating their two apartment complexes. Thuy's apartment was catty-corner Reggie's, and she was already standing outside waiting, diagonally from him.

Spotting Reggie, she waved, and he waved back.

She's looking cute today, Reggie observed. *Wonder if I should go to her, or wait for her to come to me? I don't even have a place in mind for us to go... But that's okay. I don't want to be overly eager; I think—*

The mental machine cranked inside Reggie's head again. But before his thought train could stop at the station, Thuy had already made her move, like chess, to the side of the street opposite where she was standing. She hustled across and was now on the corner directly in front of Reggie. The street separating them, at this point, was a much busier one. But since Thuy had made the first move, Reggie felt obligated to meet her halfway.

Thuy waved again, smiling.

Reggie looked to and fro, then headed across the street to meet her.

Here goes nothing, he thought as he approached Thuy with his arms open wide. He noticed people both on foot and in cars watching him. "Hey, what's up? Glad you could make it," he said, his voice raised in excitement.

Still smiling, Thuy reciprocated the hug. "Thanks! Me too! I'm so ready to eat. What'd you have in mind?"

She's from California, so might as well go to CPK, the thought abruptly popped in Reggie's head. "How about CPK?"

"Great idea!" Thuy said merrily.

They continued walking opposite Reggie's apartment and farther down the winding street of Thuy's apartment complex. Cutting through the apartments opposite where Thuy came from, they reached Hushui—the town center promenade littered with bars, date-night restaurants, boutique shops, and California Pizza Kitchen, endearingly called "CPK".

* * *

"Mmm!" Thuy uttered after biting into a slice of the hand-tossed gourmet pizza. The meat toppings, combined with herbs and peppers, played a game of pinball inside of her mouth.

Reggie looked on, pleased that she had entrusted him to order. "I knew you'd like it." He slurped the melted cheese threatening to slide off the edge of his piping-hot slice.

"It's—it's like it's spicy, but not crazy hot. And the basil—that's what really gives it that aromatic, exotic taste," Thuy mused.

Reggie shook his head, wanting to respond, but reluctant to speak with food in his mouth.

"Take your time, hon," Thuy said in a sweet tone.

Reggie finished chewing, then took a sip of his wine to clear his throat. "It's the poblano peppers," he said. "They bring the heat. But I've always ordered like this."

"What? You mean order a Margherita pizza with extra basil, poblano peppers, and pepperoni?"

"Ahh, you caught my ingredients list! Don't ride my style." Reggie smiled. "Since I didn't like eating ketchup, whenever I go to McDonalds—"

"What, wait—you don't like ketchup? Dealbreaker, I'm leaving," Thuy said, faking disappointment.

Ahh, so she considers this a date. Right on!

"Haha, just kidding. Sorry to interrupt," Thuy said.

And she has manners—God. Whatcha setting me up for? "So, whenever I go to Mickie Dee's," Reggie resumed, "I order my hamburgers without ketchup. From a young age, I noticed that when I had to order them without ketchup, they were specially made, and would come fresh. The problem is that people started screwing up my order, especially if I order alongside other people. That's when I learned the power of positive talk, particularly when dealing with non-English speaking immigrants."

"Hey! Whatcha tryin' to say?" Thuy said with a laugh.

"About immigrants, or positive talk?" Reggie laughed as well. "But seriously, have you ever heard that it's better to say what you want, than what you don't want?"

"Umm, maybe?"

"So, the point is, when I ordered a hamburger without ketchup, they would often forget—or even worse, return it with *only* ketchup."

"Oh my God, seriously?"

"Like I said, *non-English speaking* immigrants, girl!"

Thuy laughed and playfully hit Reggie's arm. "So how did you deal?"

"I started asking for a *plain* hamburger with mustard, onions, and pickles. Then later, only onions."

"So basically, what you wanted was a White Castle hamburger."

Thuy and Reggie erupted with laughter.

"Whatcha know about White Castle burgers, huh? You get high?" Reggie blinked his eyes fervently.

"Ha-ha—you know I'm from California."

Just then, the server came to deliver two more glasses of wine.

"Well, thank ye ma'am," Reggie said with a southern accent, causing the server to giggle before leaving.

"You do good accents, by the way," Thuy said.

"Well, thank you," Reggie replied.

Thuy took a sip of wine. "Mm. A good wine pairing. Pinot Grigio?"

"Yep. It's called Santa Margherita."

"How ironic. Margherita pizza and white wine with the name 'Margherita' in it."

"White wine and starch are always a good combo. That's what I like about CPK. Here, pizza isn't just drunk food."

"You can say that again," Thuy said, enjoying the rest of her slice.

"Pizza—it's not a drunk food," Reggie humorously reiterated.

"I meant figuratively, not literally," Thuy said.

The two of them shared another laugh, and after a few more glasses of wine, they found themselves joking about a variety of topics.

Finally, the bill came, with the waitress setting it on the table between them.

Let's see how she's going to handle this. Reggie pulled out his wallet and produced his credit card.

Then, to his surprise and delight, so did Thuy.

Yes! She did it!

Thuy had passed Reggie's litmus test of being a team player. Like most guys, he'd expected to pay. Nevertheless, he appreciated the fact that in this new era of cultural equality between men and women, some women chose not to use their *pussy pass* to their advantage.

"No, no, no, I got this, Thuy. You can get me next time."

"No, it's cool, I like to pay my own way," she said.

Yes! Yes! Yes! Reggie's respect for Thuy was reinvigorated. "How about this—I'll pay the tab, and you pay the tip."

"No way! We go halvsies," she said.

"Okay, if you insist."

After they finished deliberating, the waitress collected the credit card payments. Shortly thereafter, she returned with separate receipts for Reggie and Thuy to sign.

Thuy stared at her receipt for a moment, her brow furrowed. Glancing around the restaurant, she spotted their waitress and flagged her over. "Excuse me, these credit card numbers aren't mine. I have a Visa, and this says MasterCard."

The waitress studied the receipt, then looked to Reggie. "May I please see your receipt, sir?"

"Sure." Reggie handed the little slip of paper to her.

"I apologize. I accidentally charged the gentleman's card twice. I can re-run the cards and—"

"That won't be necessary," Reggie interjected. "Just hand me both of the receipts, please. Thuy, I got you. Just get me next time."

"You sure?" Thuy asked.

"We're on the same kickball team. I'll hunt you down," Reggie joked.

Relieved, waitress apologized once more and then went on her way.

Meanwhile, Reggie felt like he was making a small investment; hopefully the return would be the chance to spend some private time with Thuy in the near future.

* * *

"C'mon, boy. C'mon, Cliff! Let's get 'em!" Reggie shouted as he broke into a sprint alongside his pit bull terrier, ready to get in his warm-up run.

You're not catching up as fast as you used to. Reggie frowned as he glanced down at the dog. He remembered how Clifford used to bolt out in front of him during a sprint initially, then fall back to run side-by-side with him. But as Cliff got older, Reggie noticed he took longer to catch up, and Reggie even beat him running sometimes. It was a stark reminder of life's impermanence.

Reggie briefly remembered the words of the great late George Carlin: *Getting a dog is like purchasing a small tragedy.*

Instead of dwelling on what couldn't be controlled, Reggie slowed his pace for Cliff, the same way Clifford used to slow down for him.

After returning Cliff to his mom's house, he immediately went to his car. *I can stretch and eat breakfast at home, before heading to the kickball field,* he decided.

Sitting in his car, he fiddled with things about his direct area of control, and looked into the sun visor mirror. Catching his reflection, he saw beads of sweat dripping down his forehead and his temporal arteries bulging. Averting his gaze, he noticed the blue light on his phone blinking and checked his messages.

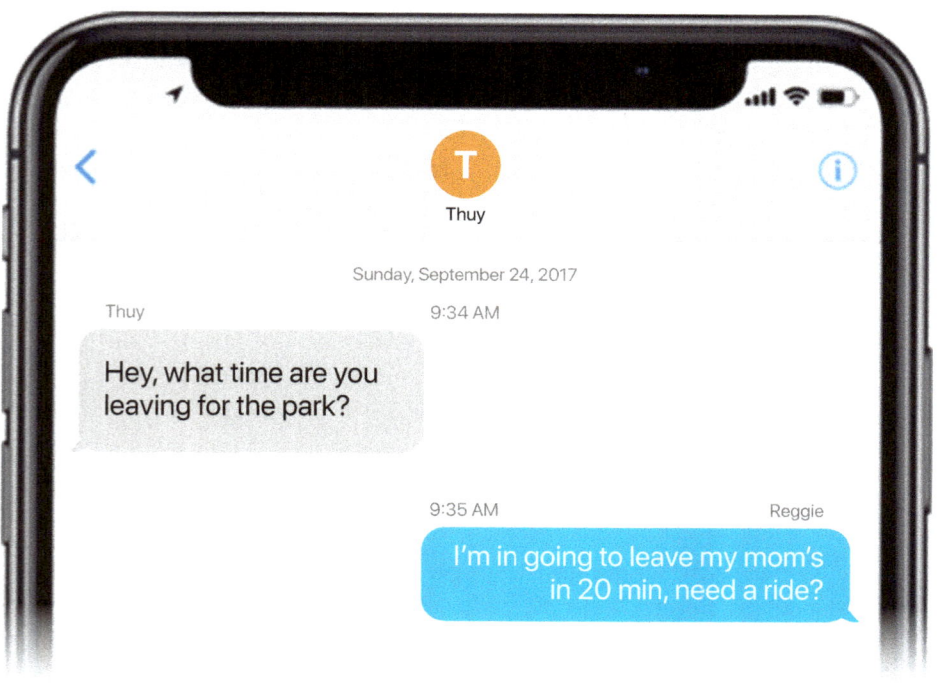

In addition to being pleasantly surprised by Thuy's initiation of conversation and contact, Reggie admired that she was taking a conscientious approach to practice. During a happy hour, Coach Neil and the team had talked about winning the coed kickball championship that season.

I'll skip breakfast, and grab a protein bar and energy drink at the gas station. I can stretch on the kickball field, Reggie planned ahead as he hit the highway to pick up Thuy. After reaching a stoplight near the gas station, he sent her a message, to which she immediately replied.

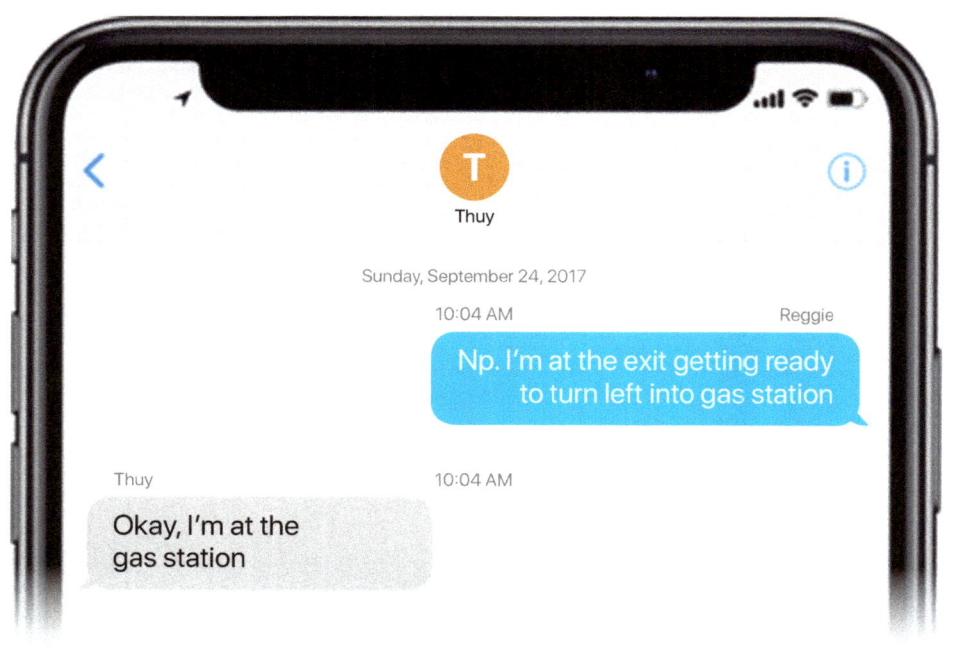

"I'm going to go in and grab a protein bar and energy drink," Reggie said as Thuy opened his passenger door to get in.

"I can grab it for you," she offered. "What do you want?"

"Let me get one of them peanut butter 'Oh Yeah!' bars, and an NOS explode drink, please."

"Explode?"

I wish I could explode inside of you. Reggie said to himself, laughing at Thuy's question. "It's an energy drink that looks like a Nitrous Oxide tank—the tanks that rice rocket racers attach inside of their cars to give them turbo boost."

"Ha-ha. Okay, I'll see what I can find. If I can't find protein bars and NOS boost, will pork rinds and grape soda do?"

"Touché!" Reggie gave Thuy a fist bump, which she reciprocated, and they shared a quick laugh, shrouded in ethnic jabs.

Shorty's pretty damn cool, but damn, she takes super tiny steps like her feet are bound, Reggie thought, watching Thuy shuffle towards the gas station.

* * *

"I really hate playing outfield. It's like trying to estimate exactly where the ball will fall. It's super hard."

"Well, what position is your favorite? *Short stop?*" Reggie laughed, taking another dig the miniature beauty's height.

She slapped his arm playfully. "I should've got you that grape soda," she replied, looking at the scenery outside the passenger's window.

Reggie grabbed his energy drink from the cupholder, took a swig, and wiped his mouth like a gangster. "When you're in the outfield, all eyes are on you," he said, adopting the style of Sonny talking to Calogero on *Bronx Tale*. "There are two major risks—one, a collision with other outfielders looking up while running towards you, and two—you dropping the ball. Even if you drop the ball, you still have to recover it and chug it back infield before the other team has a chance to score. Even with all that pressure, combined with not knowing if the ball is going to fly in your direction, you still have an advantage over me."

"Oh yeah? What's that?"

"You're a girl."

"Huh?"

"As a girl, you don't have the same pressure to perform to the standards of physical coordination like guys do. You'll be held less to blame if you make a mistake." Reggie paused to see if Thuy had anything to add or disagreed. When she remained silent, he continued. "The position of outfielder in kickball is like the position of goalie in soccer— it's the make-or-break position. All you have to do to gain everybody's love is catch the ball once if it's headed in your direction."

"You know, that's an interesting way to look at it. It's not so scary when you put it like that. A little sexist, but true, in a way."

Reggie gave Thuy another fist bump, and she reciprocated.

"Thanks for the pep talk, man," she said.

"No problem. I'm sure Coach Neil will have plenty of pep for us now that he sees we have a chance to win the tournament."

* * *

Reggie watched from second base as Darnell, the team's bruiser, stepped up to home plate. Lean, muscular, and standing at six-foot-one, Darnell was the light-skinned version of Tyson Beckford. Heart-shaped calves poked out of tube socks that would make a cabaret dancer jealous. Unlike Tyson Beckford though, Darnell had some rough features—deep set eyes, a bullet head, a square jaw, and a dimpled chin.

What else can you say about people from Pittsburg, PA? They all have that "steel-mill-will-rise-again-look".

Familiar with Darnell's reputation, the opposing team spread out and sent more resources to the outfield.

Reggie looked downfield at Dixie on third base, and signaled her to get ready to run.

Coach Neil looked at his clipboard while the other kickers stood in line. Everyone was quiet, for they all loved the sound the rubber ball made when Darnell smacked it.

Darnell put his index finger up in the air like Hacksaw Jim Duggan with a two-by-four.

The pitcher pitched a curve ball, which Darnell let pass to the catcher.

"Strike!" the umpire yelled.

Darnell took five steps backward, and the second pitch came straight down the middle. Darnell then took two big steps followed by two tiny ones before exploding in the direction of the kickball. The ball bounced slightly off a pebble on the ground, and Darnell gave his signature smirk.

Perfect, Darnell thought as he smacked the ball with the instep of his foot, right off the small bounce. The muffled noise of the rubber ball echoed throughout the field. Rather than going up high like an arc, the ball went up slightly and straight out, flying over the pitcher's head. He looked up at it like the midget from *Fantasy Island*.

Reggie took off running, as did Dixie. Fortunately, the ball landed right where two outfielders were standing. Confused at the distance the ball would travel, they scrambled to recover it.

Dixie was slower than Reggie and was a quarter of the way to home plate as Reggie booked behind her.

"Run! Run!" Reggie shouted.

Dixie scrambled as fast as her chubby body would allow.

The outfielders recovered the ball and were now throwing it infield, passing it from player to player like an assembly line. The ball finally reached infield as Darnell reached second base. Dixie and Reggie, within a step of each other, both ran to home plate.

Coach Neil gave them high fives as they shuffled to the dugout.

Darnell was three-fourths of the way to third base when the ball reached the second baseperson.

"Stay! Stay!" Coach Neil yelled as the second baseperson launched the ball toward third base in Darnell's direction.

Darnell looked back and saw that the ball was coming, tapped third base, and kept running. "I got this!" he yelled, sprinting towards home plate. He was just a few feet in front of third when the third baseperson recovered the ball and ran in his direction. The third baseperson kept his eyes on Darnell's signature pink shoes—he'd started wearing them in support of breast cancer awareness, and after getting so many compliments for acknowledging his feminine side, he'd made a habit out of wearing them.

"Darnell, jump!" Reggie shouted, spotting the third baseperson rearing back to throw the ball at Darnell.

Like clockwork, Darnell jumped and the ball aimed at his feet went under him. The catcher tried to recover the ball but was too late. Darnell had crossed the home plate.

"Yeah! Good run, champ!" Coach Neil gave Darnell a pat on the back.

Darnell turned to Coach Neil. "Oh, ye of so little faith—when I told you I got this, I got this."

Coach Neil rolled his eyes.

"C'mere, babe," Darnell then said to his young Estonian wife, Irena. She ran up and kissed him, and in turn, he picked her up, as he loved to do—throwing her around like a pampered rag doll.

You would've been tagged out if I didn't tell you to jump, you dimple-chinned prick. Reggie frowned, watching the whole exchange.

* * *

"Listen up, everybody!" Coach Neil yelled as the team gathered around. "This next inning is the last inning. You already know what to do! Irena, Theo, Dixie—first, second, and third base! Ryan for short stop. Orlando for catcher. Thuy, Darnell, Reggie—left, center, and right outfield. Kate for pitcher. Let's play ball!"

As the team hustled out to their positions, Reggie and Thuy glanced.

"Fuck, I hate outfield," she said under her breath.

"Remember what I told you. No matter what you do, you'll be fine," Reggie assured her.

"No. What you better do is catch that ball if it heads in your direction," Darnell said, interrupting Reggie's pep talk.

Thuy and Reggie gave Darnell a side-eye.

* * *

After several plays, there wasn't much action in the outfield. Most of the kickers had been women, and they hadn't kicked far into the field. Reggie observed some of their various stances and gaits, which seemed heavily influenced by their office jobs, making their knees bow inward and their toes point outward. The muscle imbalances caused them to kick the ball in various directions.

Hmm. Maybe I should try for pitcher. Even though Coach Neil would rather have a girl pitch, having a strong pitcher could strike the girls out. And by pitching just right—"

"Spread out! Spread the fuck out!" Darnell shouted as the other team's answer to Darnell—a big, burly white dude—stepped up to the home plate.

He smiled and pointed his finger in the air, imitating Darnell and obviously having it in for him. "Bring it on, buddy!" he said.

The opposing team had one out left, and the Antareans were up by one point. The tension in the air was palpable.

The big dude kicked the ball, bolting it into the air. The ark was higher than Darnell's, but far off to the left.

"Thuy! Get ready!" Reggie yelled.

"Shit, shit, shit, shit..." Thuy repeated as the ball reached its height in the sky, partially eclipsing the sun, from her perspective. She could practically see the umbra of the sun's rays around the ball. Then, as the ball began to fall to earth, its shape got bigger and bigger. "I got it! I got it!" she yelled, running towards the ball with outstretched arms.

All eyes were on her.

The ball closed in, getting bigger and bigger in Thuy's eyes .

Then, all of a sudden...

* * *

"Boom! It was beautiful, man. The arc on the ball was perfect. They should have a name for it, the same way when a football is launched from the arm of a quarterback like a scud missile and twists in a perfect spiral," Darnell exclaimed as he pounded back his beer. Irena held his arm and beamed at him with loving eyes.

Although Reggie somewhat held disdain for the way Darnell lived his life—a retail broker for Merrill Lynch, while leading a Bar/Bat mitzvah party troupe on the side—he couldn't help but respect the man. A mulatto with a ghetto name and the voice, attitude, and build of a white *Chad Thundercock*, Darnell sported a ten-years younger, thin, horse-rider-gap-having Estonian wife he'd likely gleaned from a mail order, or a Russian Jewish party. While he didn't have a formal education, he still grabbed life by the balls and lived on his own terms and faith.

Sipping beer with Thuy, Reggie nodded as Darnell continued his story.

"And then you—*you* have got to be the highlight of the game!" Darnell said, pointing in Thuy's direction. "The ball came down and out of the sky, and you caught it, smacking yourself in the face with it!"

The kickball team members laughed, remembering the way Thuy had scream, *"I got it"* right before the ball got her instead. She had put both hands up to catch the ball, yet her faced joined in to help.

Darnell took another gulp of his beer, then lifted his glass. "Everybody—a toast to Thuy, who takes the term 'use your head' to whole new levels!"

The team roared and clinked glasses.

Reggie looked at Thuy and saw that she was blushing, but jubilant. Was she embarrassed, or did she have another case of the Asian flush?

As the happy hour continued, the team celebrated their position in the bracket, and Thuy's game-saving catch. A circle had formed around her, and all kinds of people—even players from other teams—bought her drinks.

"Hey, Tweetie—" Reggie paused, realizing he'd let a diminutive of her name slip out. "Hey, I'm going to leave soon," he resumed, regaining his composure. "Are you good to go, or—?"

"Don't worry. I'm going to stay. Ashat is going to take me home." Thuy pointed to one of her roommates, who happened to play kickball for another team.

"Ah-who? Uh, never mind. As long as you're good," Reggie said.

Smiling with glassy eyes and a red face, Thuy stretched out her arms and gave Reggie a warm hug. "Drive safe."

"Thanks," Reggie said.

"Are you still going to call me?" Thuy asked.

"Of course. Since we live so close, maybe we can cook together sometime."

"That sounds great! Thanks, babe!" Thuy said just as another drink was placed in her face.

Thuy and Reggie gazed at each other for a split second before Reggie made his way to the door. Prior to exiting, he glanced back one last time to see Thuy enjoying herself.

As my grandpa used to say—it's better to leave well enough alone. Reggie turned back around and left the bar.

WHOLE **PAYCHECK**

In the dark, a digital clock with blurry blue numbers can become an inebriated person's worst nightmare.

Thuy went to bed drunk and woke up multiple times in the wee hours of the morning, finally getting up at 7:11 a.m.

Ugh, I gotta get up. Thuy propped herself into a sitting position and looked at the clock. *Am I in a time warp? It was just 4:17, and now it's 7:14? I'm losing it. I still have another hour to go. I'll just close my eyes for a bit...*

When she woke up again, it was 7:41 am.

What the fuck? I gotta get going...Whoa...

Dizzily, Thuy crawled out of bed. The room seemed to spin as she opened the blinds and turned on the lights, the illumination repelling her like an extra from the movie, *Blade*.

She stumbled to the restroom and plopped down on the toilet. As a rivulet of sweet Mountain Dew flowed between her legs and into the toilet bowl, she heard a faint "ding" on her phone. After patting herself down, she looked in the mirror. Her eyes had more bags than a spinster at Bloomingdales.

I can't go to work like this. I'm gonna call in sick.

Seeing the message-indicator light blinking, she opened her phone to call her boss, but paused upon noticing a message from Reggie, checking on her wellbeing.

Ugh, he's a cool guy. Why? Why do I meet good guys at the wrong time?

Thuy bypassed deliberating on the text message, and dialed her employer. "Hey, Bill? Yeah—hey, yeah... The reviews have been completed. I'm just—hey Bill, I'm not going to make it in today. I don't feel well. Yeah, hey, it's a woman thing, okay? Okay, bye."

Thuy hung up the phone. She hated people depending on her. Great responsibility did not come with great power.

Now that I got that situation solved, I can lie back down.

Thuy closed the blinds again and turned off all the lights. After returning to bed, she replied to Reggie's text.

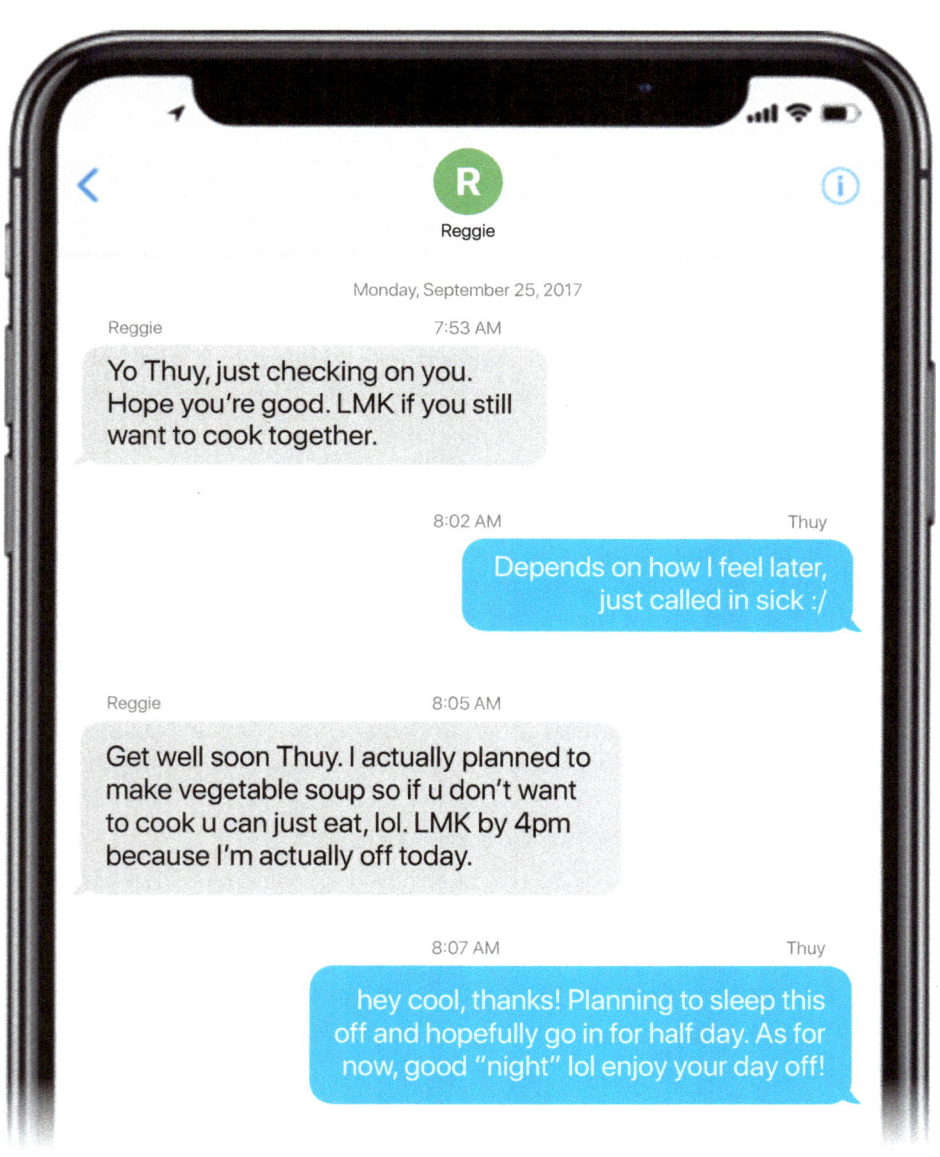

Thuy shut down her phone and drifted back to sleep. A couple hours later, her eyes creaked back open. Getting out of bed for the second time that day, she glanced around her room. She then walked into the living room, where the only sound was that of the vent fan gently whirring.

She shook her head. *I've gotta do better,* she thought to herself, determined to go into work. *Better late than never.*

Just before noon, she found herself parking outside her workplace. She looked up at the big writing that read, *Qualtech.*

With a sigh, she texted Reggie again.

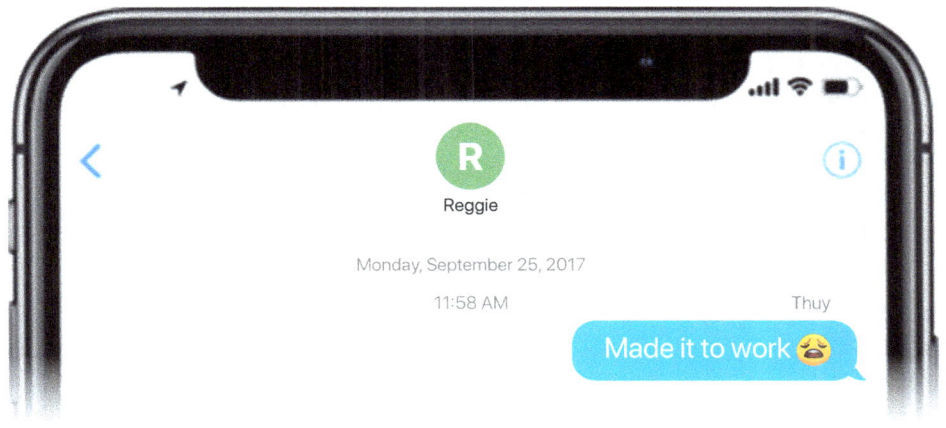

* * *

"Good morning, Miss Lieu... Well, actually, good afternoon," said one of the security guards, checking his watch.

"Ha-ha. Very funny, Russel," Thuy retorted.

"Who did you drink under the table this time?" Russel elbowed the guard beside him, and the two of them laughed at Thuy's expense.

Thuy narrowed her eyes. "Hey, how'd you—?"

"It's coming out of your pores," Russel said. "Go to the cafeteria and grab some peanuts. They'll cover the stench of alcohol and bile coming from your liver."

"Thanks for the info—and the anatomy lesson. By any chance, you got a—"

"Don't say a word. We have a whole section dedicated to you."

Russel stretched out his hand towards the lost-and-found cubby behind the security desk, featuring a small shelf full of over-the-counter medications. He picked up a bottle of Aspirin and a bottle of Dramamine, opened them, and tapped them out onto Thuy's palms. "Thanks, Russel. You're a lifesaver." Thuy popped the pills into her mouth.

After eating a miniature pack of honey-coated peanuts, Thuy headed to her locker to put on her gear—a white lab coat, goggles, and rubber gloves.

At least I won't look super tired, she thought, aware that the goggles covered a large portion of her face and obscured her eyes.

Suited up, she made her way to her workstation, giving friendly head-nods to co-workers greeting her along the way. When she reached her workstation, she noticed a pile of new folders on her desk. She turned to peer in the direction of her manager's office. Bill was watching her. Nervously, he waved.

Thuy abruptly turned back around, an annoyed scowl involuntarily slipping onto her face. *Great, just great*, she thought. *When nobody's looking, they dump their work on me. They must think I'm from a sweat shop or something.*

She moved through her tasks, sipping green tea, popping Aspirin, and gradually feeling more efficient. As her mood improved, she fell into a rhythm with her work, jamming to the music in her earphones until movement in her periphery shocked the bejesus out of her.

"Fu—" she sputtered before catching herself and realizing Bill was trying to get her attention. She removed one of her earbuds.

"I didn't mean to scare you, Thuy, I—"

"The road to hell is paved with good intentions, Bill. What can I do for you?"

"Jeez, Thuy. I—listen, I didn't expect you to be in today. I thought you were calling in sick?"

"Change of heart, Bill. Change of heart."

"Listen, I know that—" Bill paused to look at one of the group pictures Thuy had taken with her past kickball team. I know you're a passionate team player, but I get concerned about you when fall comes around and your extracurricular activities dampen your work performance."

Thuy slammed down her beaker. The hollow noise caused several people nearby to glance their way. Thuy stood and looked Bill in the eye. "Have I ever missed a deadline?"

"That's not the point, Thuy—"

"Then what's the point? See those awards over there?" She pointed to her certificates and accolades. "I didn't get those by not doing my work properly. And guess what? Still...no...promotion!"

"Thuy, the next level for you would be in a supervisory role. And in order to fill it, you'd have to lead by example. Absenteeism isn't—"

"Absentee? *Absentee*? Oh, would you call it absenteeism if I would've gone out to dinner with you when you asked me two months ago? What would your wife have said about your extracurricular activity if she found out that you hit on your subordinates?"

"Whoa, Thuy, keep it down! I was just saying—"

"You weren't saying much of anything, Bill. I'm tired of being your scapegoat. Yeah, I went to happy hour Sunday afternoon and stayed well into the evening. So fucking what! Who else are you going to give all the work your other non-efficient employees can't do?"

Bill stood silently, glaring at Thuy.

"I should have fucking stayed home," Thuy spat. "You know what? I'll take my sick day off. So much for your gratitude." She ripped her awards and certificates from the wall and threw them in the wastebasket.

"Geez, Thuy, I was just--"

"Bill, leave me alone." Thuy powered down her computer, grabbed her keys, and left her workstation behind.

"Leaving so soon? You just got here," Russel said as Thuy passed by in a rage.

Without replying, she bolted out the door and headed for the parking lot. Once inside her car, she opened her phone and texted:

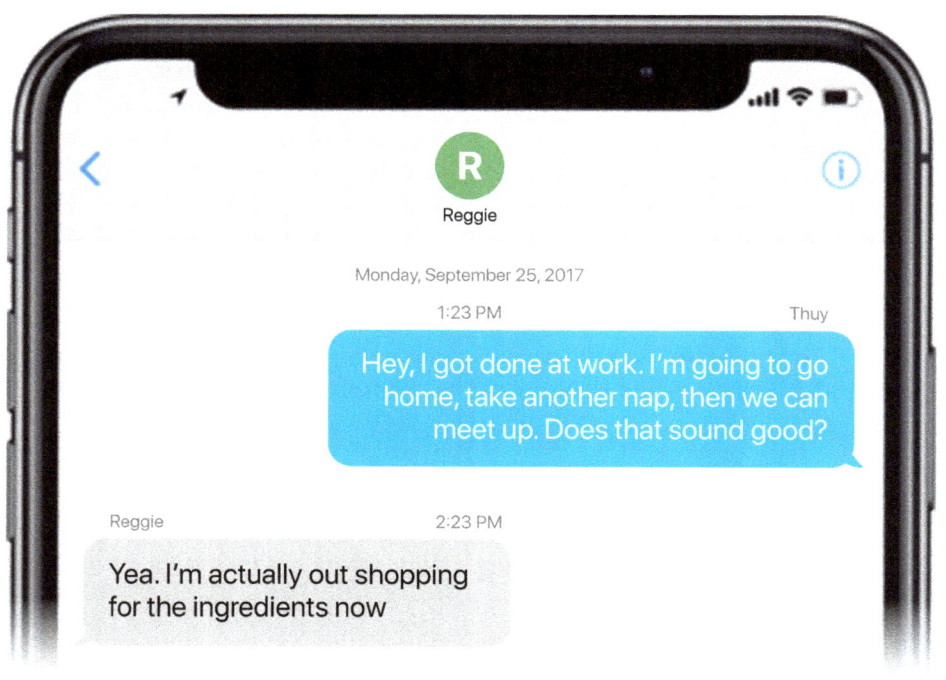

* * *

"Better than Bouillon, organic, reduced sodium, seasoned vegetable base. Grandma would be proud of me," Reggie said aloud as he picked up a glass jar of seasoning. He placed the jar in his mini cart, and continued strolling the isles of Whole Foods.

His brother, Winston—who loved to wear Air Jordans, fitted baseball caps, and diamond encrusted Russell Simmons chains—used to poke fun at Reggie for shopping here, making exaggerated claims like, *"Whole Foods' apples cost five dollars a pop."* Reggie made it a point not to argue with Winston, but noted that life was all about preferences.

From Reggie's point-of-view, the common negro was more concerned about what he put *on* his body than what he put *in* his body. Winston preferred to spend his whole paycheck on Air Jordan shoes that cost over $100, while Reggie wore simple hiking shoes made by Keen that cost $60. Hence, the $40 saved could supplement his expensive food habit.

I love shopping mid-day on my day off, Reggie mused as he returned a smile to a well-endowed soccer-mom passing by. *People shop where they are best characterized. If you want big girls, shop at Giant. If you want Wholesome ones, shop at Whole Foods.*

Reggie laughed to himself, imagining his lactose intolerant ass might be able to squeeze almond milk from the buxom beauty's natural knockers.

No time to harass upper middle-class moms now though. I got to get the best ingredients for the soup so I can motivate shorty to come over more often. Mental note—shop Whole Foods on Monday, around two p.m. if things don't work out.

After picking up the rest of the items he needed from the isles he trolled, he surveyed the inventory in his cart.

"All organic vegetables. Garnet sweet potatoes, cilantro, garlic cloves, celery, beets with tops, chives, green pepper, Chinese cabbage, quinoa, Chilean sea bass, niacin, protein powder, soup base, extra virgin olive oil... What am I missing?" Reggie peered down at the bottom part of his mini cart, where two empty glass gallon jugs resided. "Reverse osmosis purified water!"

After getting his water and going to the checkout counter to ring up the items, he looked at the cash register total. *One seventy-five nineteen! This definitely could be someone's whole paycheck.*

* * *

Standing at his kitchen countertop, Reggie washed the organic fruits and vegetables he'd purchased, and sliced them into the appropriate portion sizes for soup. In the middle of dicing green peppers, his phone chirped with a message from Thuy. Wiping his hands on a dish towel, Reggie slid his phone closer to him and opened her text.

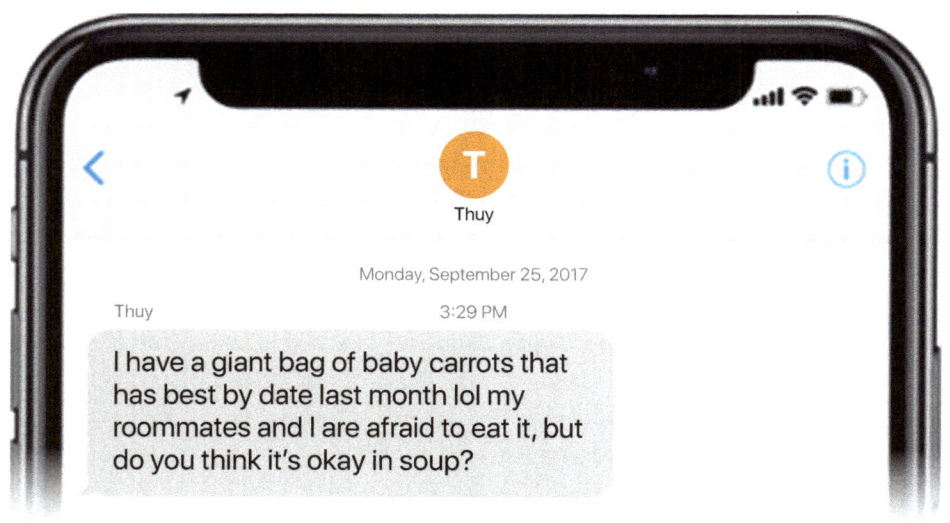

I wonder if her carrots are organic? Reggie thought. *If she's not sure about the 'best by' date, I don't want to add that shit to my pristine mix... I'll prepare the sweet potatoes just in case the carrots look unappetizing.*

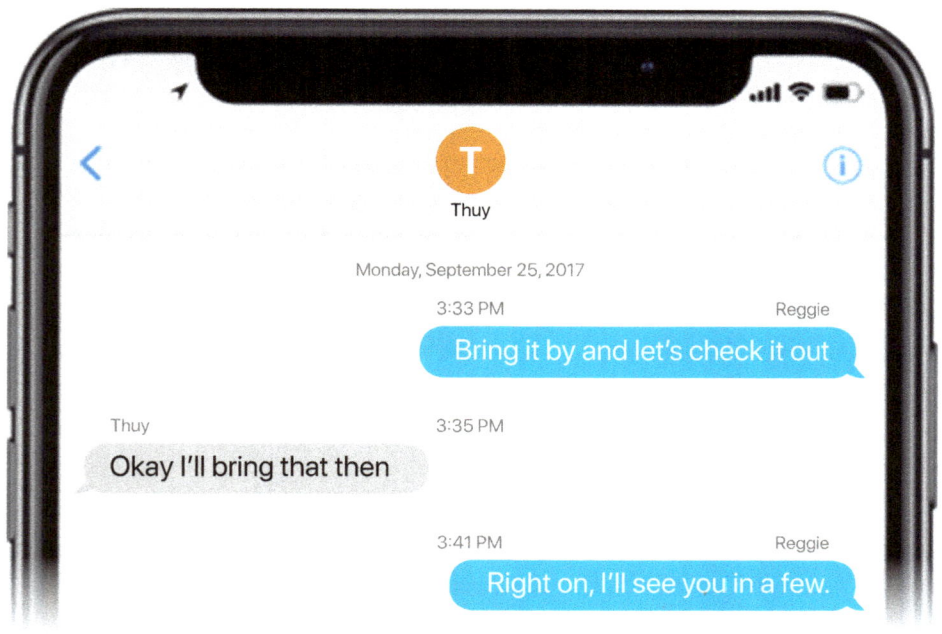

Reggie looked over the ingredients spread across his countertop. For his soups, he balanced the astringent flavor of celery with something sweet, like carrots or sweet potatoes. Carrots and sweet potatoes had a similar flavor due to their natural sugar content and carotene. But not wanting to be prude, Reggie wished he could more easily accept Thuy's offer; he wanted to encourage her to cook with him. Yet, he had reservations about the quality of the food she was going to introduce to the soup.

Reggie took out and plugged in his rice cooker/steamer combo. Dicing some garlic and adding olive oil and spices, he got a little *sofrito* going before slowly adding quinoa and water. Then he added cubed sweet potatoes to the sieve-bearing upper portion of the device. Before placing the sieve back over the boiling quinoa, he used his rice paddle to give the quinoa a good stir. Adding some of the cilantro to the spice mix, the soup's pleasant aroma began filling the kitchen. Once the upper level was situated over the quinoa, he put the top on to seal in the steam.

I'm locking the flavor in on your ass. Just in case Thuy's carrots are no good, I'll throw you in the soup and you won't need to take so long to soften.

Reggie started his soup base similarly to the quinoa, but added diced celery tops, cilantro, onion, and green pepper. He'd heard somewhere that celery tops were astringent, and that their flavor was much stronger than the stalk, which got bitter at the end. Reggie cut off the celery tops and part of the bottom. The bottom, he used for boiling in the general soup.

As he alternated between stirring the simmering soup pot and the quinoa, he threw in some chopped Chinese broccoli, celery bottoms, and beet tops.

"Looking good, looking good," he said, admiring his work.

He took a moment to check his phone, seeing that he'd gotten another message from Thuy. She was on the way, leaving her apartment.

Reggie turned everything down to a simmer and walked out to the street to intercept her. They greeted each other with a hug.

"I've always wondered what the inside of these apartment complexes looked like...The Overture," Thuy said, looking up at the big yellow-lit signs spelling out the name of the apartment building.

"Yes. The Overture," Reggie replied.

"The name sounds cool. I wonder what it means."

"I think it has something to do with music." Reggie used his electronic key fob to open the door for Thuy. They got in the elevator, and Thuy started to wiggle her nose like a bunny rabbit sniffing out a head of cabbage.

"Yeah, I know," Reggie said as the elevator hummed in the background. "The smell of cleaning supplies trying to mask the ammonia in dog urine only makes the smell worse. In fact, I wouldn't be surprised if the two chemicals bonded together to form a third chemical."

"You'd think at such an expensive place, people would have the decency to get their dogs out in time so that they don't use the elevator as a piss pad."

Reggie laughed and gave Thuy a high five.

Moments later, when they crossed the threshold of Reggie's apartment door, the aroma wafted.

"Wow! It feels like I just walked into a restaurant!" Thuy said.

"I'll consider that a compliment." Reggie walked over to put the steamed sweet potatoes into their own bowl. He then eyed the bag Thuy brought. "Let's see what you've got there."

He picked up the bag and pulled out the carrots. Turning them about in his hands, he noticed that towards the middle and bottom of the bag, the carrots appeared to be liquifying. At the very bottom, they were mushy and an off-white liquid had accumulated under them. He glanced up at Thuy. "Looks like someone beat us to the party. Here, take a look. The bacteria has already started breaking down the sugars in the carrots, producing this liquid. Not all of the carrots are bad though. The ones at the top don't have this mushiness."

Reggie grabbed two carrots, one affected and the other unaffected, and held them out to Thuy. "Here, take a feel."

"Yeah, I can definitely feel the difference. One of them feels normal, and the other feels slimy."

"Exactamundo. I also don't want to do anything to worsen your stomach, so I'm going to use sweet potatoes instead of carrots. Then later, I'll sort through the carrots to salvage the good guys from the bad bunch. Cool?"

Thuy nodded. "Sounds like a plan."

Reggie put the bag of carrots into the refrigerator, and then finished making the soup.

* * *

"Wow." Thuy stared into her empty bowl. "This was a really great meal, Reggie. It was light, but filling."

"Thanks, Thuy. You know there's plenty more. By the way, I know all about hangover soups, like congee and pho."

"Yeah, that's kind of like the big debate amongst Asian folks."

"What debate is that?"

"Which one is better for hangovers."

"Interesting. In my experience, congee is super simple and light, but pho has more going on with it, like the clippings of all the plant matter that need to be put in."

"True, but you can also get the soup broth and just noodles without all of the other stuff."

"I think congee is like what you feed starving kids in third world nations who haven't eaten a substantial meal in a long time—to avoid them eating themselves to death. Remember those commercials of the kids in Africa eating bowls of porridge?"

"Oh yeah! I get your point. Like, it's the kind of food you could feed someone who was incapacitated—"

"Or on their death bed," Reggie interrupted.

They both laughed.

Reggie wanted to give a couple more points to Thuy's culture by poking a little fun at Chinese cuisine. The irony was that Thuy and people like her were descended from Chinese people who'd migrated to Vietnam thousands of years ago.

Reggie and Thuy were still joking when the latch to Todd's door popped.

Aww shit, here comes this nigga. I hope he has some clothes on. Reggie looked behind where Thuy sat and watched the door handle turn.

Todd poked his head out of his room. Seeing the coast was clear, he slowly emerged into the living room area. "Yooo, how goes it?" he said, greeting Thuy and Reggie.

Whew, that nigga is presentable, Reggie thought, relieved. "Hey, Todd. Hope we didn't wake you. It's only, you know, about five p.m.," Reggie said, taking a little dig at Todd for being a day-sleeper. He never knew what Todd was up to, or his whereabouts. He didn't even know when Todd went in to work. Regardless, Todd was a good guy.

"Whoa. Touché," Todd retorted.

"Just kidding, man. Hey, I'd like to introduce you to Thuy."

"Hi, Thuy," Todd said.

"Hey, dude!" she replied.

Yes! She called Todd 'dude'! Reggie thought.

Todd went to give Reggie five, but Reggie put up his fist instead, simultaneously looking at Thuy to suggest she also opted for a fist bump should Todd offer a high-five or handshake.

Like clockwork, Todd turned to Thuy for a fist bump, which she reciprocated.

"Smells good in here," Todd said.

"Help yourself to some soup and quinoa. Oh, and by the way, there's some baby carrots in the fridge if you want to snack on something."

"Cool beans. Thanks." Todd opened the refrigerator to see the baby carrots sitting in their lonesome.

Thuy looked at Reggie, and Reggie grinned. The inside joke was theirs to share.

TURTLE **BACK**

I'*ll take a quick shower, and it should be ready before I hit the road,* Reggie thought as he heated some water for his tea. He opened the kitchen cabinet, but his favorite to-go cup wasn't there. Frowning, he searched the cabinet more thoroughly before suddenly remembering it had been Todd's turn to load and run the dishwasher.

Reggie peered into the front of the dishwasher. The indicator magnet that read "clean/dirty" had the "clean" indicator facing right-side up.

He must've forgot to put the dishes away. Dis nigga... Reggie thought as he opened the dishwasher. Spotting his cup, he grabbed it, along with a spoon. The items were dirty—the cup having remnants of turmeric and haritaki powder inside of it; the spoon was smeared with what appeared to be an oil-based sauce, and smear lines that ran vertically along the inside and outside of the spoon. Reggie cringed as he envisioned Todd licking the spoon like a popsicle.

Setting the cup and spoon down, he proceeded to inspected other silverware and dishes. Some were clean, while others were still dirty.

I told that jackass not to mix the clean and dirty dishes—that's why I bought the indicator. Now we have to waste energy and water to rewash all the dishes. His lazy ass don't even have the wherewithal to check to see if dishes are clean. It's almost like he licks the spoon clean or something. Frat-boy acting muthafucka.

Reggie washed his cup and the spoon with hot soapy water, got his tea mixture and erythritol ready, and took a shower. Once ready for work, he mixed his tea and sweetener, then retrieved his lunch from the fridge. He eyed the baby carrots he'd rejected from the soup and scoffed. Pulling his phone from his back pocket, he sent a text message to Todd, who he presumed was still sleeping.

Tuesday, September 26, 2017

6:40 AM   Reggie

> Todd, some of the dishes /silverware you put away were still dirty/had food on them or not fully clean. I also noticed that you don't flip the "clean/dirty" magnet back over once you've emptied the dishwasher. This may be the cause for the dirty silverware and or dishes being placed back in "general population" with others. Please try better to flip over the magnet to indicate whether the dishes are dirty/clean and also to ensure that the dishes are fully clean before putting them away. Thanks.

7:36 AM   Reggie

> BTW, help yourself to the baby carrots bro.

7:37 AM   Reggie

> Do you know where the bottle of olive oil is? Also do you have some of the plastic containers in your room?

Fuck it. It's boiled water. That'll kill any germs, Reggie thought, tired of worrying about dirty dishes. He transferred his tea from the cup to his Yeti thermos and bolted out the door.

* * *

After beating the gridlock and knocking out his morning tasks, Reggie opened the cabinet beside his work desk and peeked inside. The blue light of anticipation blinked on his phone.

Might be Thuy... He took a second to collect himself, swallowing the saliva that had gathered in his mouth. Then, grabbing his phone and swiping to activate it, he saw that he'd been mistaken.

The message was from Todd.

TW

Todd Wilson

Tuesday, September 26, 2017

Todd Wilson   10:35 AM

No luck on the olive oil, and I don't have any plastic containers in my room - also, yeah, some of the dishes weren't clean coming out of the wash, I had put most of them back in or handwashed, but it sounds like some got thru

10:42 AM   Reggie

Cool. FYI, we doing a BBQ for my stepdad soon, I forgot the exact date, but probably next week or the week after, and you're welcome to attend. I'm gonna do the ribs.

Reggie returned his phone to the cabinet, content with his interaction with Todd. Feeling restless from sitting at his desk though, he decided he could use some fresh air. He stood and took a stretch, then headed over to Khalil's office.

Khalil's door was open, but Reggie knocked anyway, exercising office-etiquette, especially since Khalil was such a paranoid person to begin with. Being a subcontractor, Khalil believed every little thing he did was liable to be scrutinized. He often spoke of how easy it was to get rid of subcontractors—hence him staying low-key like a midget's doorknob.

Responding to the knock, Khalil swiveled in his office chair to face Reggie. The chair squeaked like a tortured mouse.

"Sounds like you could use a little WD40," Reggie said.

"Yeah, they give us the old, decommissioned chairs," Khalil replied. "But what can I say? As long as that red envelope keeps coming every week, I'm good."

"Hey man, you want go out and do a couple of laps around the lake?"

"I can't right now, I got some documents to verify. But how about we hit the gym around lunchtime?" Khalil offered.

"Okay, that's cool. Go ahead and shoot me a text when you're ready," Reggie said.

"Right on."

Reggie and Khalil dapped each other up, and Reggie turned to leave.

Back at his desk, Reggie turned on his smartphone's ringer, anticipating Khalil's text. Sometime later, he heard the phone's "ding" sound.

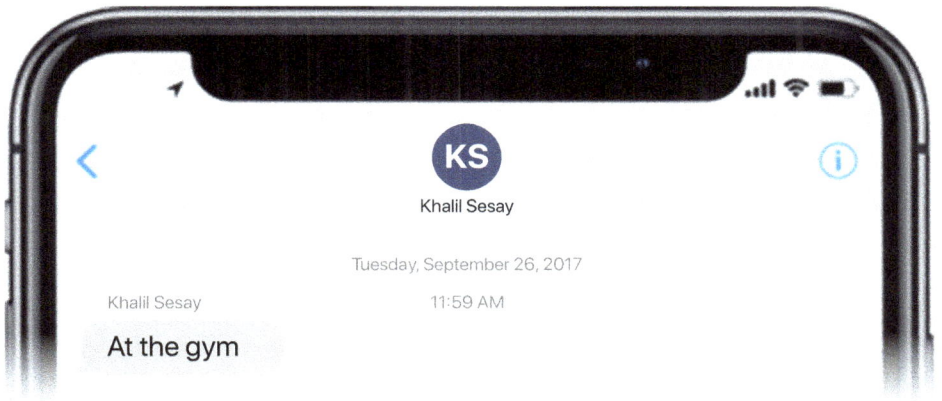

* * *

Wilhelm Properties houses many different leased governmental and contracting offices, including a workout facility. The gym was a mix between a personal training studio and an upscale gym like one would find at a Marriot Bonvoy hotel. It contained a cross-cable functional fitness trainer, several medicine balls of weight ranging from two to twenty pounds, a hexagonal dumbbell weight rack that went from five to fifty pounds, and two weight benches. The gym also bragged three 72-inch plasma flatscreens on the wall, which hovered in front of four state-of-the art treadmills. Behind the treadmills were two Octane fitness brand ellipticals that had an iso-kinetic MMA program for high-intensity interval training—Reggie's favorite.

Still wearing their work clothes, Reggie and Khalil settled for placing their unbuttoned collared shirts on a nearby hamstring curl/leg extension machine, Khalil opting to work out in his undershirt and Reggie in his tank top.

Reggie looked at the pullup bar on the functional trainer, with its groves in the close and wide-grip positions. He glanced at Khalil. "You ready to do this?"

"I'm ready."

"You ready to work?"

"Let's get it."

"All right, you know the deal. We hit the first two sets close-grip, and the last one wide-grip."

Reggie jumped up to grab the pullup bar and began his reps. After he reached ten pullups, he hopped down, and Khalil hopped up. "You gotta come all the way down, Khalil. Full range of motion," Reggie instructed upon noticing Khalil doing half-pullups.

Khalil corrected his range of motion. Being slightly pot-bellied and taller than Reggie, the pullups took more effort for him. For this reason, Reggie typically started their "midday pump" workouts with what he considered the hardest exercise.

Khalil finished his set of ten, then Reggie got on the bar and barely finished his ten. Next, Khalil got on the bar and started to struggle at six.

"Here, I'll spot you, man!" Reggie said, pushing Khalil's mid-torso up to give assistance.

"Grrrrahhhh!" Khalil grunted as he made it through his last few reps.

"Let's rest a little before doing the wide-grip," Reggie said when Khalil hopped down from the pullup bar. Pulling from his background in personal fitness training, Reggie thought over the next portion of their workout. Advice on exercise routines was something he was accustomed to giving his coworkers. "Soleus stretches. Great for range of motion in the knees and ankles. It's like a staggered-stance, bent-knee calf stretch. Have you ever seen those Kung Fu and Tai Chi masters in a cat stance with the back leg knees over toes?"

Breathlessly, Khalil nodded.

Reggie demonstrated the stretch, and Khalil soon followed suit.

"Now try to squat," Reggie said.

Khalil began to squat. As he got close to parallel, his suspicion kicked in. But determined to trust himself, he squatted a little lower, surprised by how far down he managed to go. "Wow... Even after sitting down a lot, this stretch really opens up my knees, man. Thanks!"

"Don't mention it," Reggie said as he hopped back up with a wide grip.

Both Reggie and Khalil got to eight on the wide-grip, then went to do bent-over dumbbell rows, and reverse dumbbell flies—all pyramiding the weight from lighter-weight-higher rep, to heavier-weight-lower rep. By the time they were done, they'd broken a little sweat.

They looked at the giant mirrors in front of them. Reggie stuck both his hands out parallel to the floor and observed his dorsal muscles from the front. "This workout'll give you that 'cobra backed' look. Balancing the latissimus causes anterior shoulder rotation with rear deltoid and rhomboid work, which engages the posterior chain—"

"In English, boss," Khalil requested.

"Khalil, assume you had no gym equipment and were working bodyweight training. What workout would you do to balance or counteract a pushup?"

"A pullup?"

"That's what most people think. But the opposite of a pullup is a handstand pushup. The opposite of a pushup is a row. And the only way you're going to counteract by rowing is if you have a bar that's above you—say, like parallel bars at a playground—where you can actually get up under the bar and pull yourself horizontally. The mistake a lot of people make is doing tons of pushups and pullups. Eventually, they start to slouch forward because both pushups and pullups cause anterior, or forward rotation of the shoulder. This gives a 'turtle back' appearance."

"Like Mark Wahlberg in *Invincible*?"

"Exactly."

Khalil started to walk toward the door to get his shirt.

"There's one more thing we got to knock out to make the posterior chain—er, back workout—complete," Reggie said. "Well, that's if you have a couple more minutes to spare…"

"What is it?" Khalil asked, pausing before putting on his shirt.

"You're favorite—rotator cuff cable workout."

"Fuck! Those burn like a muthafucka."

"I know." Reggie smiled. "Do them now and protect your shoulders from injury later."

* * *

Reinvigorated from the workout, Reggie returned to work with Khalil, where he made it through his tasks and later texted Thuy to follow up on their next date. Reggie was surprised at the promptness of Thuy's response.

* * *

The following day saw Reggie eagerly anticipating his date with Thuy. The hours slugged by, and approximately an hour and a half before "quittin' time", Reggie noticed his phone blinking with a new text.

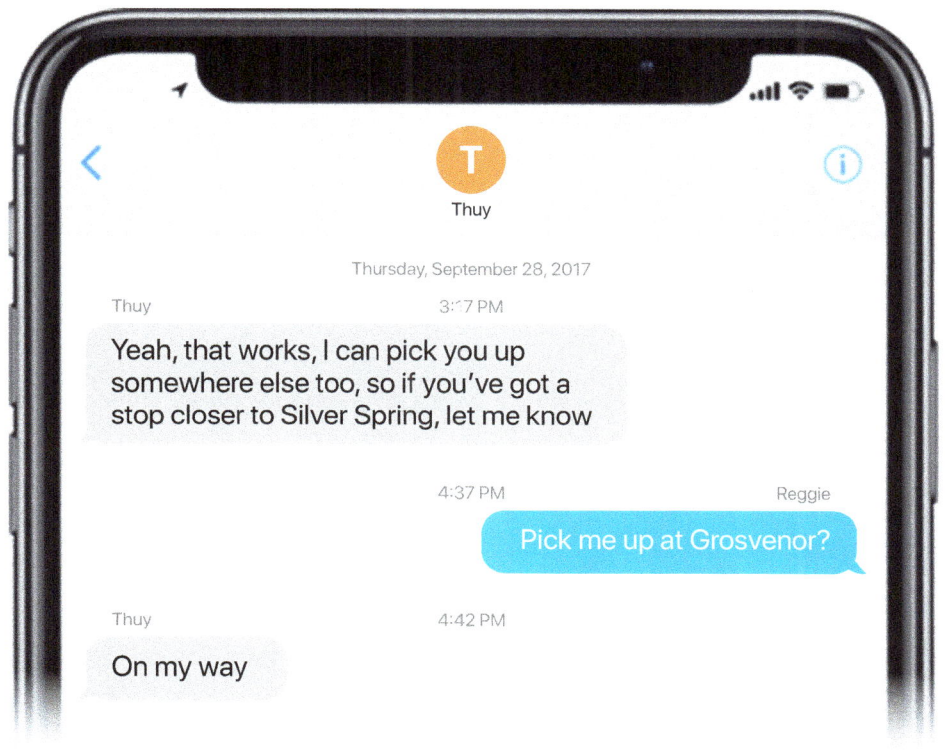

While the metro system in the Washington D.C. area is simple, the stations themselves are often complex. The two most important things people typically want to know is where to park, and where to pick up/drop off. Yet, this is rendered complicated by the many parking signs pertaining to parking spaces that only appear adjacent—creating conflicting messages about the availability of those spaces.

For example, one parking sign might read: *No parking from 7:00 AM to 9:00 AM and 5:00 PM to 7:00 PM*, while another could read: *Hourly parking from 5:00 AM to 7:00 PM*. The first sign targets people not traveling to or through D.C. for work, but rather those who are simply running errands, handling business, or possibly going to the zoo. Hence, those spaces need to be kept available for those being picked up or dropped off from work during rush hour. In contrast, the second sign targets those parking their own cars during rush hour, with the intent of returning to them after work.

Reggie waited in the overhang shelter at the roundabout driveway with other commuters. He'd always found it interesting to watch different people getting picked up, wondering who their travel companions were and what their lives were like. In the process of observing a seemingly "odd" couple, Thuy's light blue sedan swung around the driveway entrance and pulled up within a few paces of the "Kiss and Ride" sign.

I wonder if she's going to give me a kiss? Reggie thought, and then laughed to himself upon seeing Thuy looking super nerdy through her windshield. As Reggie made his way to her car, he noticed an onlooker who seemed interested in his affairs.

"Hey! Did you wait long?" Thuy asked, brushing her hair to the side of her ear.

"I'm good. I actually just got here five minutes ago, so you have perfect timing. How was your day?" Reggie said as he buckled his seatbelt. The onlooker, an older Asian man, followed Reggie with his eyes. When Thuy pulled off, Reggie briefly locked eyes with the man and flashed him a smile. The man hastily averted his gaze.

"What's wrong?" Thuy asked, noticing Reggie was distracted.

"Naw, just people are funny, that's all. So, where's this place? I haven't had Ethiopian food since I was at an Eritrean wedding seven years ago."

"A tree was in where?"

"Huh?"

"You said a tree was in a wedding. Was it in the wedding photo or something?"

"Ohhh—I said *Eritrean*. Eritrea is a country that gained its independence out of Ethiopia. It's technically the only African nation that's never been colonized. Despite being a different nationality, Eritreans and Ethiopians share similar language and cuisine—kind of like Thailanders and Laotians."

Thuy playfully slapped Reggie's thigh. "You see? You learn something new every day. That's why I like hanging with you, Reggie. You're super knowledgeable."

Reggie stared at Thuy's hand after it slapped his thigh.

Realizing what she'd done, Thuy recoiled.

"Don't worry. I'm not going to sue you for assault or sexual harassment," Reggie joked.

Thuy laughed, and Reggie joined in. Seconds later, Thuy turned on her radio just as the announcer was talking politics.

"The news..." Reggie shook his head. "There's nothing on the news but bad news."

"You're right. Let's find something light." Thuy changed the dial and a song came on.

From that moment forward, that song was forever lodged in Reggie's brain. That song embodied the post-modern sentiment that average men felt dealing with modern women—women who received so much validation from social media that one guy was no longer enough. That song—the crooning, the pleading, the wailing—was Charlie Puth's, "Attention".

Since Reggie didn't listen to the radio or mainstream media often, the song rocked him to the core. The deep synth rhythms put the listener *"in every party in L.A.,"* just like Charlie mentioned in the first verse. Furthermore, subject matter hit home. Women were now at an advantage in the mating arena, and there was nothing men could do but endure, or choose not play the game.

Beside Reggie, Thuy drove with her hands on the steering wheel ten-two, her round head and small eyes behind glasses with black frames like Bunson from *Muppet Babies*. Some people listened to songs, while others listened to lyrics. In Thuy's case, perhaps she just didn't consciously understand the subject matter. Maybe she was desensitized to it. Or maybe she only subconsciously absorbed the meaning of the song.

In stark contrast, Reggie was listening so intently that his mouth hung partially open and was in danger of catching flies. He occasionally glanced over at Thuy, wondering if she was hearing what he was hearing. But she just kept her gaze on the road, only sporadically turning to smile at Reggie.

This guy is looking at me like he lost a dog or something, Thuy thought.

"What?" she said after a moment, unable to understand his staring. "I thought you wanted to listen to something light?"

"Do you like hip-hop?" Reggie asked.

"It's okay."

"How about rock?"

"I love rock music!"

Reggie smiled and turned the station to DC 101.1. The song "Solid Ground" by the Red Hot Chili Peppers started playing.

"Wait, is that the song I think it is?" Reggie listened to the base guitar's opening riff as he fumbled with the bass and treble controls on Thuy's radio.

Thuy hunched her little shoulders. "Iono."

The drums and electric guitar kicked it.

"Yes, it is!" Reggie said. "This song is played during cinematic action in so many action movies, like *The Longest Yard*. I love this song! Do you know who it's by?"

"RHCP, I think," Thuy replied.

"RHCP?"

"The Red Hot Chili Peppers. I saw them once in a dive bar in Santa Anita. They're a California based band."

"That's dope." Reggie put up the devil's horns hand symbol. "Rock on!"

Thuy giggled, and then they both began bobbing their head to the music as they made their way through traffic.

I ALWAYS **PAY**

The consciousness of no and low-carb yuppies expands into "diversity and inclusion" by identifying traditional ethnic cuisines that fit the mold of a particular dieting fad. Another unintentional victim to this was the pseudo grain, *teff*. Teff, a poppy-seed sized grain abundant in Ethiopia and Eritrea, rose in popularity thanks to its sugar free status, and the fact that it has a low carb-to-protein ratio. As a result, left-wing, low-carb beatniks everywhere can eat healthy and virtue signal as they use their high discretionary incomes to enjoy fine dining while simultaneously serving an underprivileged community. *Injera*—a flat, spongy bread made from fermented teff—is best described as a "sourdough pancake". Ethiopians eat injera with everything, like Mexicans with tortillas and East Indians with roti.

Thuy used her injera bread to scoop up a healthy hunk of raw ground beef and minced collard greens. The sound of ground muscle tissue pressing against mucus grazed Reggie's ears, reminding him on the noises created when making hamburger or sausage patties. He watched as Thuy scooped this mixture into the fold of the bread. Just before closing it, she added a clove of garlic.

"What can I say? I love garlic," she said, noticing Reggie watching her munch on the mixture.

"Are you sure this is safe to eat?" Reggie looked down at the many striations in the muscle fiber of what once used to graze the field.

Thuy finished chewing. "Dude, I've been eating this since I got to D.C. and I absolutely love it. Eat it with garlic. Garlic is a natural anti-microbial."

"I guess I should take your advice because you do quality control for a drug company, huh?"

"Stop being a chicken and give it a shot."

"Chicken sounds nice right about now," Reggie said, earning himself an eye-roll from Thuy. "All right, here goes." He placed the combination of ground beef and vegetables into his mouth, and then noted the flavors on his tongue. "Mmm... This is pretty damn good! What's this called?"

"You, see?" Thuy said proudly. "I told you. It's called *kitfo,* and it's to die for." Thuy took what appeared to be an Erlenmeyer flask filled with a yellow fluid and poured the liquid into the two glasses in front of her and Reggie. "A toast! To cool dudes and friendship."

I wish she'd stop calling me that, Reggie said to himself. He looked at his glass. "You want to toast to orange juice? In the evening time?"

"It's not orange juice, silly. It's *tej,* an Ethiopian honey wine."

"Oh really?"

"Are you going to leave me hanging, or are you going to drink?" Thuy extended her arm and raised her glass.

Reggie smiled and raised his glass. "I'm just testing your shoulder endurance... Cheers!"

They clinked glasses and drank.

"Damn, this is pretty good too. Thanks, Thuy. I'm perplexed by how you know so much about African cultures... Did you take classes in college?"

"When I first came to this area, I started hanging out with a girl from Kenya. She took me around to different places and introduced me to different foods, and I fell in love with Ethiopian kitfo."

"That's pretty cool. What else did you learn from her?" Reggie took another sip of wine, and Thuy did the same.

"If I tell you something, promise not to get offended?" Thuy prefaced.

"Thuy, I am one of the hardest people to offend." Reggie continued in a Samuel L. Jackson-esque voice, "I dare you—I double dog dare you—to try to offend me. Speak your mind."

"Okay, here goes..." Thuy took a deep breath. "She told me—or advised me, rather—about dating black guys."

Reggie laughed mid-sip, almost spitting out his wine. Thuy was new to the east coast, where there was plenty of diversity among Blacks— not just American, but from other places as well. Consequently, he suspected Thuy must have been an easy target to indoctrinate.

This is going to be good. "Okay, I'll bite. What'd she tell you?" Reggie asked with an amused smirk.

Thuy raised an eyebrow. "You *promise* not to get offended?"

"Hold on. Before you tell me, hold that thought. Put a pin in it." Reggie motioned for the server to bring more honey wine. Then he raised his glass and clinked it with Thuy's again. Finally, he took the rest of his wine to the head. "Bottoms up," he said as the once half-full glass was empty.

"Whoa, whoa, I'd take it easy on that," Thuy warned.

"Why? Did she tell you black guys were alcoholics?"

A quizzical look formed on Thuy's face.

"Just kidding. I would really like to hear her opinion," Reggie said just as the waiter returned with another flask.

Thuy took a gulp of her wine and then steadied herself with another deep breath. "So... she said that I should *try* black guys, but not take them seriously."

Reggie let out a guffaw that caught the attention of their surrounding diners.

Thuy shifted uneasily in her seat.

Sensing the sudden awkwardness, Reggie lowered his voice to a whisper. "You mean to tell me a woman from Africa told you to get your pipes cleaned by a black guy, but not bring him home to momma?"

"Pipes cleaned?" Thuy titled her head in confusion.

Reggie made the motion of using his right hand's pointer finger going in and out of a circle created by his left hand's pointer finger and thumb.

"Oh..." Thuy said. "Pretty much."

"Well, I'm not offended by that. One must also consider the source though."

"I don't understand."

"Have you ever dated a black guy before?"

"No."

Thank God, Reggie thought in relief. He hoped to be the first to stake his claim and leave an impression. Good thing that her "slot-c" a la Terrance Popp fame may not have been completely blown out.

"Imagine this," he said. "We both live in France, and I've never dated a French-born Vietnamese girl. Then I make friends with a Korean guy who says you shouldn't take Vietnamese French women seriously, only—" Reggie made the in-and-out motion symbolizing sex again. "Don't you think that information could be somewhat lopsided? While Koreans and Vietnamese are both Asian, that doesn't necessarily make the Korean man a trusted source for all things Vietnamese, especially in terms of women."

"Good point. I didn't think about it like that. But in real life, I'm not into Asian guys."

Oh, you're one of those... Reggie decided not to ask why. He knew the trend of Asian women and white guys was pretty much a regular thing now. "The same rationale applies to a black Kenyan woman, and black men from America—in America. Since you don't have a black American female friend—" *Also, thank God for that,* "You don't have someone close enough to the source to give you somewhat reliable anecdotal data."

"But since Koreans are also Asian, the Korean guy could use his experiences with other Koreans to guess how Vietnamese women would act," Thuy countered.

"In theory, yes—especially if the woman in question was born in Vietnam. But the Korean guy has three things working against his assumption. One, the disparity between Koreans and Vietnamese *within* the Asian culture. Two, the difference between Korean culture and French culture. And three, synergistic differences that occur between the junction of a French person whose family generations past are Vietnamese."

"So you're saying my Kenyan friend is not accurate—not just because she's not American, but because black people in America aren't Kenyan?"

"Pretty much. And not to go too deep down the rabbit hole like David Carroll, but Africa is not just one big, happy continent where all people are dark-skinned, hold hands, and sing kumbaya."

Thuy burst of laughter escaped Thuy's throat.

"But," Reggie lifted his pointer finger in the air like Sherlock Holmes getting a clue, "that's not to say her observations regarding Black Americans are unfounded. In all honesty, I can't say she's one-hundred percent wrong for trying to protect you. It's just that you have to consider the source and the motivation for *why* she would want to tell you that—under the auspices that she considers herself Black."

The gender war will not be televised.

Reggie paused for a moment, and then decided it best to keep the topic on the current ethnic dialogue, where he and Thuy could hash out their differences rather than go into the gender piece— a piece that would likely deny Reggie a piece of ass. He would, however, continue taking his daily dose of red pills, as prescribed by Sandman. "There's one thing I want to touch upon, Thuy."

"What's that?"

"Well, it's more like a confession…"

"A confession, already?" Thuy smirked. "Ooh, this must be good."

"Don't block off your calendar just yet. I just want to speak on something that happened earlier in the day."

"What?"

"Remember you caught me looking distracted after you picked me up? Well, I had locked eyes with an Asian guy who'd been watching me get into your car."

"You 'locked eyes' with him," Thuy said, a hint of teasing in her voice. "What? Did you think he was attractive or something?" She giggled at her own joke, the buzz from the wine making her cheeks rosy like the kids on boxes of Christmas cookies.

"Ha-ha, very funny," Reggie retorted. "I just think it's interesting because you know, most Asian women—"

"Aren't going out with Asian guys? Yeah, I know. It's kind of—well, I dunno… It's a thing. I guess I should, right? But it's like… I dunno." She shrugged. "I just have my likes and dislikes."

"Well, one—I wasn't going to say that. I was going to say, most Asian women go out with white guys. And two, it may be your thing, but it seems to be an overall trend. I felt like the guy was looking at me like I was doing something wrong."

"Guys like that get on my nerves. It's like they think they own us or something."

Reggie opened his mouth, but then closed it. He was aware of the unfair, unidimensional portrayals of Asian men in media, but decided to not cape for them at the moment, lest he work against himself. The topic could be revisited at a more advantageous time. "I can dig it." Reggie lifted his glass to clink with Thuy's.

"To doing your own thing," she said.

"To doing your own thing," Reggie echoed.

After another clink of their glasses, they continued their meal.

* * *

Churches in general—but Black American churches in particular—usually have a kitchen area and extended cafeteria seating. The fixings are somewhat semi-industrial, having industrial sinks with extra-large basins, and stoves with stainless-steel finishes. But the refrigerators are often family-sized. The hallways are usually narrow, and the bathrooms house one toilet each, considering most Black churches were either built or usurped from a time past, when Americans were generally more religious. As demographics changed, populations grew and shifted, technology increased, and traditional family roles and composition disintegrated, white people "evolved" out of Baptist-style churches. Then black people, often "late to the party", took over these abandoned churches. It was not uncommon for these churches to be housed in a narrow building with multiple levels, often appearing as a house with a large front porch.

Reggie noted all of the aforementioned characteristics about the Ethiopian restaurant as he leaned back in his chair, nice and buzzed, observing his surroundings. It took him back to times past, with Meemaw dragging him to one of her all-day Seventh Day Adventist church services.

Good ole Grandma.

Reggie briefly reminisced on fond memories of times past while waiting for Thuy to return from the restroom since she'd left her purse behind. The staff had already bagged the leftovers and removed the used plates.

"You ready?" Thuy said, finally returning from the restroom. She wiped off the lenses of her glasses with her shirt, brushed her hair to the sides of her ears, and affixed the spotless spectacles.

"I'm gonna go to the bathroom too. I'll be right back," Reggie said.

"Okay."

Thuy put her credit card on the tab.

"Hey wait," Reggie put his hand on the bill, "Let me pay the tip."

Thuy snatched the bill from him. "That's not how this works. It's my turn!"

Even in the new era of female independence, Reggie still carried the chip of "the man should at least pay something" on his shoulders. Reggie relinquished his grip although he was partly concerned about how he'd be viewed by others; he didn't want to fall into the stereotype of black guys mooching off women, especially of other races. He swallowed and pushed back his self-consciousness, deciding it was nobody's business but their own how they handled things.

"Right on," Reggie said and then headed to the bathroom while Thuy took the bagged leftovers in one hand, the bill in the other, and approached the counter to pay.

"Here you go," Thuy said as she put the tab on the counter.

A tall, skinny, older Ethiopian man likely in his 60s slid the tab from Thuy's side of the counter to his own. He had shriveled fingers with round tips, like ET trying to phone home. As he rung up the register, he looked Thuy over suspiciously. "You have the kitfo and tej, yes?"

"Yup. And it was delicious. Thank you."

"And you sat at that table over there, yes?" The man pointed in the direction where Thuy had sat previously.

"Yep," she answered.

"There was somebody else there... Is everything okay?"

"Dude, everything's fine," Thuy said, a little perturbed.

"Okay. Glad you enjoyed the food." The man handed her the receipt. "Please, come back soon."

"Thanks." Thuy shook her head and walked out to her car, smartphone in hand.

Not far behind her was Reggie, who'd emerged from the men's room. Not seeing Thuy, he walked to the exit. As he looked around, he noticed the Ethiopian man at the counter watching him.

"Did you see my friend?" Reggie asked the man.

"She went outside."

"Cool, *amasa ganalo,* my brother." Reggie gave the guy a head nod.

"She paid, you know," the man responded.

"Huh?"

"She paid," the man repeated. "She paid for everything..."

Reggie paused, simply staring back at the man without responding.

"Whenever I go out with a woman, I always pay," the man said smugly.

Nigga, you ain't me. Reggie gave the guy another head nod and a smile. Then, he exited the building. *Hatin' ass nigga.*

Reggie approached Thuy's car, seeing her inside looking at her smartphone. When she noticed him out the corner of her eye, she unlocked the door. The car was already running.

"You ready, Thuy?" Reggie said.

"I'm ready," she replied.

"Let's roll."

* * *

A blue light shone through the darkness surrounding Reggie. He turned toward it, watching as it grew wider and more defined, resembling the illumination from a smartphone. Once Reggie was within five feet of it, the light stretched into the shape of a flat-screen, and silhouettes of black hands began to move across it.

Oh, that's just the 17" media control touchscreen in Khalil's Tesla, Reggie realized as his eyes adjusted to the darkness around him. Soon, the rest of the vehicle came into focus.

The fall season was upon them, and the sun had yet show its face on that side of the parking structure. The area was engulfed in twilight, darkening the parking lot and its surrounding buildings, including Reggie's office. With people being sparse at that time of morning, the area resembled a post-apocalyptic movie setting.

Khalil was sitting in his sleek white Tesla, playing with the controls like he typically did before work. Always vigilant, he glimpsed Reggie in his periphery and rolled down his window. "Ayo, Reggie! What's going on, man? Why you in so early?"

"Nothing much, Khalil. Just wanted to get a jump on things, you know."

"I can dig it." Khalil fist-bumped Reggie through his car window before Reggie continued on his way to the building.

Once inside and logged on to his computer, Reggie completed his expense reconciliations and made notes about the service areas whose operating budgets had yet been forecasted. The time on his computer monitor's lower right corner read 7:07 A.M.

Reggie compared the historical costs of different services and products used by the service areas, and then looked at the major categories featuring the largest expense pockets used by those service areas. To get an idea of the costs, he went online to compare what the service areas were using regarding technology, to what was on the market and the analysis on how the technology itself would grow. Additionally, he took note of the ways previous technological growth had increased costs. He then applied the percentage of the growth rates to current costs, forecasting them into the future. Lastly, to support his predictions, he saved the article links discussing such changes to a folder.

It was 9:42 A.M. when approaching footsteps, the scents of the different perfumes, and the aroma of Shatner roasting coffee beans in his cubicle distracted Reggie. He averted his eyes from his computer screen and stretched. Done with his analysis on one service area, Reggie decided he would apply the same technique to all of the service areas under his jurisdiction.

He hopped up from his chair and made his way to Ishmael's office.

"This analysis is spot on, Reggie," Ishmael was saying moments later. "And the idea regarding benchmarking our government customer against other government organizations and scaling it for employment level is spot on too!"

"Thanks, Ishmael," Reggie replied. "I wanted to ensure that I wasn't only providing an analysis of our customers' expenses over time. Analyzing their actions across agencies at a given point in time can provide a picture of how they're doing, especially regarding the new products and services they decide to take on."

Ishmael shook his head as he looked over the documents Reggie had provided. "How did you pinpoint what those other agencies were buying?"

"Ishmael, my good man, I still have contacts at the GSA who work in IT procurement. I worked at a temp agency at the GSA and made a few good contacts there."

"This is brilliant work, Reggie. You're really on the ball today."

"Thanks, man." Reggie smiled to himself as he walked back to his cubicle.

Could it be that his date with Thuy had put a pep in his step?

Just as Thuy crossed his mind, he looked at the time. *Damn! It's already 10:20! It'll be lunchtime soon... Maybe I'll drop shorty a message to see what's up.*

As Reggie picked up his smartphone to text Thuy, his mental chatter kicked in:

Don't do it. Let her drop the first line.

But what's wrong with just testing the water a bit?

Y'all just went out the other night. Give it a rest. Maybe she'll hit you up.

What if she's busy? I know—I'll just send her a message. If she doesn't respond, I'll leave her alone.

Dude, what are you doing? This isn't high school anymore. You're a grown man. Men usually initiate the conversation. If she doesn't want it to continue, she'll give you a closed answer. Send her a text. It lets her know you're interested and keeps fanning the flames a little.

What flame? Y'all didn't even kiss yet.

Like I said, this isn't high school anymore. No need to rush things.

But isn't she like, a party girl?

I'm not sure. But even if she is, women usually dictate the pace in the beginning. Shut up and let me handle this!

Thanks to his mental deliberations, ten minutes passed before Reggie finally sent a text. Then he waited, although he received no immediate answer.

Fuck it. I'mma go for a walk, come back, knock out a couple of service areas, then it'll be lunchtime.

Reggie stored away his things, including his phone. Then he locked his computer. On his way out the building, he spotted Khalil coming his way. They bumped fists as they met.

"Hey man, I see you're on your grind today. You've been looking busy ever since you got here,"

Khalil said.

Reggie stared at the zigzag patterns in Khalil's dreadlocks; he probably spent more money on braids than most African women did. "Yeah, I think maybe I have a little fire lit under my ass since I started seeing shorty."

"A woman'll do that to you."

"Yeah, but I'm just feeling things out right now. It still the exciting phase. It's like we're boxers trading jabs—not landing any power shots for now, but it's like on that 'who-calls-who' and 'entice-and-withdraw' tip."

"Yeah, I can dig it. Where you going right now?"

"I'm about to go outside for some air. Want to join me?"

Khalil looked back and forth, checking no one else was around. "All right, let's go."

"Bet."

* * *

Once Reggie was back at his desk, he unlocked the cabinet containing his cellphone.

Yes!

The blue light in the upper right-hand corner of the phone was blinking. Seeing Thuy's name, Reggie held his breath in anticipation for a moment.

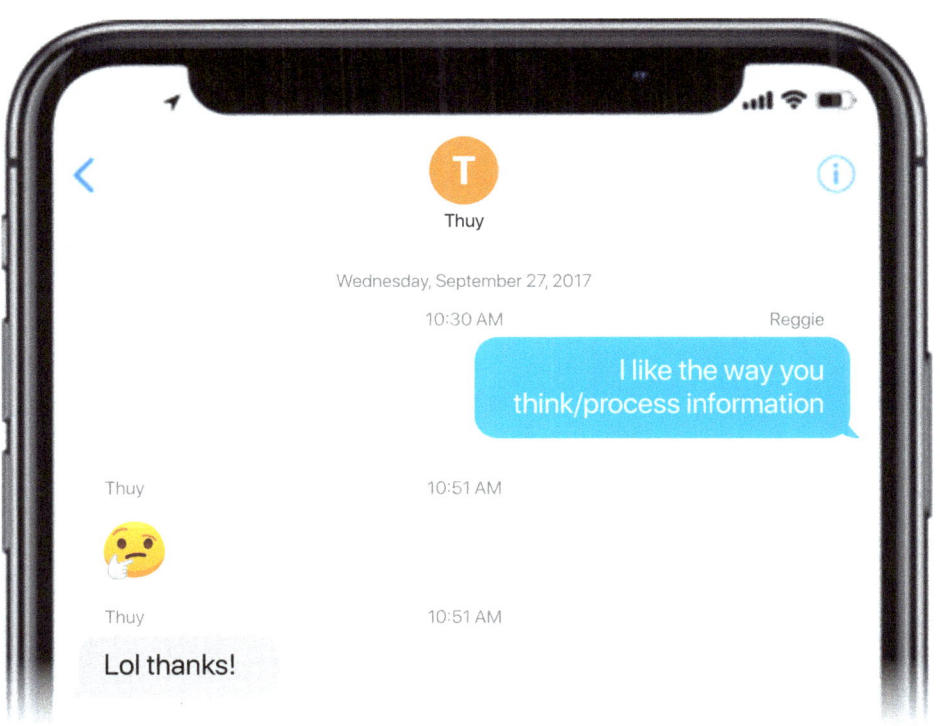

Reggie started to type a reply, but then backspaced all of his words.

Naw, I'll let her have the last word and get back at her tomorrow.

He put his phone on silent and returned it to the cabinet. He then opened his computer, pulled up his spreadsheets, and got back on task.

Not long after lunch, once Reggie had shucked-and-jived with people about the building complexes, he returned to his cube and put his wallet and keys back in his cabinet. Inside, the blue light was blinking on his phone again.

Naw, it can't be. She wouldn't have hit me back without me replying first...

Nevertheless, he hoped that was precisely the case. He unlocked to his cellphone to check texts.

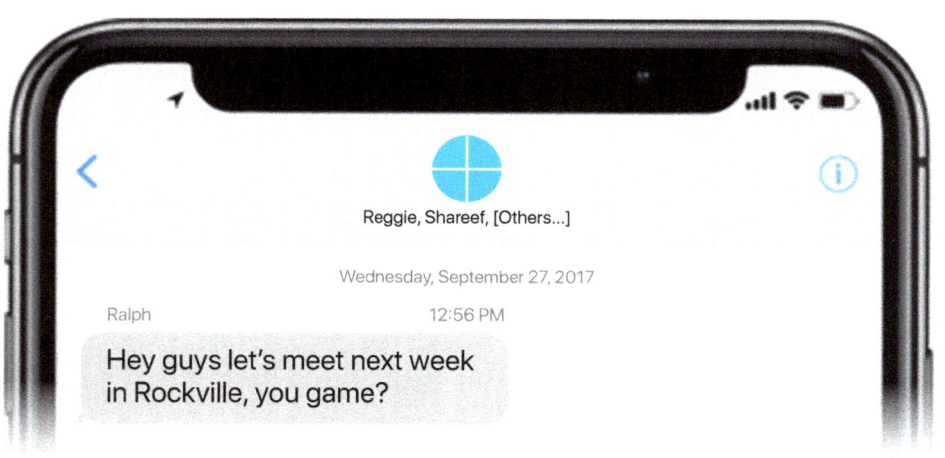

Hell yeah! Smiling, Reggie typed his response.

HYPOCRITE

I f you spoke with Ralph Hatagiko on the phone, you would never think you were talking to an Indonesian guy who grew up in a predominantly black neighborhood. His parents instilled work ethic and discipline in him, and had him attend ROTC in high school. In the early 2000s, Ralph got Reggie a job at Wireless Essentials, an AT&T wireless reseller that operated out of a mall kiosk and was being manned by one person at a time. Ralph was initially Reggie's manager, but after going on to find other work, he still kept in touch with Reggie.

Eventually, they ended up going to college together, and Ralph introduced Reggie into his circle of friends. Their favorite pastime— getting ten cent wings and mugs of Yuengling Ale at Hard Times Café, a local sports bar.

Ralph eventually married Missy—a super busty, porcelain-skinned, feminist he'd met in college. Unbeknownst to Ralph, Reggie and another friend, Tyler, saw his wife's tits. Here's how it happened.

* * *

Hermosa Beach, California, 2005.

Ralph had gone to work for the day, but had allowed Reggie and Tyler to hang out in his condo, leaving them to their own devices.

Within the quiet condo, Reggie stirred awake, stifling a yawn as his stomach released a loud growl. Climbing off the couch, Reggie rubbed his eyes and squinted at the beams of sunlight coming through the living room blinds. Blinking rapidly, his eyes slowly adjusted and he caught sight of Tyler, who was still snoring in his sleeping bag on the living room floor.

Keeping his footsteps quiet, Reggie trudged across the floor, heading for the kitchen positioned adjacent to the living room.

His stomach still gnawing with hunger, he was prepared the raid the fridge. But instead, he stopped right in his tracks.

Reggie's eyes widened, stumbling upon a vision he knew wasn't meant for his eyes, but was there nonetheless. "Hey, Tyler..." Reggie's dumbfounded voice drifted through the condo. "Tyler, check it out!"

"Hmm?" Tyler mumbled sleepily from the living room.

"Yo, Tyler, you gotta see this, bro!" Unwilling to keep the sight to himself, Reggie jogged back to the living room, approaching Tyler to shake him awake.

Tyler's brow furrowed with irritation and his eyes popped open. He stared up at Reggie. Before he could say anything though, Reggie dashed back to the kitchen, knowing a curious Tyler would follow.

"Ho-ly smokes... Do I see what I think I see?" Tyler's eyes widened to the size of sausages, and all traces of his previous tiredness disappeared. He stared at the refrigerator door—or what was stuck to it, rather.

"Yep, I think so. And it's a beautiful sight. You think we'll get struck dead for this?" Reggie asked.

Tyler rubbed his chin. "Not necessarily. Feminists bathe in achieving power through sexuality."

"Well, I guess not wearing a bra allows things to...hang."

"Well, I'll be damned. Tickle my White Christian male privilege!"

Reggie and Tyler snickered as they continued staring at the polaroid on the refrigerator door. The photo displayed a side-view of Missy, naked from neck to buttocks. It was classily done, showing her baby bump—the kind of picture expecting couples took to capture the beauty of a woman as she goes through pregnancy. But what Reggie and Tyler couldn't stop looking at was the full, graceful, elongated, milky-white breasts with nipples like cherries on top of a mountain peak, perkily pointing at the blue dome of the sky.

"Should we tell Ralph we saw it?" Reggie asked.

"Nah, that would be distasteful," Tyler said.

They admired the picture a couple minutes longer, and then went about their day.

Later, once Ralph had returned from work, the picture had been taken down. Reggie presumed Ralph must have been mortified over forgetting to take it down in the first place. And surely, he had to have known there was no way Tyler and Reggie had missed it, considering they'd been in the house all day.

* * *

Yesterday's text message from Ralph had come as quite the surprise. It had been a while since the college friends had gotten together, and Reggie was excited to catch up with Ralph. But Ralph had been super busy—now a father of three who often worked overtime as a contractor for one of the largest consulting firms in the area.

After his morning meetings at 8:00 A.M. and a restroom break, Reggie returned to his desk and checked his phone for any updates on the meetup. Surprised, he found the following:

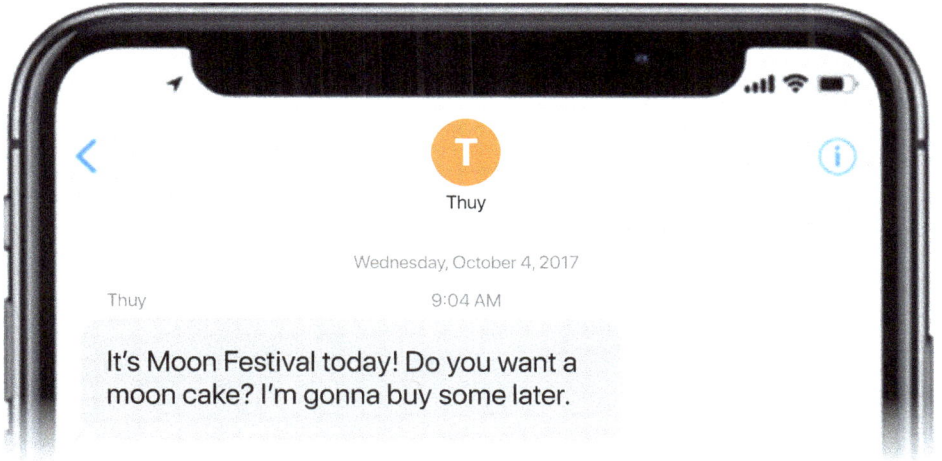

Yes! Hell yeah!

Reggie had to put his hand over his mouth to keep from exclaiming out loud. This was an unexpected victory—Thuy initiating conversation, with a tone of excitement, no less. Apparently, pulling back a little bit worked wonders.

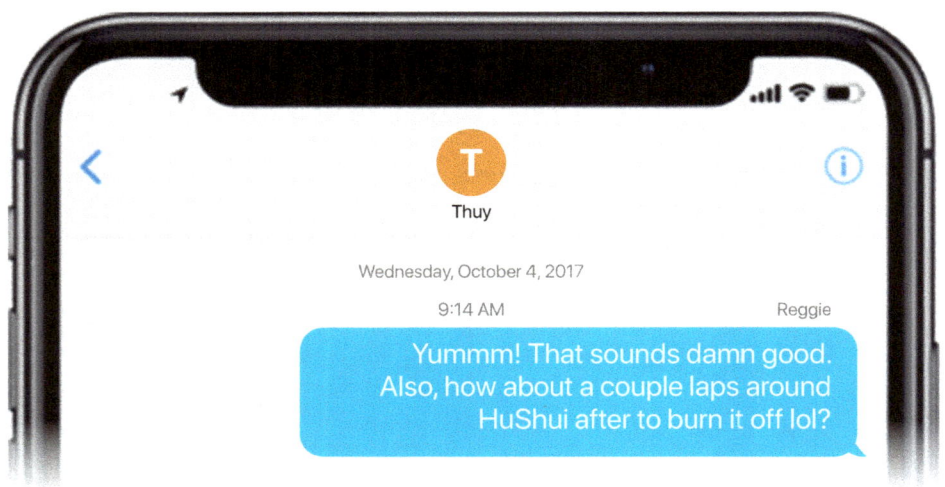

Reggie waited a minute or two, failing to consider how he could fit Thuy into the schedule since Ralph had yet to confirm a time for their meetup. He simply knew that some way, somehow, he would make it all happen.

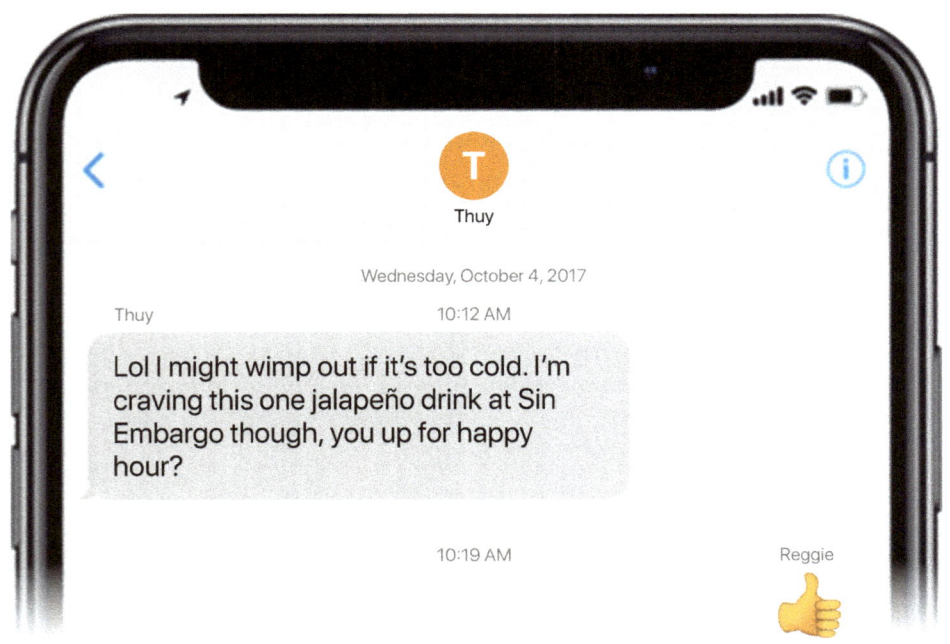

* * *

Later in the day, Reggie's phone went off again. His mind immediately jumped to Thuy, but when he checked his messages, it was Ralph.

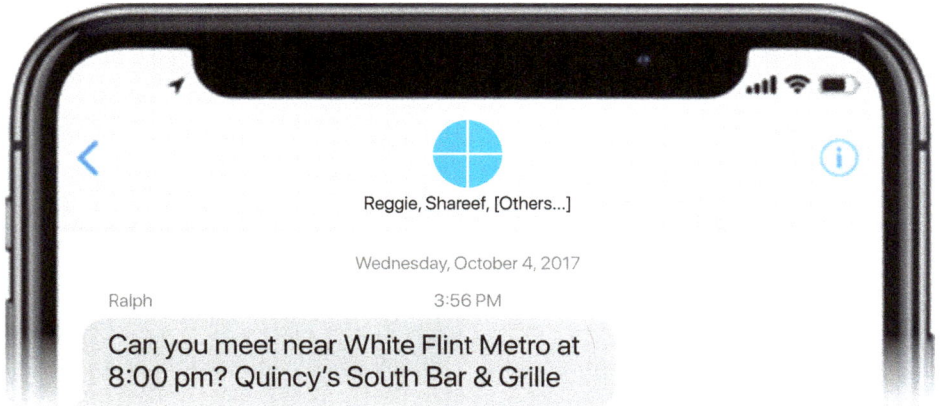

So, if I meet Thuy between 6:00 and 6:30, I can spend an hour with her—maybe even just sport her around the town center, then head out to Rockville at 7:30. Besides, shorty and I haven't really gotten into anything heavy yet. There's no telling where her head is at. Let me get Ralph to give me a little more leeway on the time...

His fingers flying over the keypad, Reggie texted back:

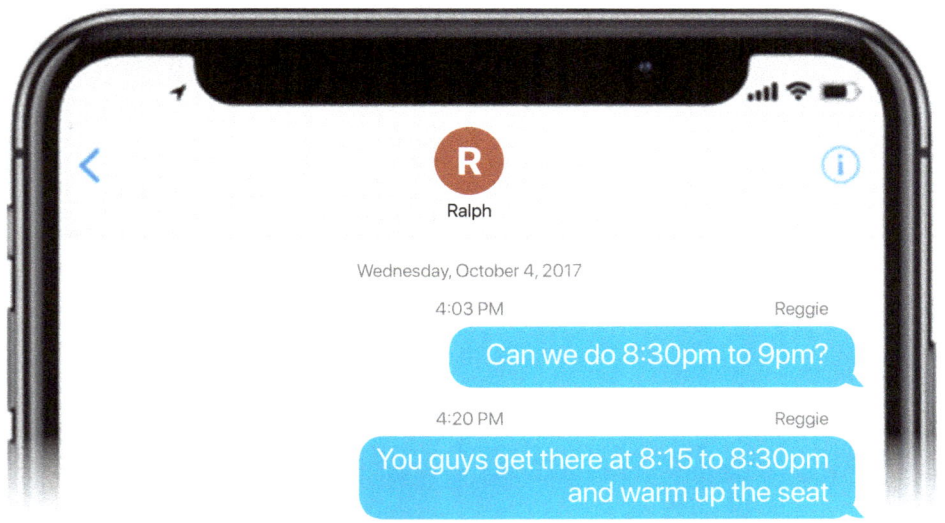

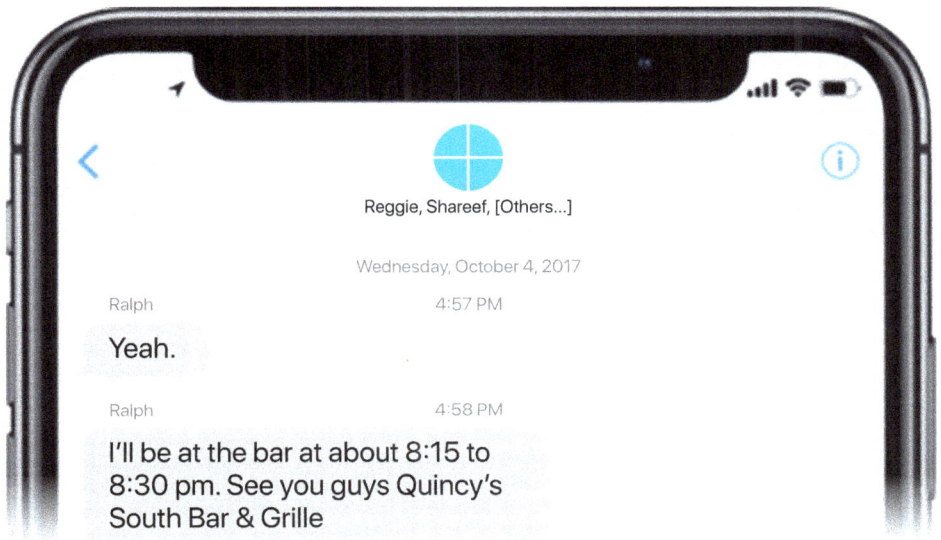

The last couple of texts came in just as Reggie was in his car, driving out of the parking structure like a bat out of hell to leave his workplace behind. After maneuvering like an extra from *Fast and Furious*, he reached the parking garage in his apartment, only to be blown by the following text:

Fuck! She's on that shit now! Reggie rolled his eyes.

A year ago, his brother, Winston, Jr., had become a father. Like any good grandmother, their mom subsequently stepped in to help. With Winston and his girlfriend out-of-town, Reggie's mom needed someone to walk the dogs while she tended to the baby.

Originally, there had been only one dog at his mom's house—Clifford, who originally belonged to Reggie and was well-trained. But later, Winston, Jr. came across another Pitbull puppy that was up for adoption and snagged it. Winston, however, never put in the time to train the dog. Hence, the dog's temperament was a lot feistier than Cliff's; as a result, walking him was a challenge.

Their routine was to take the dogs around the side of the condominium public area, an area Reggie mentally deemed "dog toilet", and let them shit between the street and sidewalk. People had to tip-toe through that area as if walking around land mines, lest they leave an imprint of their shoe's brand names on piles of gooey dog droppings.

Reggie decided the operation was simple. He needed to get to his mother's house, which would take about ten minutes. Then, he'd walk the dogs around the corner, let them shit, and take them back into the house—adding another then minutes to his excursions. After that, he would take a 15-minute drive to Rockville.

He tried wrapping his mind around adding 35 minutes without rushing Thuy.

The dogs needed to be fed an hour before walking. With this in mind, Reggie calculated that he needed to tell his mom to feed the dogs once he was within 50 minutes of getting to her house.

He replied to her text.

* * *

"Ah, shh, shh, ah shh—fuck it's cold!" Reggie shivered in the icy shower. Working to stimulate his brown fat stores, he hoped Wim Hoff and Mike Mutzel weren't leading him astray. Regardless, what Reggie liked most about cold showers was how they brought him into the present.

"Ahhh...." Finally, Reggie's body adapted to the cold, and the bottoms of his feet warmed and tingled. He stayed in the shower just long enough to push past his limit. Afterwards, he dressed quickly, sprayed himself with cologne, and texted Thuy.

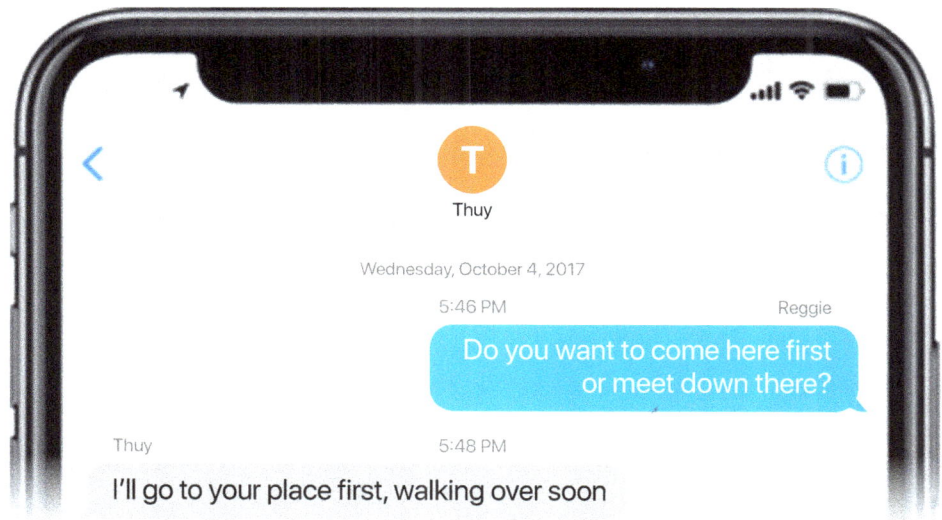

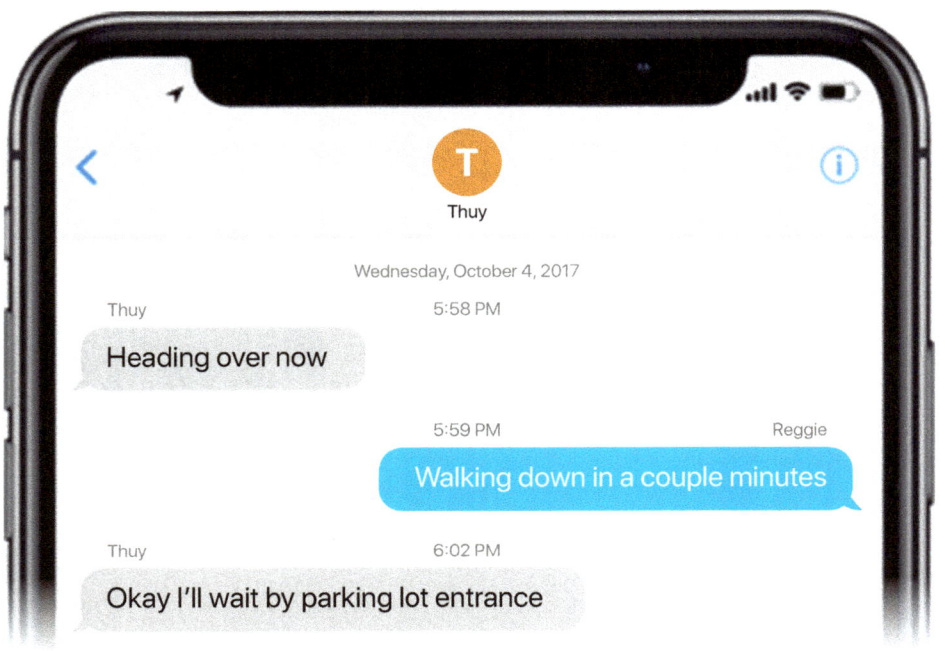

Reggie met Thuy as she approached the parking lot entrance. He extended his arms and she gave him a warm hug that felt a little tighter and longer than just a "buddy-buddy" hug. Reggie felt her breasts press against his solar plexus.

Now we're getting somewhere. He smiled, knowing Thuy couldn't see him smiling due to her height.

She took a light whiff of his cologne. "Mmm, you smell really good."

"Well, thank you m'dear. Now, where are the mooncakes?"

"Oh, they're in my car. Want to get them now, or after happy hour? Just to let you know, I'm forgetful after a couple of drinks!"

"How 'bout I take the mooncakes up to the apartment and we come back for them after hanging out? I promise, I won't eat them all."

"Sounds like a plan."

They walked over to Thuy's car, and all the while Reggie felt slightly on-edge. He wanted to fit everything perfectly into the evening.

Thuy opened the car door and retrieved a tin box depicting the moon, a woman wearing a robe, and a white rabbit.

"Looks like an elaborate setup," Reggie said, looking at the box.

"Mid-autumn festival is a big thing back home. But since none of my relatives are here, it's just me and my roommates. And you, of course."

Reggie's spirits soared, pleased that Thuy included him as one amongst her circle. He just hoped that wouldn't include getting *friend-zoned*.

Thuy handed Reggie the box, and he nonchalantly went back up the elevator. As soon as it reached the top floor, he sprinted towards his apartment, put the mooncakes in the refrigerator, and briefly looked at Todd's door.

Keep your grubby palms off, Todd. This ain't community property, Reggie thought before sprinting back to the elevator to return back to the town center.

* * *

Sin Embargo was the Cuban-themed restaurant in the town center. It reminded Reggie of Miami's *Havana 1957,* only bigger and with a larger central American influence, as they served guacamole dip. Almost every Latin-themed restaurant had to include Salva-Mex components—the "chips and the dips" so to speak, as the bowl of guacamole was surrounded by tortillas, fried plantains, and yuca chips. The wood-grained shelves containing the many types of rum served were a testament to the Cuban theme, and the dishes that included black beans –*habichuelas* –were numerous.

Reggie watched as his spoon sunk like the Titanic into the ocean of black beans, pork pieces, and black bean starch. "Hmm, tastes like there's cumin in it. A good, but unexpected accent," he said with a nod of approval after tasting the soup.

"Yeah, Ashat uses it all the time when he cooks," Thuy said as she used a Yuca chip to scoop some guacamole into her mouth.

As she crunched and munched, Reggie reflected on how lots of Asians smacked when they chewed, fully immersing themselves while eating. Thuy's smacks were cute—like a baby suckling on a bottle, losing the grip of the nipple in its gums, and smacking at air to resume the rhythm eating.

The server approached their table. "Two jalapeno mojitos?" she asked, confirming their drinks. Reggie and Thuy nodded, and the server placed the drinks on the table. *"Buen probecho,"* she said before taking off, shaking her *caderas* as she walked away.

"Welp, here's the drink you've been craving, Thuy. Cheers."

"Cheers," Thuy replied.

They clinked glasses.

Reggie sipped deeply on the drink, and started coughing. "Damn! That's got a kick to it!"

"Ha! I told you to try some of mine before ordering a whole one!"

"No, I actually love it!" Reggie said. "The sugar cane inside keeps it sweet, while the jalapenos make it spicy. Makes you conflicted about whether to keep drinking it."

Thuy smiled and nodded as they each sipped some more between eating.

"So, you stoked about your upcoming trip to Miami?" Thuy asked.

"In the past three years, I've made the pilgrimage to Miami Beach once per year."

"You don't get bored of going to the same place year after year? What's down there?"

"For me, it's the perfect place to unwind, run on the sand, swim, and eat at all of the restaurants on this one promenade they have down there."

"What kind of food do they have there? "

"Let me see—Cuban, Brazilian, Spanish, Italian, Mexican, a seafood place, and a crepe place. Sorry, no Vietnamese food."

Thuy laughed and jabbed Reggie in the shoulder. They sipped on their drinks for a little, then the image of the box of mooncakes returned to Reggie's mind.

"Why is there a woman with a rabbit flying in front of the moon on your box of mooncakes? Is she a fertility goddess or something?" Reggie asked breaking the silence.

"Or something," Thuy said vaguely.

Reggie paused, checking to see if she was being smart-allicky.

Thuy smiled, sensing Reggie's stare. "The woman's name is *Chang Oh,* and she was the wife of a great archer and architect, *Hou Yi.* The story is something along the line of him performing great feats, not limited to using arrows to shoot out the sun's light and building a palace for the emperor. He was rewarded by the emperor with a small bottle of immortality medicine, or juice or—" Thuy paused, interrupted by Reggie's phone suddenly vibrating on the table like a lowrider pancaking.

"Apologies, sweetheart. Hold that thought. Let me check this, it's probably my..." Reggie swiped the phone open and his suspicions were confirmed.

Mom. Fucking bugaboo! I told her I was going to let her know when it was time. What the fuck does she want now?

Her ass will have to wait. I told her I was going to let her know when!

"Are you okay?" Thuy asked, sensing Reggie's frustration.

"Oh... Yeah, I'm good. It's just my mom. She can be a... um, she can be persistent at times." Reggie chuckled.

Thuy busted out laughing. "Trust me, I know the feeling. My mom can get on my nerves too. Sometimes they don't get it when they're being overbearing."

Reggie raised his glass. "Cheers to annoying moms!"

"Cheers!" Thuy said, clinking her glass against his.

"Now, please continue with what you were saying," Reggie said politely after taking a sip of his drink.

"I lost my train of thought. I told you I'm forgetful after a couple of drinks." Thuy poked out her bottom lip, looking like a Pikachu with tits.

"You were saying the emperor gave Hou Yi some sort of elixir," Reggie said, refreshing her memory.

"Right! I remember now! So anyways, he was so excited to receive this gift that he rushed home to share it with his wife, Chang Oh. She was so excited that she drank entire bottle—"

"Wait, so this dude gets a unique gift of immortality to share with her, and her selfish ass drank the whole thing?"

"What?"

"Never mind. Sorry to interrupt. This drink has a kick to it. Keep going, please."

Thuy rolled her eyes and resumed the story. "Chang Oh started to float up toward the sky. She grabbed everything she could to keep from floating, but nothing worked. The last thing she grabbed was her pet rabbit. Hou Yi tried to hold on to her too, but couldn't. So she was doomed to live eternally without her husband, her only companion being her pet rabbit." Thuy took a deep sip of her drink.

"Damn, it sounds like a spinster story on steroids, but with rabbits instead of cats," Reggie said.

Overcome with laughter, Thuy nearly spit out her drink. "In Asia, that's like one of the biggest fears—to be over thirty and unmarried."

"And what about you? Are you afraid?"

"I lived that life. I've done that, and I'm good. Dude, I was raised in America, so I'm adapted to life here without the heavy expectations of Asian culture. Besides, my first husband was a white boy."

"True. But the fact that you know the story of the mooncake lady must mean you've retained some of your culture."

"Please don't call me a hypocrite, but I'm Vietnamese when convenient."

"Hypocrite," Reggie joked.

They laughed and drank more.

"The names *Hou Yi* and *Chang On* don't sound like any Vietnamese names I've heard," Reggie said after a moment.

"That's because they're not. They're Chinese. The original kingdoms came from Southern China into what is Vietnam today. I'm actually forty percent Chinese."

"Interesting. You learn something new every day."

"Like my last name, Lieu, spelled L-I-E-U, is the Vietnamese version of the Chinese name Liu, spelled L-I-U."

"Okay, I get it. So names like *Tran* are the Vietnamese version of *Chan*?"

"See? I knew it! I knew it!" Thuy exclaimed.

"You knew what?"

"That you're smarter than you look!"

Reggie laughed. "I'll toast to that." They clinked glasses for the umpteenth time, and Reggie took a long swig of his drink. "Wait a minute…" He narrowed his eyes at her. "You're not saying that because I'm black, are you?"

* * *

The conversation between Reggie and Thuy continued to flow, touching many subjects—race and politics in particular. Yet, Reggie's buzzing cellphone gave their conversation the *coitus interruptus* treatment. Reggie looked down.

Fuck.

"Hey, Thuy, sweetie… Let me take this real quick. It's my mom again."

"Okay, babe."

Reggie stood from the table and left the restaurant's seating area. As he retreated to the general area to call his mom, he abruptly turned his head back to the table to look at Thuy. She was sipping more of her drink.

Hollup… Wait. I'm trippin'. Did we just call each other by pet names? I got to keep shit cool here.

* * *

"Ma, go ahead and feed the dogs now, I..." Reggie's voice trailed off in frustration as he paced back and forth, talking to his mom while a guy smoking a cigarette nearby appeared to eavesdrop on the drama.

"We talked about it, but never agreed on specific dates, so I..."

"Well, I'm ready now. Do you want me to walk the dogs or not? Just go ahead and feed them."

Annoyed, Reggie held the phone away from his ear while his mother rambled on the other line, her babble drifting through the air.

"It doesn't matter when you feed them, ma," Reggie said, exasperated. "You just *think* they need to shit after an hour. You know why? Since you feed 'em once per day and you only let them out to shit in the evening, they are just pooping out yesterday's meal. It's not like their digestion is so fast that they eat and then need to poop an hour later, especially Cliff's. No, the issue is nobody wants to take responsibility for the fact that...hello? Hello?"

Fuck.

Reggie's mother was raised in Southeast Washington D.C. She was the type of woman to ask someone for a favor, then gaslight them for not moving fast enough. Amongst her childhood friends, she was the most rational. She was smart and moved among international people at her job. At times, she even spoke the French she'd learned in vocational school during her youth, until the programs instituted by Marion Barry landed her a job in the local government. Working throughout high school, she used the referrals she gained for her service to get a job in the federal government. And like Sylvester Stallone in *Cliffhanger,* she climbed the GS scale until she reached a 12, then stepped sideways along that scale as she moved through time. Taking advantage of different programs during the Clinton administration, she purchased a house that got her "out of the hood and into the woods."

* * *

As Reggie returned to the table, Thuy was thumbing through her phone.

"You know, it's good to hold your phone at eye level so you don't put a strain on your neck," Reggie said as he approached.

Thuy looked up. "Oh, hey. Thanks for the tip. Doing quality control all day definitely takes a toll on me." She self-consciously rubbed her neck.

"So, here's the deal. I know we talked about walking around while snacking on the mooncakes, but I've got to leave here in the next thirty minutes or so because I have to go walk the dogs," Reggie explained as he retook his seat.

"I didn't know you had a dog. Well, I didn't see one around you, anyway."

"My mom has my dog. The newer apartments had restrictions against certain breeds, so I left him with her. For a while, he was the only dog there until my brother decided to get one."

"Oh. What kind of dog do you have?"

"A Pitbull."

"I love Pitbulls! They're so adorable. They really get a bad rap."

"Hmm, you know," Reggie said after a pause, "I was trying to do a couple things later on, including but not limited to going to another bar to meet some college buddies, where their specialty drunk food is funnel cake fries."

"Dude, I love funnel cake!"

She's going to stop calling me 'dude' one day.

"Okay, cool. Now, I need to run to my mom's real quick to walk the dogs. Just in-and-out. Grab the dogs, walk them around the corner, let them do their business. Then we'll head to the bar and I'll introduce you to some friends. Are you good with that?"

"Okay," Thuy said.

"Okay?" Reggie said, his eyebrows raised meaningfully. He swallowed, hoping Thuy caught what he really meant. The trip to his mom's was strictly for walking the dog, not introductions. While he didn't think his mom would have a problem with Thuy, he just didn't want Thuy to feel any sense of relationship pressure. Nevertheless, having Thuy along for the ride appealed to him.

"Okay!" Thuy said, replying to his last inquiry.

They asked for the check, and as they waited Reggie drank his previously untouched glass of water.

Thirty minutes later, they were out of the bar and in Reggie's car.

JUST **JONIN'**

The parking lot and community courtyard was dimly lit by lightbulbs encased in globes sitting atop rectangular wooden posts—still intact from the 1980s when the community was first built. Reggie parked his car in the loading zone in front the townhouses, where residents dropped off their trash and recycling, and emergency and maintenance vehicles temporarily parked.

The townhouses were beige with coffee-colored trimmings, matching the color scheme of the wooden posts and light-globes. The warm yellow tint from the lighting, juxtaposed against the beige and dark brown colors, sung a soft monochromatic symphony.

Reggie disembarked his car and looked over at Thuy. "Remember, in-and-out."

"You act like we're gonna rob the place, dude!" Thuy joked.

Stop calling me 'dude', Reggie thought to himself. He looked over to Thuy again, his austere gaze bringing her down a notch. Nonetheless, Reggie realized he was probably taking things too seriously. In attempts to prevent an interaction between Thuy and his mother, Reggie was being too pushy. He needed to just let the night flow.

Reggie released the tension on his eyebrows. "Good luck with that. I pity the fool who tries to rob *my* mom." He smiled and Thuy smiled back.

They both got out of the car and soon, were entering Reggie's mom's house.

In the middle of a call, Reggie's mom held her cellphone in one hand while cradling Winston's baby with her free arm.

Reggie gestured for Thuy to stay at bay, remaining in the doorway.

Thuy looked over at Reggie's mother and waved.

She smiled, giving a quick wave with the phone-holding hand before returning the device to her ear and resuming her conversation.

Meanwhile, Reggie moved farther into the house to unleash the dogs from their posts. They barked excitedly upon noticing Thuy. Clifford looked up at Thuy with his big brown eyes and raised his paw to offer like a handshake.

"Aww! You're so cute!" Thuy said, leaning down to accept Cliff's handshake. She then cupped the dog's head in her hands and scratched behind his ears. Enjoying her affection, Cliff leapt up and licked Thuy's face, causing her to giggle.

Time to get these guys walked and head back to Rockville, Reggie thought, pleased the dogs had lightened the mood.

Reggie gave his mom a nod and she reciprocated the gesture. Reggie could tell his mom seemed annoyed with him, but there was no time to try to soothe the mix-up they'd had. Besides, her moods were often all over the place, and Reggie couldn't be concerned at the moment.

* * *

"That was fun," Thuy said, looking in Reggie's direction. The dogs had been walked, and the two of them had now returned to Reggie's car.

"I'm glad you like Cliff. He's a real cool dog. I think you'll also like my other friends. They're pretty cool too."

"If anything, I'm going for the funnel cake, babe."

Reggie smiled. "You know, I like when you call me that.. But not so much when you call me *dude.*"

Thuy laughed. "Being from California, we use 'dude' a lot. I say it to girls too. I'm sorry, that flew over my head—what did you say you liked me to call you?"

Reggie nodded absentmindedly, realizing Thuy likely used pet names and nicknames randomly. The word 'dude' annoyed him, but he didn't want to overreach and insist she called him 'babe' from now on. Their relationship wasn't solid enough for that yet. "Never mind. I was just messing with ya... Hold on, let me text my boys and let 'em know we're on the way."

Reggie pulled out his cell phone, opening the text thread for his friend Ralph.

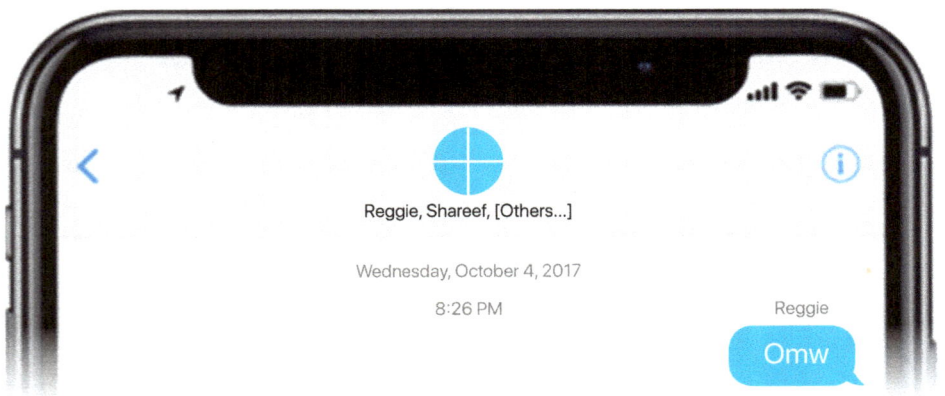

With the text message sent, he cranked the car engine and drove off. A minute later, the phone started to chimed with incoming texts. Reggie checked and sent off quick responses at stoplights.

Reggie smirked and suppressed a chuckle over the fact that he'd referenced Thuy as his 'little homie'. Chancing a glance at her, he saw that she was staring out the passenger's window, taking in the evening scenery.

* * *

"You miss one-hundred percent of the shots you don't take," Shareef said before raising his drink to his mouth and gulping beer down his gullet. His face sagged at the jowls.

Reggie cringed at the sounds of Shareef's gulping. *This nigga looks like Tommy Sotomayor mixed with a Georgetown Hoya dog,* he thought, staring at Shareef from across the table. The guy had terrible table manners, but Reggie's friends had all decided to go out to a local bar for food and drinks anyhow.

Shareef narrowed his eyes at Reggie as if somehow reading his thoughts.

Reggie averted his gaze, feeling slightly awkward. He was well aware that Shareef seemed to be going through a dry spell. He'd been getting a lot of rejection lately. In contrast, Reggie's head in the clouds from having Thuy with him. She continued to impress him. Even now, he admired how she was such a good sport, hanging out with the guys.

Reggie had noticed the way Shareef had eyed Thuy when he introduced her to the group. He wasn't worried though. Reggie's judgmental ass figured Shareef was no competition.

As for Ralph—he was already married and had his proverbial cow at home. He had been with Missy throughout college, and their parents knew each other through church, creating community ties. It takes "a village" as they say.

Many, like Captain Picard, thought the final frontier was marriage. But Reggie, being red-pilled, knew otherwise.

Reggie turned toward Thuy. "How you doing over there?"

"Good," she said. "You guys have some of the most interesting conversations I've heard, especially about the one-hundred percent of the shots."

Reggie chuckled. "With a lot of guys, meeting up with girls is a numbers game. It's likened to the game of hockey according to Wayne Gretzky, hockey extraordinaire. He came up with—"

"You guys order the funnel cake fries?" a brunette waitress said, cutting Reggie off as she carried over a tray of what looked like French fries covered with confectioner sugar.

"We sure did. Set them right here, please." Reggie pointed to the space on the table between him and Thuy, who was seated to his left. Ralph was his right, and Shareef was across them.

The waitress set down the food.

Thuy wrinkled her nose at some red dipping sauce the waitress had left behind. "Is that ketchup?"

"No. It's raspberry marmalade. They just make it look like cheese fries with ketchup rather than a traditional funnel cake. You dip it into the marmalade like you would dip fries into ketchup—or like most people do. I personally don't like ketchup."

Thuy grabbed a funnel cake fry, dipped it into the sauce, and devoured it.

Shareef watched her out of the side of his eye and smirked.

"Hmm, these *are* really good!" Thuy said.

"I'm glad you like them," Reggie said. "I don't usually order the raspberry dip. I usually just order mine plain, or with maple syrup."

Thuy took another funnel cake fry and dunked it in the raspberry sauce. She then held it in front of Reggie's face, using her other hand to catch any would-be spills. "Here. Try it."

Is this chick actually feeding me funnel cake fries? Reggie blinked, surprised, but liking it. *He* opened his mouth, allowing Thuy to insert the funnel cake fry. The flavor tingled on his tongue. "Hmm. Tangy. It complements the powdered sugar though." Truthfully, he still preferred maple syrup, but wanted to keep the contact with Thuy going.

And it did. As the night went on, Thuy and Reggie sipped from each other's drinks. Each time they shared, Reggie felt his trust with Thuy growing.

"It's almost like a jelly donut," Thuy said, continuing to enjoy the funnel cake. "Did you eat jelly donuts growing up?"

Reggie wiped his mouth with a napkin and took a sip of his drink. "Not really. Although I loved powdered donuts. I used to eat them, then leave the powder on my lips and go to the mirror because I thought it looked like Day-Glo lipstick."

Thuy laughed and proceeded to crunch on another funnel cake fry. She was as giddy as a kid getting overpriced ice cream from the ice cream man.

"It's that good, huh?" Reggie asked.

"*Very* good... And I'm laughing at the thought of you as a kid pretending to have lipstick on."

"Reggie's always had gender expression issues," Shareef interjected, seemingly unable to help himself.

"Oooh!" Ralph said, his tone instigating.

Thuy burst with laughter.

Reggie cracked a smile. "Oh, so we gonna start that shit now?"

Shareef took another swing of his beer. "Oh yeah, we gonna start that shit now."

"Aww shit," Ralph said as Reggie and Shareef both stood from the table.

"Be back," Reggie said to Thuy before following Shareef away from the group.

Thuy cast a worried glance over toward Ralph. "Oh my God, are they going to fight?"

Ralph shook his head. "No, they're just jonin'. It's pretty funny. They've been doing this since college."

Thuy titled her head in confusion. "What's *joning*?"

"It's like *Punk'd,* but with insults."

"Oh..." Thuy said, looking on and catching snippets of the exchange between Reggie and Shareef.

"So you got jokes, Shareef?" Reggie asked.

"Yeah, I got jokes," he replied.

Reggie nodded, accepting the challenge. "Okay then. Well, Shareef, the reason you miss one hundred percent of the shots you *do* take is because you're so ugly. You so ugly, your mama had to breastfeed you through a straw!" Reggie heard Thuy snickering back at their table. He turned to look towards her, a grin on his face. "As a matter of fact, Shareef gets it from his mama. Shareef mama so ugly that when she went in for a checkup, her gynecologist kept sticking his fingers in her mouth!"

Ralph and Thuy exploded with laughter that rang through the whole bar. Several onlookers who'd overheard the comment began to hold back their own laughter.

"Okay, okay," Shareef said, a bit louder than necessary to ensure onlookers could hear him too. "So you wanna bring mamas into this, huh? Well, we all know your mama. She's fat--"

"She is fat," Reggie nodded in agreement.

"—and she's brown skinned," Shareef continued. "Got them black bumps and blemishes, looking like a chocolate chip cookie with eyes."

The onlookers, the majority white, unashamedly released their laughter. Some had stopped eating altogether, in favor of gawking at these two black men cracking jokes about each other's mothers.

"Not only does your mama look like a pockmarked dalmatian, she's got acne problems." Shareef looked at the crowd, pleased to have a riveted audience. "His mamma's skin got so many pimples, she fell asleep in the bookstore and when she woke up, a blind man was trying to read her face!"

Ooohs and *ahhs* sounded throughout the crowd.

Thuy watched in astonishment as Reggie geared up to launch his next attack. Like Shareef, he too, began to address the crowd. "Well, we can all see that Shareef is Black. And not just as in African American, but as in extra crispy."

Practically everyone in the bar's eyes widened, and the laughter grew.

Ralph pulled out his cell phone and started recording the show.

Reggie held up his hands, palms forward, to silence the crowd and let them know he was ready to continue his act.

The crowd hushed.

"Shareef so black that when he hops out of the car, the oil light comes on!"

Laughter abounded.

Thuy, however, shifted squirmed in her seat. While everyone else was laughing, she couldn't help noticing Shareef no longer looked too happy. She was worried that the *joning* match would escalate into violence—as most things between black males looking to one up each other often did.

Nevertheless, Reggie kept going, despite sensing Shareef's discomfort. "Not only is Shareef black, but he's black and ugly. He gets it from his mama. His mama so black and ugly that she could only get a date on Black History Month!"

Roars of laughter echoed through the bar, and Shareef's visible discontent mounted. His jaw clenched, Shareef looked around at white people laughing at and mocking him.

"You got something to say?" Reggie asked, waiting for Shareef's comeback. The laughter around the bar died down as all the spectators did the same.

Yet, Shareef was silent—and Reggie decided to take advantage of that silence.

"Shareef so black, if you put his ass in a bottle, he'd be a Pepsi with teeth. Nigga's smile so bright, it's like *Close Encounters of the Third Kind*!"

Shareef balled his fists...

"Hey Reggie, I think he's had enough," Ralph intervened.

"Had enough? Had enough?! This nigga don't want it with me!" Reggie exclaimed.

Thuy's anxiety intensified. She recognized the effect alcohol and pride was having on the two men in front of her. They were making fools of themselves, and it didn't look like they were going to stop anytime soon.

"That nigga Shareef looks like the aftermath of an orgy between Boo Berry, Digums the Frog, and the Crunch Berry beast!"

The mostly white crowd guffawed, enjoying the insults far too much. Hanging on to the every word of the lighter complected, more attractive, Reggie.

With his fists still clenched, Shareef took several steps in Reggie's direction, decreasing the distance between them. Invading his personal space.

Reggie gave a mock shudder. "Aww. Wittle Shaweef don't wike me?" He turned his back to Shareef to address the crowd. "Hey guys, Shareeeef don't liiiike it—"

"Rock the Casbah! Rock the Casbah!" the crowd roared in response, catching on to the song reference and clapping.

Shareef lunged forward at Reggie, and Reggie instantly pushed him backward.

Just as Shareef prepared to take a swing at Reggie, Ralph hurried forward grabbed him.

"Easy, fella. Easy..." Ralph said.

* * *

"I told him not to start. I *told* him he didn't want it with me!" Reggie said as he banged his hands against the steering wheel.

"I know, babe. But you had him where you wanted him already. Why did you have to overdo it?" Thuy said. Rather than looking at Reggie, she stared out the car window. In the distance, she could see a flickering streetlights, blinking like a strobe-light and making it look as if a party was about to take place on a desolate street corner. It must've been a short circuit.

Reggie sighed in frustration. "Why? Because Shareef tries that shit every time, that's why. And Ralph knows it. He always tries to one-up me. You know what? You don't understand. You'll never understand. Niggas... People like Shareef don't get it, so they push and they push until..." Reggie's voice trailed off as he stopped at a light. He looked over at Thuy, noting her disapproval. He sighed again. "You know what? You're right. I probably went a little far tonight. I didn't intend for it to turn out like this. I know that it wasn't cool for me to punch him in the solar plexus after Ralph grabbed his arm. I know that it was embarrassing to be asked to leave. I apologize. Maybe I –"

"You know what?" Thuy said, cutting him off and finally looking at him. "It's cool. Shareef did start it. Seemed like he was hating on you."

Reggie blinked, surprised. "Thanks for understanding."

"I don't condone you taking it over the top though," Thuy reiterated.

"I know. Maybe I had too many jalapeño margaritas. They were pretty strong. Good thing we split one." He glanced in Thuy's direction again. "I also want to thank you for walking with me afterwards to 7-11 for coffee and a talk. That was really cool of you." Reggie pulled into the parking structure and parked alongside Thuy's car.

"It was nothing, babe."

She called me babe again, not dude. Reggie smirked. "So, you good to drive?"

"C'mon, Reggie. I live, like four blocks away. And with the sobering conflict, a walk, and coffee, not only can I make it home, but I'll probably be up for a few hours."

"Maybe go to Harris Teeter and cop a couple of Tylenol PM or pop a Bendryl and call it a night?" Reggie suggested.

"We'll see," Thuy chuckled.

"So, talk tomorrow?" Reggie asked.

"Sure."

"Okay." Reggie swallowed and took a deep breath. *It's now or never,* he thought. Then, before he lost his nerve, he leaned over to kiss Thuy on the lips.

But she turned her head, offering him her cheek instead. "Not tonight, dude."

Fuck! She called me dude again.

Thuy disembarked the car and left Reggie wondering what had just happened.

Welp, back to the drawing board, Reggie thought as drove up the many ramps of the parking structure.

* * *

Why the fuck is this nigga eating his pie backwards? Reggie watched Raulin nibbling on the crust of a slice of key lime pie.

Raulin glanced at Reggie from the corner of his eye. "I like my pie, like I like my *wee-mon.* I eat them from the back." Raulin laughed at his own joke, his tongue curling backward like a snake licking soft serve ice cream.

"You's a nasty nigga," Reggie said.

"Oh, the pleasures of life, my friend."

Raulin and Reggie shared a laugh as they raised their glasses and toasted to life and friendship.

Spending time with Raulin provided Reggie with a much-needed break, not to mention some humor. Unfortunately, their paths only intersected when it had to do with eating, drinking, or Raulin's favorite—chasing women.

Raulin and Reggie had been friends since their teenage years when Raulin worked in a boutique pizza restaurant in the same mall that Reggie worked in a retail store. Later, they attended community college together. While Raulin stayed in the restaurant industry as a bar tender, Reggie had moved on and ended up in an analytical field.

Reggie now worked the standard workweek, with weekends off. In contrast, weekends were Raulin's prime money-making days; his "weekends" were Tuesdays and Wednesdays. Hence, Reggie could only entertain a couple of drinks, since he had to be up bright and early the following day.

Raulin, on the other hand, worked nights and could easily sleep in. He also had the same ways as when he was younger—a side effect of working in a field where his peers were usually in their 20s. Keeping up with his clientele, Raulin stayed out and partied with younger people during the week even though he stuck out like a sore thumb in a crowd full of millennials.

In addition to being both out-of-touch and out-of-time, Raulin had a huge head and face, resembling a second-rate Robert Kiyosaki due to his Japanese, Bolivian, Peruvian, and European backgrounds. Raulin adhered to European styles and culture though, preferring to wear either FCUK shirts with the Union Jack emblazoned on them, or sporting Diesel pants with zippers and shit. And his absolute favorite was narrow square-toed boots that curled up on the ends, just like Raulin's tongue when he laughed.

"In the summertime of my life, I was caught up with Arlene and her shit. That was the best time to get into the Washington DC real estate market," Reggie said.

"Exactly," Raulin said.

"That's when the housing market was cheaper, and you could get loans—"

"*Stable* and cheaper."

"Right, stable *and* cheaper. But I didn't have anybody that was making any moves to give me sound advice. For example, my cousin Cee and his folks started buying in Baltimore because they started watching *The Wire*. They thought Baltimore would be the next big thing, although the school systems in the city suck ass. But I decided to look into it." Reggie paused to sip his drink and continued. "One seller tried to sell me a house with a family already occupying it so that I could receive the cash flow. But it was sandwiched between two abandoned boarded-up houses... Did I tell you this story?"

Raulin shook his head. "No."

"Me, Arlene, and the agent—I think the guy's name was Tom—"

"Is Tom the guy who drives the corvette?"

"No, he's nobody that you know," Reggie said. "Anyway, Tom took us into this house for a tour. As we walked into the dining room area, I saw this baby on the floor. In his diapers, on the floor. And there was a tray with pizza. You know, like when you put pizza in the oven?"

Raulin nodded. "Yeah."

"He was crawling on the tray. And on the tray were roaches and silverfish. You know silverfish?"

Raulin titled his head, not fully understanding.

"They look like little *milipedes*. You know, little bugs. And they're like, silver."

Raulin shook his head. "Umm…"

"Uhh—*plata*. The color *plata*. You know, those little bugs. Those freakin' *insectos*."

"Uhh, yeah," Raulin said, tired of Reggie trying to describe the bug and wanting him to get to the point of the story. If Reggie would have said "los milpies" instead of "millipedes" Raulin would have understood him.

"The baby was crawling around on the floor and lifting up the piece of pizza with bugs all around him. So I looked at the woman, and she didn't even care! I thought to myself, '*I can't buy a place like this. I can't be a slumlord.*' You know a *slumlord,* right?"

Raulin didn't answer. His Spanish vocabulary didn't have the word 'slumlord' in it.

"You have your place in Wheaton, right?" Reggie asked.

"Yeah."

"You don't just let roaches, rats, and all that shit come in—no—you have it cleaned out so it's decent."

"But that's the responsibility of the tenant," Raulin said. "If they don't care about it—like I say, if I'm walk there and they say it's an infest of roach, I'ma will blame them. They don't care about it. You know, one time I fumigated there because they told me, '*Oh there's some roaches you gotta watch out, blah blah blah.*' So I going to fumigate over there. I'm going to put half and half."

"Right," Reggie said.

"That way it costs you, it costs me," Raulin explained.

Reggie nodded. "Right, right."

"You gotta care."

"Right."

"Because otherwise, we can't environment."

"Right, right!" Reggie laughed, partially because Raulin's accent was thicker than an obese stripper in Atlanta sipping a malted milkshake, and partially because while Raulin didn't enunciate every word, the spirit and meaning of his message was still communicated. Reggie was grateful for friends like Raulin and didn't want him to change for anything in the world. "You're absolutely right! I wasn't thinking like that. I was thinking about—"

"Those motherfucker finish with all that," Raulin interjected. "There's no rush. There's no fuckin' rush. There was incubation of roaches and rats. You guys leaving trash. Leaving diapers outside. That the reason rats coming. And it's about this is...this is... Forget it, man. Well, they was different mentality—"

"Like me. I'm not going to deal with it," Reggie said.

"In my view, I no care because I'm no living in there," Raulin said with a wave of his hand.

"Right, but—"

"You gotta make sure. Think about the property. It's easy to combat that thing. You just put a smog and just cost you two-hundred dollars."

"You're right, you're right. I wasn't thinking about that back then. Good point 'Lin," Reggie said as he finished the rest of his beer.

WHITE **GIRLS**

I probably bombed, and she's not interested anymore. I'll just send her one last message and arrange to return her mooncakes. Then I'll let her go on about her business, Reggie thought as he composed a text while at a stoplight on his way to work.

He was used to being in situations where he had to let people go. Although he was super attracted to Thuy and had enjoyed their time together, he presumed letting her go would be easy since he hadn't invested too much in their dating. Plus, they'd taken turns paying when they went out, so he didn't feel like he'd been used for free meals like some other bitches *tried* to do.

As a prelude to stopping the communication, Reggie figured he'd send a "touch n' go" message—one he didn't expect Thuy to answer immediately--but would pave the way to cutting ties between them.

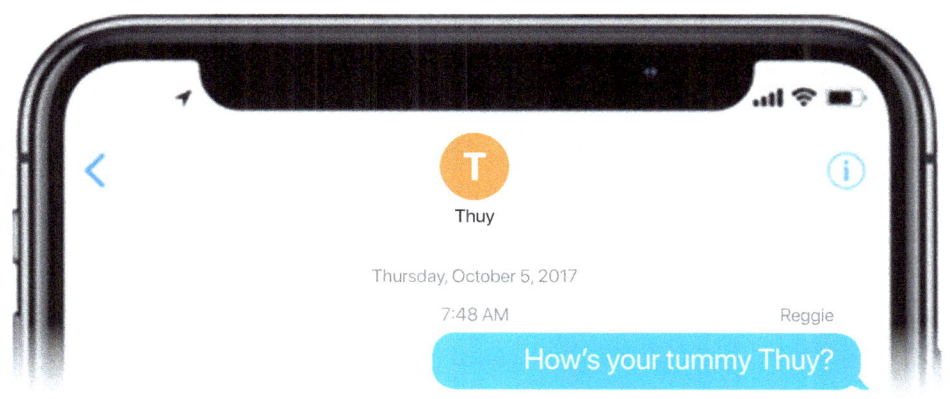

* * *

Seated at his work desk, Reggie fired up his computer, and the calendar app greeted him with a ding. He read the accompanying message: Fiscal New Year Celebration at Jonny B. Goode's.

That's right! Today's the happy hour!

Having more to focus on than worrying about Thuy provided Reggie a sense of self-control. He glanced at his phone, but the blue light of anticipation wasn't blinking. So with a shrug of his shoulders, he resumed working.

A couple hours later, however, the blinking blue light flashed in Reggie's periphery. His breath quickened. Just as he'd suspected, it was Thuy.

* * *

The evolution of the dive bar was a sight to behold in the late 2010s. Masses of millennials got what they asked for—open air meeting places with up-regulated "cleanliness" and menus that contained vegan and vegetarian choices. American restaurants innovated in order to welcome two major types of crowds—the regular "rough and tumble" group who wanted a drink after a hard day's work (or no work at all), and the office workers who wanted to "cut loose" every so often.

Johnny B. Goode's was that place.

The group seating had the wood-and-brass look of traditional saloons but featured isolated islands. It was in one of these places that Reggie and his teammates sat about with stomachs grumbling from the post-lunch/pre-rush hour insulin drop.

After the group had ordered appetizers and returned their menus to the waitstaff, Ishmael decided to open his big mouth.

It never fails... Never fails... Reggie said to himself as Ishmael droned on about stats regarding the finance team tightening their budgets, and their customer ending up in a surplus. Ironically though, the goal was to get as close to zero as possible, for being under budget was sometimes scrutinized under the same microscope as being over budget.

In reality, the team spent more time babysitting Ishmael and his insecurities than hand-holding customers for the sake of getting them to follow recommended budgetary patterns and restrictions.

The waiters approached with everyone's drinks while Ishmael carried on like a reverend at Sunday dinner with a group of hungry black folks eagerly waiting to dive into a basket of fried chicken at the center of the table. Just like the reverend making everyone wait as he said grace and acknowledged the many things God had done for the church, Ishmael rambled on about the budget team.

"Just like we take care of our clients and stakeholders, we take care of our team. Work hard, play hard, that's what I always say." Ishmael raised his 34 oz beer mug full of Landshark, the drink shaking in his hand as his shoulder impingement interfered with his wrist's stability. "What would I look like right now if I didn't show appreciation to my team for all of the hard work they put into this fiscal year?"

Like a goldfish swimming in a bowl of foamy piss, to be honest. Reggie smirked. From where he sat, he could only see Ishmael's face distorted through the beer mug.

The team, including Reggie, raised their glasses to schmooze their slave driver for another season of assuaging Ishmael's OCD ass when everything always turned out okay.

"Happy New Year! Eat, drink, and be merry!" Ishmael exclaimed.

"Happy New Year!" the team echoed in unison, with Shatner's radio voice—like the kind that the dispatch officer had in Ice Cube's song *Ghetto Bird*–being the loudest among them.

Reggie immediately took to his drink and laughed to himself, noticing the odd glances they were receiving from people in their vicinity. Most people associated New Year's Day with the first day of January, not October. Ishmael should have said, 'Happy Fiscal New Year' to avoid sounding like a jackass. But hey, Ishmael got to celebrate two New Year's Days, presumably making him extra cool.

Reggie looked about the place and the team. The team was almost purely composed of minorities—four African Americans: Reggie, Denise, Sadie, and Kayreen; two Asians: Bon Phan and Freddy; two Mexicans: Felipe and Ishmael; and a Middle Eastern Lebanese/ Jordanian: Linus. Shatner was the only non-minority on the team, which technically made him a minority as Ishmael's token white guy.

Ishmael was a master of manipulating mainstream racial narratives, and Shatner was his secret weapon. No successful financial base shop, in the abstract sense, can be run without a meat-and-potatoes, nuts-and-bolts, soup-to-nuts, tie-wearing white man. Shatner—Reggie called him "Scatner" in his mind because he was full of shit—looked like the result of an orgy consisting of William Shatner, Sam Kinison, and Robert Palmer. He sported the traditional *Men in Black* meets Mr. Smith from *The Matrix* look. He had two outfits—a navy-blue blazer with tan khaki pants, and a black blazer with black slacks—that he paired with either a burgundy or a black tie to give the impression of owning four outfits. Depending on the day, he either looked like a CIA agent, or a pall bearer.

After all the shop talk and other bullshit coworkers discuss while consuming appetizers and free alcohol, the momentum of happy hour began to wind down. People started texting loved ones and planning how to hump around the beltway traffic to get home.

Reggie grabbed his smart phone and formulated a text.

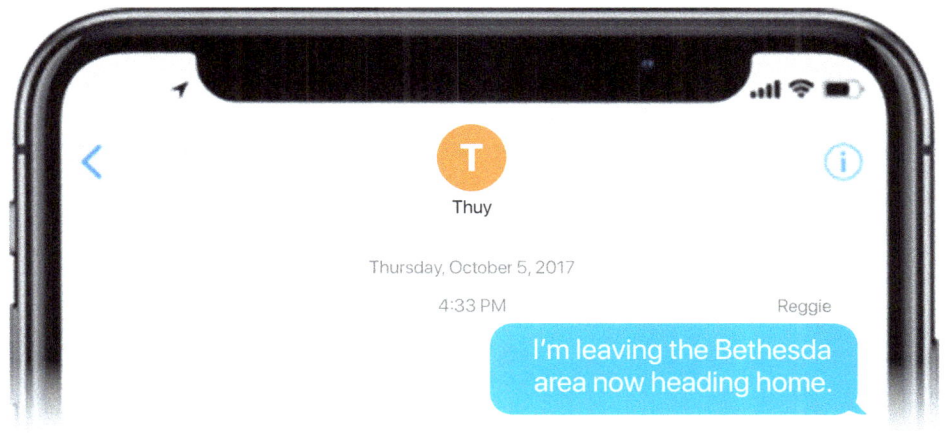

* * *

Since Reggie's car's Bluetooth wasn't working properly, he did like *Baby Driver* and listened to music from YouTube through his earphones. He pulled into the garage way while Phil Collin's *Easy Lover* played.

Ahh the 80s, when all the rockstars partied like rockstars. I betcha they had— Reggie's thought halted as a notification came through on his phone. He saw that it was Todd, informing him that he'd just acquired some "extracurriculars".

"Whoo hoo!" Reggie cheered aloud. He quickly responded to the message and let *Easy Lover* play once more from the top as he strutted to the apartment, where Todd happened to be in the general kitchen area.

After a brief greeting and chat, Todd disappeared into his room, and then reappeared with what Reggie had been anticipating. Shortly thereafter, like boxers returning to their corners after a bout, the two of them retreated to their own rooms on opposite ends of the apartment.

Thank God for roommate style apartments and the privacy they provide, Reggie thought as he pressed the lock on his door.

He reflected on the last live conversation he'd had with Thuy, in which she indicated wanting the rest of the cakes back.

I'll give her back her stuff and send her on her way. She's cool people, but for the time we've been hanging out, nothing is really coming from it that I can't get on my own. Feeding me the funnel cake fries looked good on me, I'll

admit, since she's a cutie. But it's time for me to go back to focusing on me.
I'll catch shorty on the kickball field.

Reggie changed out of his work clothes and into more comfortable attire. He intended to pay Thuy for his mooncake, having no intention of taking advantage of the situation since his mind was settled about discontinuing his pursuit of her. As far as he was concerned, dating her may have come to naught.

Awaiting Thuy's reply, he figured he'd rub one off before meeting her to totally take the anticipation of sex off the table. A little "post-nutt clarity"—an idea he and some buddies had kicked around when one of them was mulling over whether to see a girl he wasn't really into just for sex. One of the other guys suggested, *"If you're not really into a chick*

but you're horny, jerk off first. If you still want her, go for her. If not, stay away. That way, you keep yourself from making what could be a regrettable mistake."

There was a lot of wisdom enshrouded in that statement. But more than anything, the fact that men were almost always held accountable for their interaction with women was at the forefront of Reggie's mind.

As he mulled over all of this, Reggie fumbled with the small knot on the baggie Todd had given him. After finally getting it open, he put "Sarah" on his "command center" table. He was ready to party with the "white girls".

After spreading half of Sarah out and dividing her into three, he stepped back and admired his work. Her perfect white skin, with its granular crystalline glimmer and hint-of-diesel aftertaste, drove many men off the deep end. Just ask Al Pacino's *Tony Montana*.

His armpits starting to sweat a little, Reggie rubbed his hands together in anticipation. Next, he poked his head out of his bedroom door to see if Todd was still in his room. He indeed was, and upon knowledge of this, Reggie headed for the kitchen.

There she was, sitting on the counter in her blue-bottled glory. Svetlana was his Russian beauty. He held her by the waist, lifted her into the "Skyy", and admired her curvature from below.

Tiptoeing back to his room, Reggie snuck a peek at Todd's door again. Since his door was always closed, it hard to know whether Todd was sleeping or gaming. Either way, there was nary a sound.

Reggie shuffled back to his own room, closed the door, and set Svetlana beside Sarah on the table. Although Svetlana technically belonged to Todd, Reggie was sure he wouldn't mind him taking her out on a date for a little while.

Now, there was one last white girl to include, and her job was rather important. Her name was Keri, and her role was to make sure everything went smoothly—literally. Ever since the 80s, Keri had been keeping the flour-kicking ash of negroes everywhere at bay. Keri was so very, very... greasy.

Fuck a live chick. I can always rely on my Russian MILFs to be there for me, Reggie said as he clicked on the latest "Russian Matures" link. Up popped a myriad of thumbnails—from older women in lingerie nighties exposing tufts of pubic hair, to women with large areolas that sat atop massive mammaries. One caught his eye—the one with the curly auburn hair, wide hips, and pouty lips shaped like an "O". She had to be the absolute cutest. But the one that always haunted his dreams was the blonde-haired Florence.

Reggie poured a shot of Svetlana and then took a sniff of Sarah. As Sarah made her way to the back of Reggie's throat, his tongue tasted of aspirin; Reggie thought it tasted like aspirin because of what Julienne Moore's character told Mark Whalberg's character in *Boogey Nights*. Ironically, Reggie was about to embark into mom versus boy territory.

Now to be fair, Reggie vindicated himself in that these people were just actors. Still, there was always an inkling of wonder regarding whether somewhere in the mountains of Russia existed an incest epidemic. It was taboo, it was hot, and the computer bots didn't help. The scouring little creatures titillated the mind of the post-modern lonely man—a man who'd been shunned by mainstream expectations of females in masses and consequently turned inward to his mind, where graphic images and fantastical stories of others' gratification met his sexual needs. Tech companies knew this, so they upped the ante with thumbnail suggestions that took one from plain-vanilla missionary sex, to *bukkake* harems.

With so many choices at his fingertips, Reggie's method was to take a few strokes of his peen here and there, click through some of the videos, then find one hot enough to make him lose his load.

One of his favorite stories was of Flo and Benny. Benjamin was this Russian ripped teenager who often wore pimp sunglasses, socks, and brandished a swollen, blood-engorged flesh scepter that was ready to plunge into Florence's plump, porcelain-skinned body. Flo—the tasty, nasty, mature Russian red-head mommy—was armed to the nines with tactical tits and an ass that wouldn't quit. It was like she was sent by Gorbachev to start a new cold war, aimed at defeating the USA by draining the *jing qi* from its fighting-age men.

Reggie kept one browser open with Benny and Flo in the background for later. He then opened another browser on the side by dragging the folder label; he didn't want to lose his place. Every video he watched, he compared with Benny and Flo to see which would get him off more. He took care not to sniff too much of the other white girl, lest he create more vasoconstriction than necessary. He stroked some, then clicked more thumbnails.

One on the side, featuring the image of a mature cartoon woman's body, caught his eye. He realized it was erotic parody clips of *The*

Simpson's and *Family Guy*—Marge getting ready to do Bart, Homer and Lisa getting at it with Flanders on the side, monster cock Chris and Meg Griffin from *Family Guy* getting busy...

As he stroked, he got harder.

Cartoons?! Hell naw. But wait...

Reggie spotted an odd, anthropomorphic clip of a female succubus with a superhero's body—complete with horns and claws—having sex with a man in bondage from the viewer's perspective. He opened it up, and a new window opened with a barrage of thumbnails underneath and around it.

The wide world of *hentai* opened to him.

Here we go. Reggie took another sniff. His pupils dilated. Was it the coke or the myriad of images? The cause remained unknown.

The veins on the cartoon's cock and the vaginal lips of the demon woman seemed to grip, slip, and maneuver in tandem. The squishy sounds and the visuals made Reggie stroke more urgently as he imagined some otherworldly being propagating with him.

Holy fuck, she's got hot tits.

His stroking became faster and he started to feel a buildup of semen in his ducts. He backed off, stood up, and slapped his cock. He paced back and forth, and then gripped his knee before going to the closet to get a pillow. On his way back down to the floor, he grabbed the roll of paper towel he kept in his room. He threw the pillow in front of his command center and placed his knees on it.

Ahh, that's more like it. Now, let's get back to business.

Reggie saw another hentai clip of two women, both with buxom, muscular, hourglass-shaped bodies and round bubble asses. One was miniature sized and white, and the other was black and Amazonian. He opened it, and his jaw dropped, unprepared for what he was about to see.

The miniature white cartoon woman stretched her womb around the black woman's huge member. The scene was grotesque yet stimulating, as the animators took care to show the outline of the big woman's cock in the stomach of the little woman as she moved up and down on it. Then it happened—the big, black transwoman exploded inside of the little white woman, the semen leaking in rivulets down the side of her dick. Some of the semen gushed out at what appeared to be toward a third wall, so the viewer could feel like the cartoon's orgasm was going to reach the real world.

Reggie was amazed by how turned on he was. He had just done two lines, and his cock was harder than Chinese calculus. On the other hand, when using cocaine with alcohol, a third, more exuberant molecule, cocaethlylene, shot through his bloodstream, enhancing his euphoria. This euphoria created an enhancement in his senses—colors became brighter, the guttural sounds of the many thumbnails and pornographic ads reached deeper into his soul, and the erotic imagery swept him away. He empathized with the actors and actresses. He found that the same way men empathized with two lesbians having sex despite not owning a vagina, the feeling intensified when one of te women had a cock; the feeling of exploding inside of a wet, musty love cavern was one of the most natural highs around.

I gotta turn this anime shit off. It's fucking with me big time, Reggie thought, feeling that he was 75% to the way of his PONR.

Then he saw it—a thumbnail with a huge, round, peach-shaped booty and a woman who appeared as if her neck could do a 360. He also saw the words "Brazilian Rafaela Ferrari", and that was all he needed. He clicked on it. As the movie began to open, he stopped it midway and stood, pacing a couple times to let his excitement go down and relieve the pressure on his knees.

He glanced around his area. The pillow he'd been kneeling on had what appeared to be drops of water; his inner thighs and buttocks were wet and he'd been sweating out his ass. He looked at his setup; he had a small baggie of white and one line left on the table.

After I finish that one, I'm done for the night. Then I'll take shorty back her shit.

Reggie stared at the lone uneven line of *devil's dandruff*, and then looked at *Manuela*. She was smudged with the greasy lotion. His cock was greasy too. He used his right hand to feel his pulse. It was slightly elevated, but nothing alarming.

Returning to his command center, he put more lotion on his hands to finish his arduous task. He took a shot of vodka, and clicked back on the Russian's page to see more action with Flo and Benny. As the young man plunged his love muscle deep into the pink-fleshy peach of the tender mature beauty, his guttural sighs echoed throughout the scene. Reggie empathized and began to beat his meat. But Reggie had already given too much of his attention to Flo and Benny over the past couple of years, and the newfound anime excited him more. The porn industry knew how to up the ante.

He paused on Flo and Benny, looking at Flo as her mouth made an "O" shape.

If there's nothing good on the other thumbnail, I'll come back and you can get it all, my little babushka.

While Reggie became increasingly aroused by the anime, he was also slightly disturbed, considering some of the clips and body proportions were not common in the general human population. He looked back at the opening video of the Brazilian woman. It was a side view of her from the waist up, kissing a shirtless muscular man. Her face somewhat resembled Ariana Grande's, but more mature. Her lips were rosy pink, and her cheeks appeared rouge. Her tits were plump and perky, and sat high on her well-built frame.

As the camera panned about her body, her ass was the perfect plump healthy shape—two large round ovals joined together that made her lower back tapered into an upside-down heart shape. The man had palms full of her ass.

Although the people in the video were exotic, the beginning was natural. Reggie did half of the line on the table and waited a little to swig the vodka. He fast-forwarded the video to where they appeared nude, and realized the woman was trans.

The first time Reggie saw a transwoman who turned him on was Yasmin Lee's "Kimmy" in the movie *The Hangover 2*. Same specs, different model. Great ass, hips—apparently everything feminine, tits and all. Especially the ass. But the peter threw Reggie off; the Brazilian woman had a huge cock, rivaling the size of the man she was with.

Reggie suddenly found himself more confused than turned on. At least Yasmin had a baby cock.

Reggie fast forwarded to the point where they started fucking. The man inserted his cock into Rafaela's perfectly waxed gloryhole, that was ensconced by two muscular gluteus maximi, and went to work. The view was super anatomical—as Rafaela took all of him, she made long sensuous glides and kissed the man at the same time, the two of them being face-to-face. Though Rafaela's guttural moans had a deeper tone to them, the view of the muscular legs and ass, and the man being gratified filling Rafaela up to the hilt, somehow inspired life into

Reggie's cock as he imagined being engulfed and squeezed by a hole that was probably burning hot like a furnace.

Reggie took a swig of vodka and finished the last half of his line. Then, the world accelerated. He was so close to his computer that the images burned on his retina as Rafaela switched positions. She was now reverse cowgirl riding the man! Rafaela was facing the camera with her tits and her monster cock swinging as she bounced up and down on the man underneath. At the juncture of the two porn stars, Reggie saw, in the following order—legs, taint, balls, taint, balls, cock, hips, tits, and smooth muscle. It was a lesson in anatomy if he'd never had one before.

Rafaela said something in Brazilian Portuguese to the man underneath, and the man screamed "Vai! Vai, vai, gushstoso…"

Rafaela began to stroke her cock. Her light, fleshy skin turned pink from the blood engorgement. It was a sight to behold. Her mushroom tip threatened to make Princess Toadstool a second-rate hooker.

Reggie stroked, and then it happened. All three of them came together—Rafaela, the man, and Reggie. The man emptied himself into Rafaela's ass. Rafaela shot a huge creamy load that first had little droplets that flew out—almost as a warning—then finally a big gooey, mucus-looking load that shot out in a fabulous arc.

Reggie envied how this transwoman had enough nutt and a large enough hose to expel that amount of ejaculate. Empathizing with the release of ejaculate, huge breasts, pouty lips, moans, and her bright red perineum, Reggie let his emotions go. He quickly grabbed his paper towel with his trolling hand, put it immediately in front of his dick, and let his explosion muck up the paper towel. He completely emptied himself as he stroked out every last drop and shuddered as his hand reached the tip of his dick.

No rainbow-colored flags, intertwined gender symbols, protests, or lessons in pronouns necessary. Reggie had gotten a full education of gender expression, identity, and sexual orientation, all in one porn session. He kneeled in his squalor for a little like Eddie Murphy's character in *Boomerang*, not wanting to move immediately after orgasm. He just closed his eyes and enjoyed the rush of chemicals flooding his brain, including oxytocin—the binding hormone which gave him a warm, tingly feeling all over, and caused him to bind to the images now burned into his retinae.

Then he remembered he needed to deliver the mooncakes to Thuy.

He looked at his cell phone and saw the blinking blue light of anticipation, though there was no anticipation anymore since he had just squirted it out onto a paper towel.

Fuck! It's 6:20 already? What the fuck?

CCS

Reggie always marveled at how coke made time speed up. Granted, part of the issue was that he'd also gotten lost in the porn maze. He had been exploring the world wide web—and himself—for almost an hour. Finally seeing Thuy's text, he responded.

Reggie hopped in the shower to clean himself up, his head still buzzing with the pornographic images and moans echoing in his ears. As he dressed, he realized he no longer cared about making a good impression as he did before, considering Thuy was pretty much going to be in the friendzone.

* * *

As Reggie made his way towards Thuy's apartment, the sun had already started to ease below the horizon, painting the sky with beautiful twilight colors.

Reggie shook his head, trying to free himself from the trance he was still under. Once the gas station came into view, he dialed Thuy. "Hey, I'm out here," he said in an unexcited tone.

"Okay, I'm on my—"

But before Thuy could finish responding, Reggie hung up.

Hurry up and get here soon. I don't feel like standing around, holding this box of mooncakes like an idiot.

Five minutes later, Thuy trotted over. "Hey!" she said jovially.

"What's good? Here you go, your mooncakes and ten dollars for what I ate," Reggie said, although he hadn't really eaten two mooncakes. He just wanted to get the night over with so he could get back to life as usual.

Thuy tilted her head curiously. "Who put the bug up your butt, Mr. Killjoy?" she said, sensing Reggie's emo vibe.

Reggie suppressed a laugh, though not at Thuy's joke; he simply found her word choice ironic since he had just been glimpsing of all types of butts. "You know," he said, cracking a smile, "you stole that line from Homer Simpson when he told Flanders about himself. And why you looking at my butt anyway?"

Thuy laughed. "Just wondering why you're rushing me. Why don't we grab some green tea and go for a walk?"

"So you want to go for a walk with Mr. Killjoy?" Reggie shrugged. "Well, at least you didn't call me *dude*."

Thuy giggled. "C'mon, *dude*. My treat."

"All right, all right," Reggie said, figuring a walk with Thuy was probably a good idea. He could sober up, listen to her chitchat, then head back home to get some rest.

Thuy went into the gas station and resurfaced with a large bottle of green tea. Reggie glanced at her hands; she was carrying the box of mooncakes in one, and the green tea in the other.

She only bought one bottle of SoBe green tea? Reggie thought, feeling slightly miffed. Though he found the gesture eyebrow-raising, he stretched out his hands as she came his way. "Here, let me take that for you," he said, reaching for the mooncakes.

"Thanks, babe," she replied, handing them over.

Babe? Did she just call me 'babe'? Let me see what she's talking about... Drink tea and talk. She's probably just bullshittin'.

Reggie and Thuy proceeded to take a stroll around the lake, taking in the many happenings along the lakeside restaurants. As they walked, Reggie noted the various glances they garnered from people passing by—older Asian folks in particular. Reggie debated whether it was the box decorated with traditional Chinese characters in his hand, or the fact that he was walking with a cute Asian woman that caused all the attention.

Is she catching this? Reggie glanced sideways at Thuy, seeing that her head was slightly tilted back as she gulped some of the tea.

Noticing Reggie in her periphery, Thuy smiled, then handed him the tea.

Reggie looked around self-consciously, but accepted the drink because as with the funnel cake fries, he viewed the gesture as an offering of trust and intimacy.

After walking a little while longer, Thuy broke the silence between them. "You know my deal, but I'm going to reiterate. I was in a relationship, married for the better part of my twenties to a guy in the military. I just got to the Washington D.C. area last year from California, looking to start over. But mainly, because of my schedule, I never really got a chance to date and explore and meet other people. But I also just don't really like letting people—uh, guys—get close to me. That's why I might seem wish-washy at times." Thuy shot Reggie a cautious glance.

Reggie nodded, acknowledging what she'd said, but not biting at her words.

Unexpectedly, Thuy grabbed his arm and gently pulled him over to the side. "How do you feel about what I just said?"

Reggie paused, looking at Thuy and the backdrop behind her. He was still high, and the merry-go-round lights shimmering off the lake in the distance distracted him somewhat. He forced his gaze back to Thuy, making eye-contact.

It's now or never, so might as well get this over with... Let her reject me real quick so I can go back home to my computer and my bed. I'm maxed-out for tonight.

"I'm a little drunk, so don't take this the wrong way," Reggie began. "I've been feeling you from the jump—er, from the first time we started hanging out. I understand your situation. You're starting to get out there and don't want anybody tying you down, but you still want to meet people and hang out. As you said, *explore*. But at the same time, the only way you're going to be able to explore and meet people is if you let them in. And yes, I had a feeling that you had a wall up because you kept calling me 'dude' and acting hard. It became really annoying, trying to figure out whether you wanted to give me a chance and start some of this exploring with me."

"Acting hard?" Thuy snickered. "I've been through some stuff and you're right—I do have a wall up. But yes, Mister... What's your last name?"

"Jenkins."

"Yes, Mr. Jenkins, I'd like to see how things go with us."

It's now or never... Reggie stepped forward, entering Thuy's personal space. "So, Miss—what's your last name?"

"Lieu."

"I think we could definitely go on some wonderful adventures together, Ms. Lieu."

"Oh yeah?" Thuy stepped closer to Reggie, moving into his personal space as well, until they stood face-to-face.

"Yeah." *It's now or never,* the thought repeated in Reggie's head. He then closed his eyes and moved to kiss Thuy, giving her a peck on the lips that she reciprocated. Afterwards, he backed up to look at her.

She smiled at him.

Encouraged, he gave her another peck before slowly opening his mouth. Thuy parted her lips in response, permitting Reggie to slip his tongue through. He caressed her tongue with his, tasting the inside of her mouth. Their heads pushed each other's a little, and Reggie opened his eyes to see if Thuy's were still closed. Finding that they were, he continued his tongue-fu attack.

Then, just as Reggie began to close the kiss and exit Thuy's mouth, she pulled him back. He left his bottom lip in her mouth as he closed segment

the kiss, then pulled out. Their lips made a suction sound, like they were vacuum sealed.

Thuy took a deep breath. "Too much tongue, Mister Jenkins."

Reggie blinked, slightly taken aback. He'd thought her passion had matched his. "Okay, cool," he said, figuring they were probably done making out for the night. He nodded and averted his gaze from Thuy. "Yo, Thuy, it was good hanging out with you, and I hope we can do this again soon."

"Aww, does wittle Weggie have a curfew? Does wittle Weggie hafta go beddy-bye?" Thuy mocked playfully.

"Maybe you wouldn't mind telling me a bedtime story and tucking me in, Mommy?" Reggie said, deciding to play along although he was at least three to five years older than Thuy.

"What story would you like to hear, son?"

"The story about the three little pigs—especially the Vietnamese one. The one that ate the whole crispy duck…"

Thuy slapped Reggie on the arm, and they both laughed. Shortly thereafter, they began walking towards their living spaces.

When they approached the intersection where Reggie and Thuy were to part ways, Reggie paused, feeling emboldened and wanting to test Thuy. "So, are you going to tuck me in or what?"

***

Butterflies raced through Reggie's stomach. He had expected Thuy to turn him down, but instead, she accepted his request and followed him home like a cute stray cat. Reggie remained quiet most of the time they walked together, occasionally smiling or nodding at Thuy, with her mirroring the gestures.

I've already shot off my best load and then some, I don't have any Rhino pills, I still have coke in my system, and now I gotta perform sexually. And I'll likely have to use condoms. Fuck! Maybe I'll just start, tell her I'm super tired, eat her out, and call it a night. Or maybe she'll want to dip when she discovers that my soldier doesn't want to salute. Fuck! Why now? Maybe I can just make out with her, cuddle, and say that I think we shouldn't rush into sex—but then I'll sound like such a bitch…

They entered Reggie's apartment, and Reggie was relieved that Todd was nowhere in sight. Todd sometimes liked having late evening conversations when he was high, rambling about random, loosely interconnected topics.

Good thing I cleaned up after myself, Reggie thought as he opened the door to let Thuy in his room. The only telltale signs that he had be using internet porn was the lone bottle of Keri lotion on the table next to his closed laptop, which was in front of his bedroom window. Reggie had returned the bottle of vodka and put the coke away before going to meet Thuy.

"This is you, huh?" Thuy looked at Reggie's room from a panoramic perspective.

"Yup," Reggie said, hoping she wouldn't single in on the bottle of lotion he'd left behind.

"Keri? They still sell this? I haven't seen this lotion since the nineties. I tried it, but it's too oily for my taste."

Reggie clinched his perineum as he looked for a deflective comment. "Yeah, but I get ashy feet that tend to crack, especially in the winter. I find that putting it between my toes helps a lot."

A brief pause slipped over the room as Thuy simply stared at Reggie.

"TMI?" he guessed.

Thuy cracked a smile. "My cousin owns a nail salon. Trust me, I know about the agony of the feet."

Reggie watched Thuy approach his command center—er—computer table, and glimpse the view of the restaurants and town centers below. The moon happened to be out and nicely hovered in the upper left corner of the window frame, right above the Sin Embargo restaurant, still bustling with people.

"Dude, I can see everything," Thuy marveled.

The word 'dude' stung Reggie's ears again. But since they had shared a kiss, he was okay with it. He walked up behind Thuy and wrapped his arms around her waist. "Look down. You see those lights? That's MyThai," he said, gently rocking her from side-to-side. He bent to kiss her neck. "So every time you eat there, you're eating *under* me."

"Ha-ha. You're a funny dude," Thuy retorted.

Reggie kissed Thuy's neck again, and she leaned back, giving him more access. He proceeded to kiss upward to her cheek, making her wriggle like a kitten enjoying a back rub.

"Hey, babe?" Reggie spun Thuy around to meet him face-to-face. "Don't call me 'dude'."

Thuy smiled widely, and they began to kiss. This time, there were no complaints as Reggie's tongue twisted around Thuy's like King's Dominion's *Anaconda*.

Fuck, I'm still spent, and my condoms are in the bathroom, Reggie thought as Thuy started unbuttoning his shirt. Furthermore, Reggie was still somewhat concerned about CCS, especially since he had been doing coke earlier. He eyed his wastebasket, which contained most of the batter-colored load he'd squirted out earlier.

CCS, or Condom Collapse Syndrome, was the psychological and/or physiological phenomenon that happened when a male, hard as bricks, became soft as cotton after putting on a condom. It usually impacted men who'd previously been in long-term, committed relationships where they felt psychologically tied to their partner. After a breakup, confidence and self-esteem suffered, making these men uncomfortable with themselves, especially in the presence of new people.

One of Reggie's childhood friends, Rodrigo, said he never stopped using condoms, even when he met his first wife. However, once he got used to her, he went raw and was hooked. After his divorce, one of his methods to get used to using condoms again was masturbating while wearing one. But to some, the practice was no avail. They could be harder than a DeBeers diamond, but if you so much as threw a condom in the same room with them, they went Limp Bizkit. And once CCS was experienced, it created a self-fulfilling prophecy of dread.

These thoughts swirled in Reggie's head as he and Thuy were under the covers, naked, kissing and fondling one another. As he touched Thuy's love box, his hands became eyes, seeing that Thuy's pussy was a peach with a syrup filling, and bald like an eagle. Her legs were muscular, and the adductor muscles that ran inside her thighs felt as if they belonged to Chun Li. Her skin was like satin.

A war raged between Reggie's self-deprecating thoughts and the present moment that had him semi-hard. Amongst the mental chatter, Thuy started to pull on Reggie's cock with smooth, up and down strokes. As Reggie kissed her, he leaned his weight onto one elbow and knee as he played with Thuy and positioned himself higher up on her body. She caressed him from balls to tip, using gentle motions.

The soft and sensual feeling got Reggie's nerve ends firing, and slowly but surely, he began to harden. Reggie's confidence began to build.

"Umm, yeah, babe. That's it," Thuy said, looking directly into Reggie's eyes. They gazed at each other, smiling.

Then Thuy started to do the unthinkable. She moved Reggie's hand, opened her legs, and began to guide him in.

Reggie pulled back a bit. "Hold on, babe. My condoms are in the—"

"I don't like condoms," she said.

Should I trust this broad? I mean, statistically speaking, she's less likely to have something. But if I force the issue, not only do I risk turning her off, but I might get soft. But I don't want to get her preg—

"Don't worry, I'm on birth control," Thuy said, somehow reading Reggie's mind.

He nodded "okay" and pecked her on the lips. They then looked at each other as she slowly guided him in.

Her face crumpled as she could just barely get his tip in. "Ah, you're big," Thuy said mid-kiss as she squirmed about.

"No, you're small." Reggie chuckled as the sky opened up for him like the beginning of *The Simpson's* episode. He wasn't even at his hardest and she felt super awesome at the tip. He removed her hand. "Let me, babe."

Thuy nodded, removed her hand, and caressed Reggie's lats.

Reggie began, holding the base of his cock and dipping and dabbling his tip in the entrance of her love cavern, alternating that motion with brushing the *one-eyed bishop's* face up against her clit. Thuy began to squirm and make soft moans. Then slowly, his mushroom tip poked in the entrance of her love cave like Casper the Ghost sticking his head through a wall before entering a room. Although he had sufficient "headway" to enter her entirely, he decided to play at her entrance for a bit, making Thuy's breath quicken.

In her ardor, Thuy pulled Reggie closer, but he resisted and continued teasing her. Still holding the base of his cock, he talked to himself.

C'mon, c'mon, please! Don't do this to me now! Why now? I know her pussy is bomb, but why couldn't this have come to me when I was ready to hit it like I wanted to? Fuck. C'mon man! Stay in the game!

Reggie's cock was only at 70% stiffness, and he noticed that as he played with Thuy, he experimented with a full entrance somewhat to his chagrin. Thuy's pussy was so tight that Reggie's cock bent even when he dipped the head in. He was essentially buying time, but to Thuy, it was a torturous foreplay session that could turn her into a full explosion if only he could give her what she was yearning for.

But be as it may, Thuy liked it. In her mind, Reggie was an experienced gent, a "tongue fu" master. But in all actuality, Reggie was actually a "hentai pimp", watching cartoon and other porn, and busting his nutts off like a meltdown at a peanut factory—leaving him somewhat empty and unable to fill Thuy's order.

C'mon, c'mon… Just get a little bit harder. We can do this. We just have to get through this night. Then next time, we'll be ready. It's now or never!

Reggie moved his head faster and faster at her entrance. Still holding the base of his cock, with all of his might, he thrust forward. To his amazement, she felt so good inside that he inflated to 80% hardness. Thuy broke from kissing him, letting out a moan that made him a little bit harder. Although he still wasn't at his best, he had a fighting chance.

Employing a strategy, he first used his pubic bone to push against Thuy's as he was deep inside, preventing himself from emphasizing the retraction of his foreskin and becoming overly stimulated. When feeling the need for more stimulation, he pulled back a little, stroking at her entrance to get harder before going deeper.

"Oh my God, oh my God, oh my God, oh my God…" Thuy lied, knowing damn well she didn't believe in God. She was a Buddhist. But as her pleas and moans began to build, they turned into aspirations and puffs of air. She was reaching her peak. To Thuy, Reggie seemed like a pro.

This will be the acid test. Fuck it, we're either made for each other or not! Reggie thought. He then went kamikaze, putting most of his weight on his elbows and stroking deep into Thuy while ensuring he was "riding high" on her pubis mons to create friction with her clit.

Thuy dug her fingers into Reggie's back. They shared a fuck-face and Thuy nodded her head yes.

"You ready, babe?" Reggie asked.

"Uh-huh," Thuy said, out of breath.

Reggie gave Thuy everything he had left in his shaft, but a one last "hoo-rah".

"Ayieee!" Thuy screamed as she Rhonda Rousey'd Reggie into her naked full guard.

"Fuuuuuuuuuck!" Reggie yelled as he let his remaining nougat flow. He couldn't believe he'd nutted twice in one night. Not bad for a guy approaching 40.

In unison, Reggie and Thuy sighed in relief.

Reggie let his head fall to the side of Thuy's. With his eyes closed, he felt all of the sensations of the chemical cocktail being produced by his brain.

Thuy let her thick little calves fit on the humps of muscle on Reggie's butt. She released the grip of her inner thighs, sure that she had drained him.

As her legs rested on his back, held together lightly by interlocking feet and ankles, she turned to the side and smiled. She eyed the silhouette of the lone bottle of Keri lotion against the backdrop of the windowsill and the lights of the town center below. She knew what he'd been up to and was surprised he had been able to go all the way through with his task. Thuy gently power tripped about how her pussy was able to squeeze blood from a rock.

"Did you cum good, bae?" Reggie asked, raising his head to face Thuy's.

She nodded, smiled gently, and kissed him. They shared two kisses before Reggie couldn't hold his head up any longer. He sank down into the bed, and his body released itself into Thuy's grip as she delicately stroked the back of his head and neck.

They lied for a while, until finally, the blanket of the night covered them into a deep slumber.

THAT'S **ALL YOU**

With a glide in your stride and a dip in your skip, got daytons on the mothaship... Reggie sang to himself as he traipsed through the office hallways, listening to Ice Cube's *Bop Gun*—a hip-hop remake of George Clinton's *One Nation*. Passing acquaintances, he nodded, smiled, and gave dapped-up handshakes.

"Yo, Moe!" Reggie greeted as he entered the café area.

"Reggie, what's goin' on, *bahddy*?"

Reggie grabbed a couple overpriced protein bars, then turned towards Moe, who stood behind the counter. "You're going on, my dude. Gimmie my regular, and I'll also take a side of bacon."

"Your wish is my command, bahddy. Hey, Gabriella—one side of bacon," Moe said to his employee while he put two green tea bags into a tall paper cup with a cardboard guard around its waist. Moe pulled the lever on the hot water machine and glanced at Reggie. "You're in good spirits today, no?"

"How did you guess?" Reggie said, looking up from reading the total carbohydrates count printed on the back of his birthday cake flavored Quest Bar.

"Because when you walked in, you had this big smile on your face, like you were in a good childhood memory," Moe answered as he finished pouring almond milk into the green tea mixture.

"Moe, you ever see the movie, *White Men Can't Jump*?"

"Is that ah, the movie ah, with that Black guy who does karate with vampires?"

"Yeah, Wesley Snipes. Although *Blade* came out after *White Men Can't Jump*."

Moe nodded. "I think so. He was playing basketball with that bird-nosed guy, right?"

It never occurred to Reggie that Woody Harrelson had a bird-shaped nose. When picturing crooked noses in Hollywood, Owen Wilson more readily came to mind. Reggie laughed, thinking that Owen Wilson was the result of Matthew McConaughey losing a fight. "Yeah, I guess. But anyway, they had a saying—*even the sun shines on a dog's ass some days.*"

Moe secured a sippy top onto Reggie's hot tea, and Gabriela dropped off the bacon. She exchanged smiles with Reggie.

She's juicy as fuck, but I need to be easy. Moe always hirin' them phat jointz, Reggie thought, looking at the healthy-shaped Guatemalan woman as she walked away.

Moe looked at Reggie, exchanged glances with Gabriela, and raised an eyebrow. "So, I'm guessing, my bahddy, that you would be the doggie, no?"

"Yes, my buddy, yes! I'm going to Miami tomorrow!" Reggie paid Moe, grabbed his purchases, and bolted for the door, unable to take one more 'buddy' from Moe. Along the way, he passed onlookers who seemed puzzled by his sudden burst of energy.

"I'll have what he ordered," said the customer who'd been behind Reggie.

Reggie chuckled on his way out the door and then sprinted up the carpeted stairwell leading to his office section. Reaching the entrance, he touched his badge against the sensor, and the door beeped and opened for him. He got to his cube and set his morning treasures— green tea with almond milk, double bagged for extra caffeine, two low-carb protein bars, and bacon—on his workspace table.

Since Reggie had started eating out with Thuy, he'd been struggling to discipline himself into ketosis. So instead, he settled for low carb. He looked at his receipt, reading, *Moshen Hamidzai Inc.*

Ahh, so that's what Moe's real name is, Reggie thought. *You don't meet a lot of Middle Eastern guys with the name Maurice.*

He sat down and logged onto his computer, where he was met with the annoying Microsoft Windows prompt: *Don't turn off computer as it is updating.* Using this as an excuse to check on Thuy, Reggie took out his phone. Oxytocin was still pumping through his veins from last night's encounter.

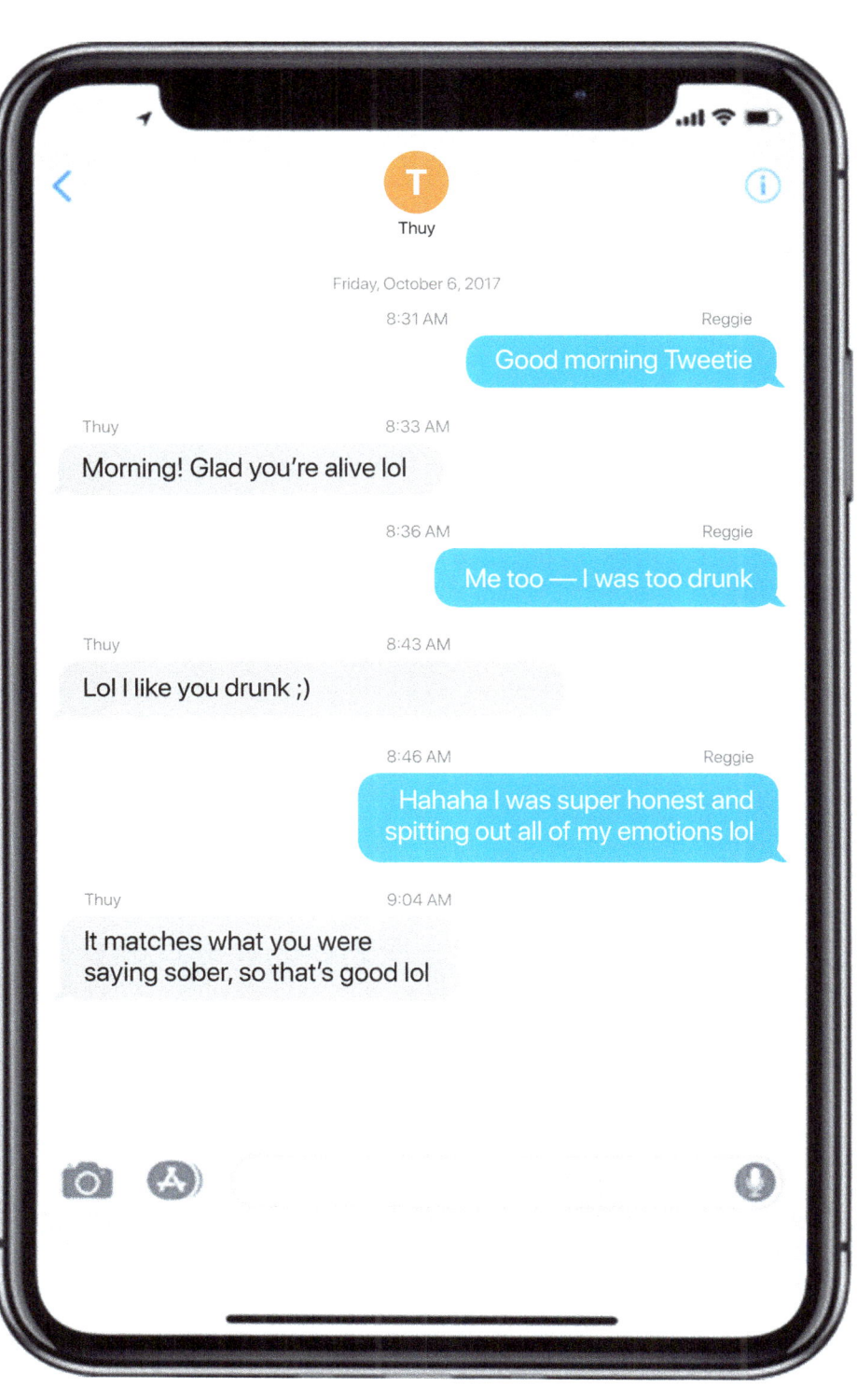

Reggie smiled, appreciating the fact that Thuy recognized the consistency between his words and actions, and hoping this would score points with her where gaining trust is concerned.

Letting her have the last word, he set down his phone and got to work with renewed vigor. Yet, less than an hour later, there was a knock on the side of his cubicle entrance.

"When you get a chance, please come see me," Denise said, strutting by.

Reggie nodded, finishing his current task before grabbing a pen and notepad and heading after Denise.

Seated behind her desk, Denise sipped her coffee as Reggie entered her office.

"This is what I need you to do," Denise said. "Ishmael has to present his analysis to the board tomorrow and needs the data from the different service areas regarding average expense levels over the last ten years."

Reggie scribbled her request on his notepad. "Got it. Anything else?"

"No, that should be it. When do you think you can get it to me?"

Reggie checked the time. "By lunchtime. That way, if there are any other ways you want to present the data, we can do it by close of business."

"Sounds like a winner."

Reggie returned to his desk and set to work extracting the necessary data into Excel spreadsheets. He isolated the columns and used the VLOOKUP and SUMIFS formulas to acquire the necessary data. He then used the chart feature to display the expense levels as bars on a graph, with the average expense level running through the bars as a line. Done by 11:15 a.m., he patted himself on the back and emailed his work to Denise.

Reggie's day continued with more tasks, a few meetings, and thoughts of Thuy.

He liked letting Thuy have the last word so that he could pick the conversation back up later. Ready to do just that, he retrieved his phone and responded to Thuy's last reply regarding his sober and drunk words matching.

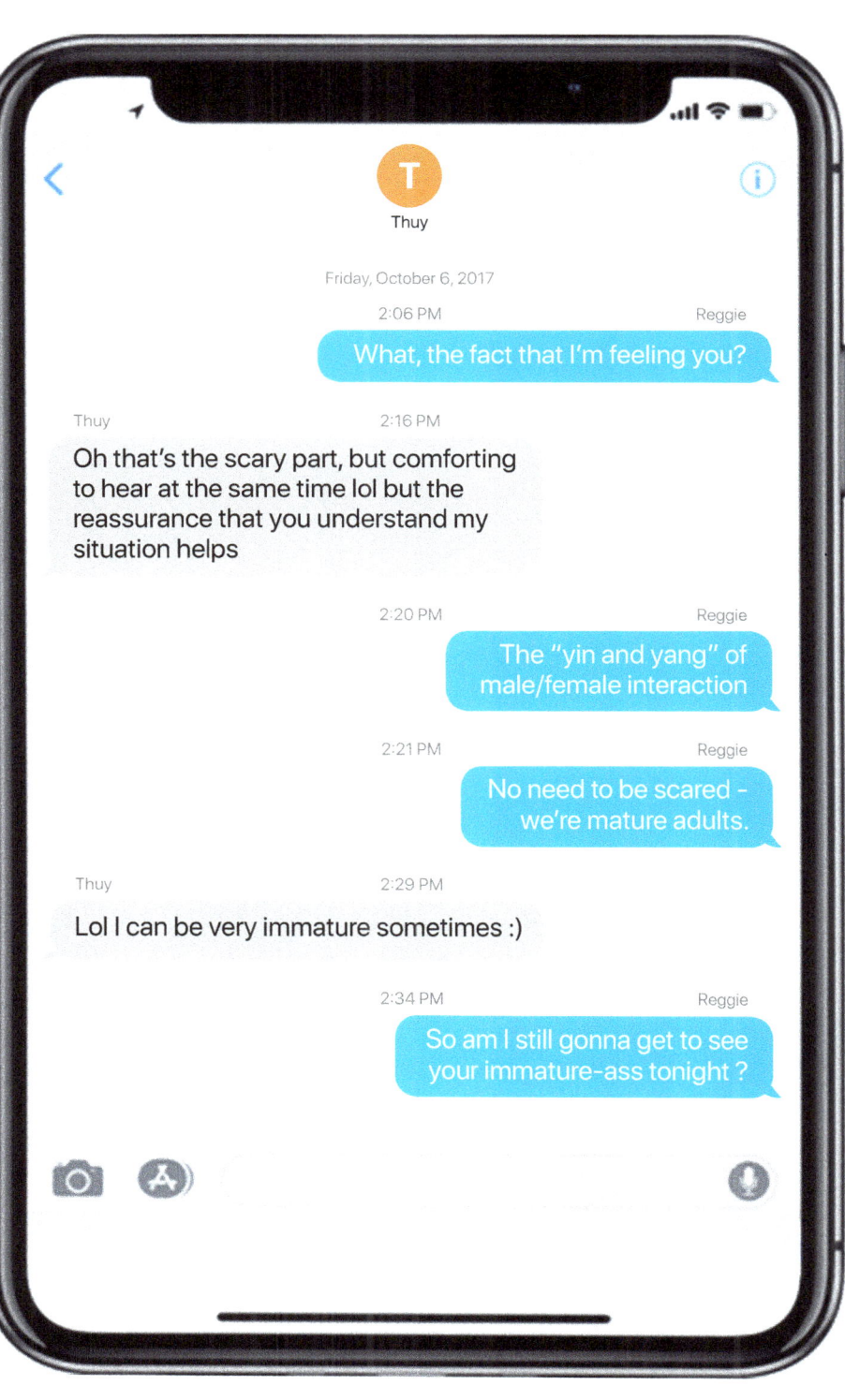

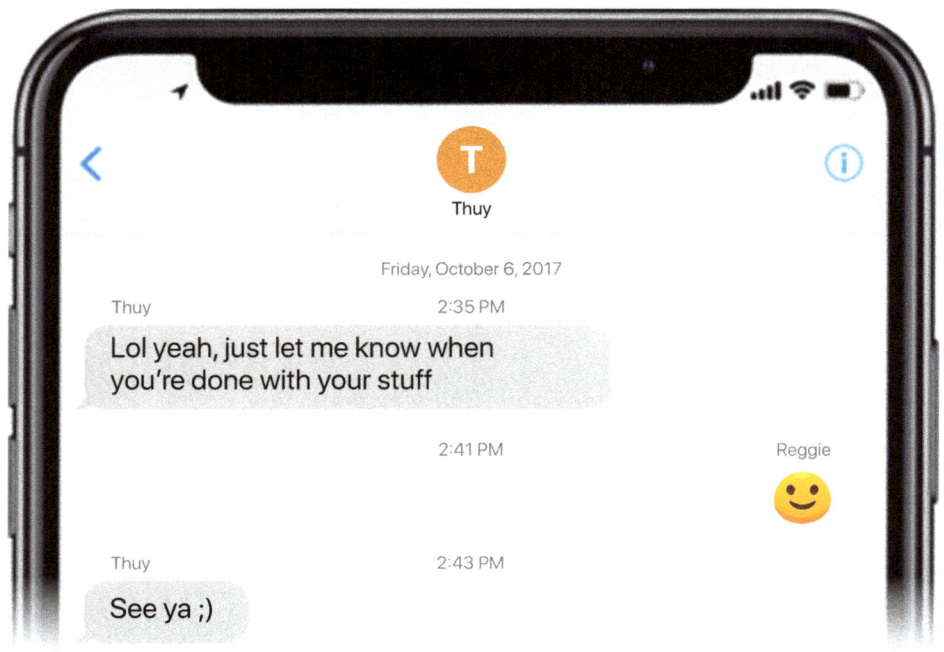

Reggie smiled, ending the conversation just as a ding sounded on his computer. He put his phone away to read the message he'd just received from Denise, complimenting him for compiling the data exactly how Ishmael needed.

Reggie's smile widened. *Another day another dollar.*

He shut down his computer, his workday coming to an end.

Besting rush hour, Reggie arrived home and changed out of his work clothes. He then started packing for his Miami trip, tossing underwear into his suitcase and putting toiletries into a plastic bag for TSA inspection.

Just then, his phone dinged with an update from Thuy.

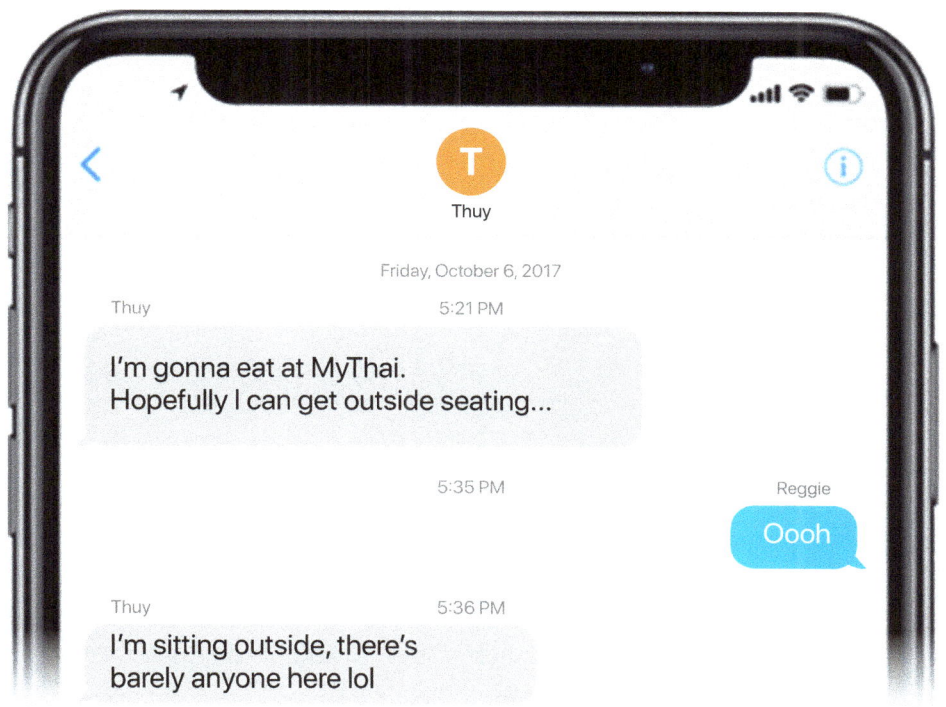

Reggie bolted downstairs to the town center restaurant area, spotting Thuy sitting outside with the evening sunlight shining on her dark hair. Facing his direction, she smiled and wiggled her fingers at him in a wave.

Not before long, they were seated together, enjoying their meal.

"Are you stoked about your trip tomorrow?" Thuy asked before picking up some beef and rice with her chopsticks and inserting them into her mouth.

Reggie smirked. He enjoyed watching Thuy eat. She, like other Asian people he'd met, liked to smack her chops when eating. When the guys Reggie knew did it, it ranged from annoying to outright unbearable. But Thuy's smacking was light, like a kitty cat lapping milk from a saucer.

"Oh yeah," Reggie replied. "The only time I go out dancing is when I hit Miami Beach. I haven't been really feeling the electronic house music scene in D.C. Plus, Miami has a good mix of different ages, since people from all over vacation there."

"I didn't know you were into dancing," Thuy said.

"You want to know something funny? The guy who taught me how to dance was Vietnamese."

Thuy blinked. "What? Really? So, no offense, but black people are known for rhythm and dancing. Asians... Well, they're known for playing tennis, ping pong—"

"And the piano?" Reggie interrupted.

They laughed.

"Yeah, the piano," Thuy said..

"But here's the thing," Reggie said, "when he taught me to dance, it was more club-techno style, and incorporated breakdancing. And while breakdancing has elements of personal style and pizazz, some of the signature moves are technical and/or acrobatic—and Asians are known to be good technicians. I think China has its share of acrobatic feats. *Shen Yun* comes to mind."

"That's interesting. I never really thought about that."

"We started clubbing early in high school. We used to go clubbing on Thursday nights when the *Zei* club was open, and people would dance on top of speaker boxes and stuff. What about you? You like to dance?"

"I didn't really do much dancing in my late teens and twenties. Some of my friends would go clubbing, but since I was, you know, an army wife, I was either a homebody or going to bars with my ex. It became a routine after a while."

"I can imagine."

* * *

The sheets stuck to the back of Reggie's lower half. He was on top of Thuy, and this time, Thuy was aggressively kissing him—using her tongue to flail him like a stingray that just got stepped on by Lizzo.

For someone who used to say, "too much tongue" you sure are tasting the fuck out of my mouth, Reggie thought, unable to resist a smile that caused the kiss to break.

"Whatcha laughing at, babe?"

"More tongue, Miss Lieu. More tongue."

Thuy rolled her eyes and smacked Reggie's bare bottom.

Reggie put his finger down there to test. Yep, her oven was preheated.

Thuy reached down to Reggie's nether regions and grabbed a handful of nuts like she was at a cocktail party.

Thuy put him inside, little by little.

"Ahhhhhh," Reggie sighed in relief.

"Uhnngh," Thuy groaned in agony, wincing as she stretched.

Yes! Now I'm going to hit it like I was supposed to. Reggie smiled as he began to spiral his hips, keeping his penis relatively centered, but moving his pubic bone about Thuy's to create stimulation for her while avoiding "in-and-out" movements that would turn him into a "nutty" professor.

"Oh my God, babe. Oh my God, babe..." Thuy said as Reggie seemed to be winding her up like a major league softball pitcher.

Her breathing quickened, and Reggie slowed his motion. He took a deep breath in and then exhaled, gazing into Thuy's face. "I don't want you to cum too quick, bae," he said, giving her a few honey smacks like a frog on a cereal box.

Thuy smiled and embraced Reggie as they took a moment to enjoy just being and not rushing to orgasm. Reggie loved that her teeth were straight and white—he briefly got a flashback of what Linh would have been like had she gotten her teeth cleaned.

Snap out of it, Reggie, he said to himself, returning to the present moment. Feeling Thuy's pelvic contractions, he started to swirl his body again.

Thuy put her hands on his hips and stopped him. "Hey babe, let's do it like this," she said, guiding Reggie to move his legs outside of hers. She closed her legs, effectively making herself tighter.

Reggie grimaced as her already cozy parts became claustrophobic.

"I want to feel every inch of you, babe," she said, seeing Reggie's face wince.

He nodded.

I'm gonna make this man cum so fucking hard, Thuy thought, a mischievous grin slipping onto her face.

Knowing what Thuy was up to, Reggie shifted his weight onto his forearms. Lifting his pelvis, the top of his tip and shaft contacted the top of Thuy's love cavern. The pressure between Reggie's lower abs and erection stimulated the top of her sugar wall. Thuy turned her head to the side and squinted as Reggie gave her a sly grin of his own.

Aww fuck! A wave of pleasure rode up Thuy's body like a Hawaiian surfer hanging ten.

Stroke after stroke, Reggie staved off the need to explode by playing the music of Faze-O's "Ridin' High" in his head, for that's essentially what he was doing—riding high on her twat and using his shaft movement rather than foreskin retraction to cause stimulation. He maintained control until...

"Gnuuh, oouuah, oooh, yeah...fuuuck." Thuy dug her nails into Reggie's triceps.

"Yeah, that's it, babe. Let it go," Reggie said, acknowledging the arrival of Thuy's love train at Gazmville.

I wish he would shut up. There's no way I'm gonna let a guy control me. There's no way— "Uuagh! Uuagh, uuagh, uuagh, fuuck, fuuck..." Thuy shouted, completely letting herself go.

Now that's the way I want to hit it. That's what's up, Reggie thought.

Thuy sank deep into Reggie's bed, becoming one with his mattress as it started to contour to her body. Reggie's cologne, body sweat, and warm breath engulfed her. She went somewhat limp, and Reggie rested his body partially on his knees while still rock-solid inside of her.

Reggie felt a warm viscosity, like syrup and butter heating together on a griddle before being poured over a stack of flapjacks.

Uh huh, that's that nutt. Tweetie done got a real good one. Reggie kissed Thuy's neck and cheek.

In ecstasy, Thuy opened her eyes to find Reggie at her smiling. *Asshole! Made me fucking come again!* "Whatcha laughing at?" she huffed.

"You!" Reggie playfully put his finger on the tip of her nose. "You thought you were gonna get me with that position."

Thuy laughed. "You got me, babe. You ready to get yours?"

"I'm ready."

Reggie got back to work. Instead of distracting himself, he fully felt Thuy through and through. The squeeze of her legs and the wetness of her love pushed Reggie to the point of no return. His semen, built up like new construction, was now poised for release.

"Ah-ah-ah-Fuuuuuck!" he announced as his he blasted off like Buzz Lightyear—his ball juice filling her to the brim. He fell onto Thuy, completely spent.

Thuy caressed the back of Reggie's sweaty head and neck as if she had just given birth to him. The sweat of their bodies leaked into every crevice and crack—the sweat from Reggie's buttocks dripped like the "techniques" Biggie Smalls spoke about in his song "Ready to Die".

After trading jokes and small talk, Reggie finally withdrew from Thuy, and she got up to find her underwear and clothing.

Removing the bedding revealed a milky white substance where Thuy's bottom half had been.

"That's all you," Reggie joked, pointing to Thuy's leukorrhea.

"No way! That's you!" she said, jabbing Reggie in the arm.

"There's no way that could've been me. I was too deep inside of you to have dripped out that fast."

Thuy playfully slapped Reggie's arm again, and they embraced for a quick kiss before Thuy resumed collected her things from the floor as if on a treasure hunt.

"So, tell me more about your Miami plans," Thuy said, prompting a brief conversation about Reggie's traveling plans until her eyes suddenly went wide.

"What's wrong?" Reggie asked.

"You were right. That was me on the bed. And you—you're leaking out!" Thuy turned and made a beeline for Reggie's bathroom.

Reggie laughed, watching the little naked woman's butt cheeks as she ran like a kid who'd stolen something. *You did it again, man. You done did it again,* he thought.

APACANEEGOHRS

I *wonder if Thuy's in bed already,* Reggie thought as he stuffed the rest of his necessities into his duffle bag. Taking a quick break from packing, he reached for his phone.

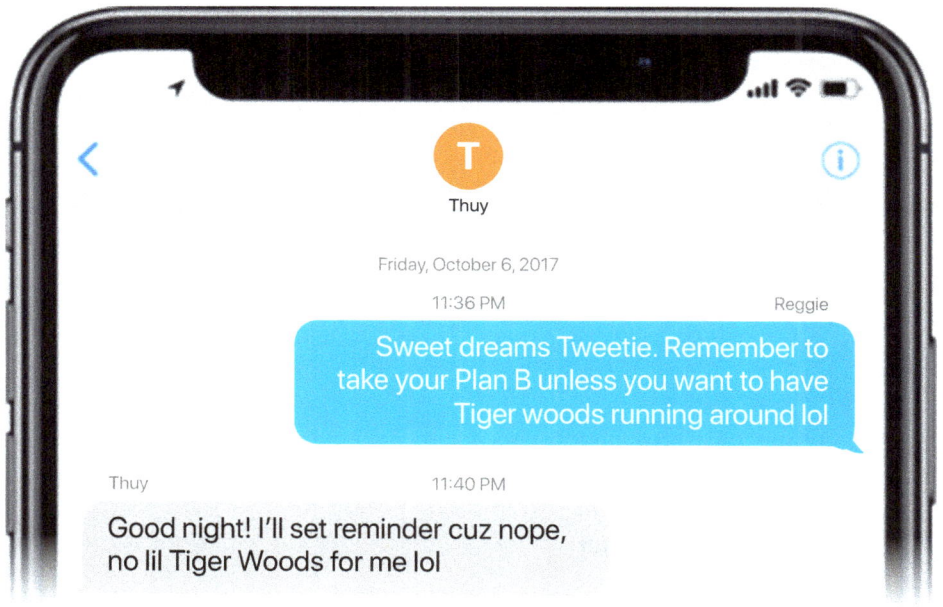

Reggie laughed, powered down his phone, and went to bed.

* * *

Excited and ready for his trip, Reggie woke early the next morning. Restlessly, he double-checked his duffle bag, making sure he hadn't forgotten anything. And just when he was certain he had everything he needed, his phone chimed with a notification.

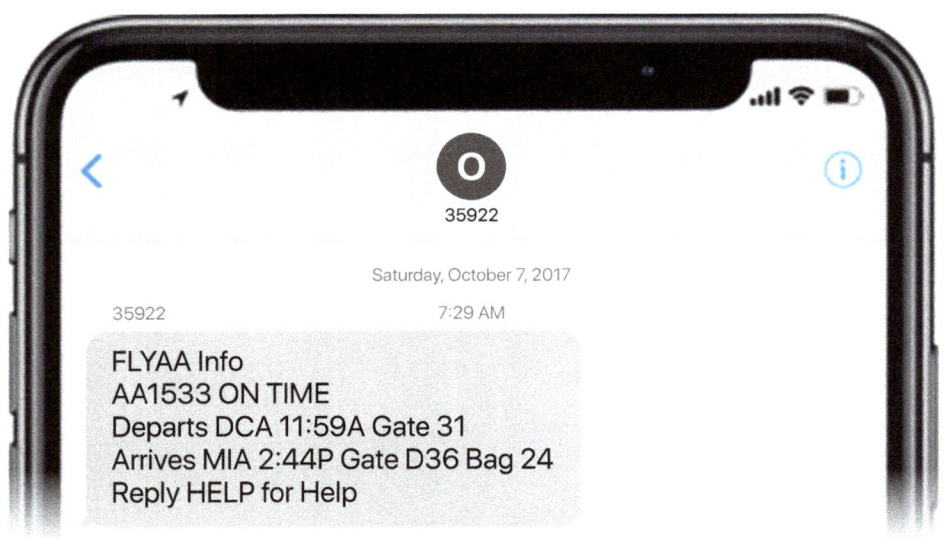

Cool. I'mma head to the metro early and get a jump on the day.

Before heading out, Reggie scrolled through the texts on his phone and realized he didn't reply to a message that he received from his friend, Jeff.

I wonder how Jeffrey's been. It's been a while. He's usually up early. I'll give him a shout-out.

Reggie and Jeffrey hadn't hung out much since Jeffrey had started a serious relationship with a Chilean woman he'd met in the spring. Although they'd had their ups-and-downs, Jeffrey was no quitter and was in it for the long haul.

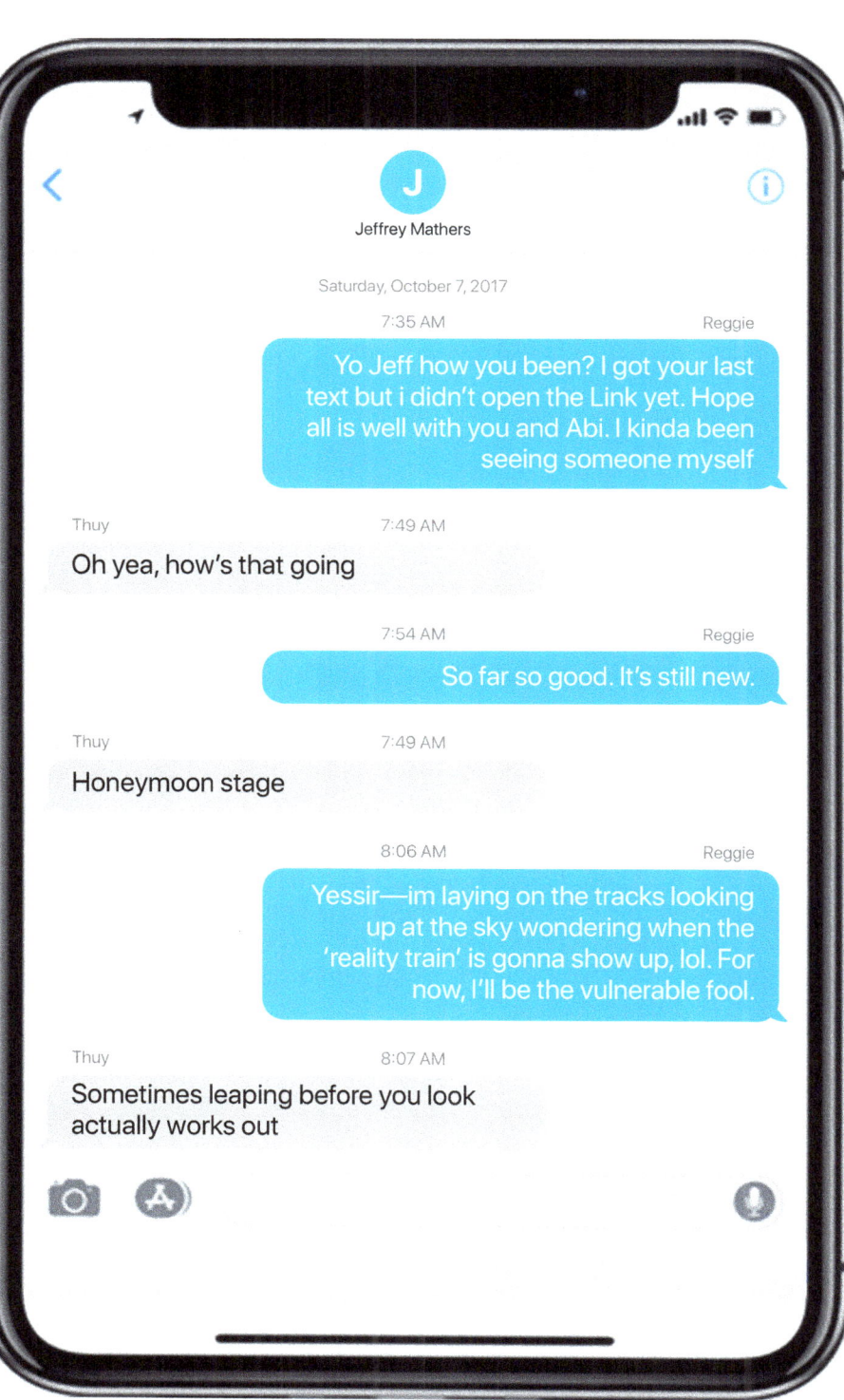

* * *

At the airport waiting to board the plane, Reggie sat across from his long-time buddy and butcher of the English language—Raulin. With an intense look on his face, Raulin was focused on his phone, although he was doing nothing more than updating Facebook with new statuses and selfies to let his friends and followers know he was traveling to the Sunshine State.

Reggie took out his own phone, figuring he'd touch base with Thuy to check the temperature of their relationship.

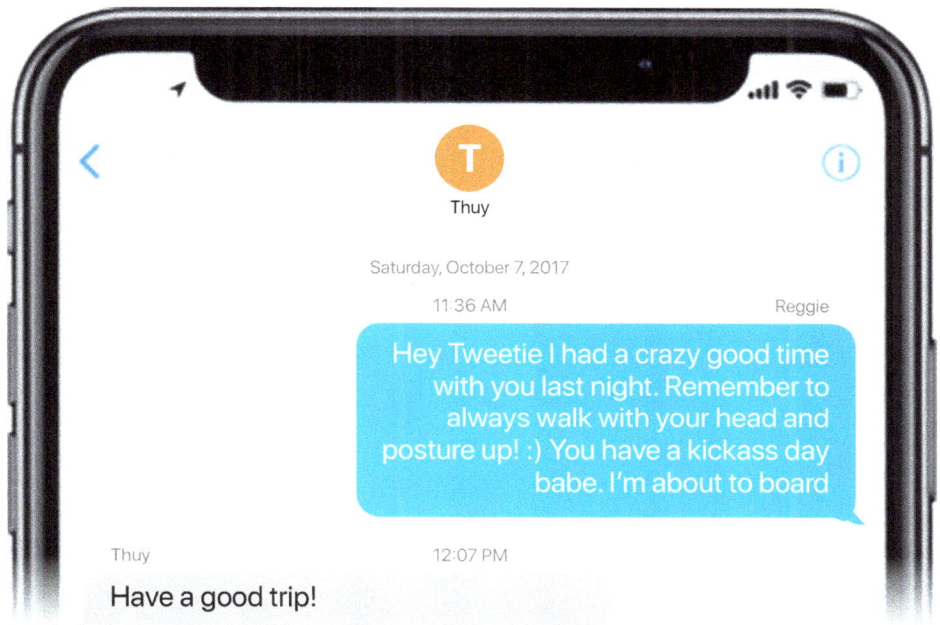

Reggie smiled. A little while later, he found himself on the plane and putting his phone in airplane mode at the request of the flight crew, as they went into relaying emergency instructions. And although Reggie attempted to pay attention, he already yearned to listen to the isochronic tones he'd stored in his phone.

The airplane window was on Reggie's left, and Raulin was on his right. As the plane took off, Reggie observed the many reds, oranges, and browns of autumn above the nation's capital. When the airplane reached over the clouds, it was like being in another world. The thick blankets of cotton hanging in midair obscured the ground, and the sun shone above them like a rolling cumulus tundra. Reggie tuned in to the music in his phone, following the patterns of the clouds. The soothing music transposed against the friendly sky rocked him into a slumber.

* * *

As the plane descended into Miami International Airport, the browns, oranges, and reds of the Mid-Atlantic area became green, while the coastline sported the blues and whites of the ocean and sand. The wakes of speedboats and jet skis seemed to be glued together in a stop-motion picture frame, the theory of relativity practically observable to the naked eye.

The plane touched down, the pilot's voice droned about crosscheck and the usual verbiage, seatbelts popped open, and the dings from indicator messages sounded through the plane as more people turned their phones back on.

I've always wondered what that meant, Reggie thought, reflecting on the pilot's "crosscheck" statement. Like Parker Lewis, he made a mental note to Google the word. Checking his phone, he saw that he had a few missed messages:

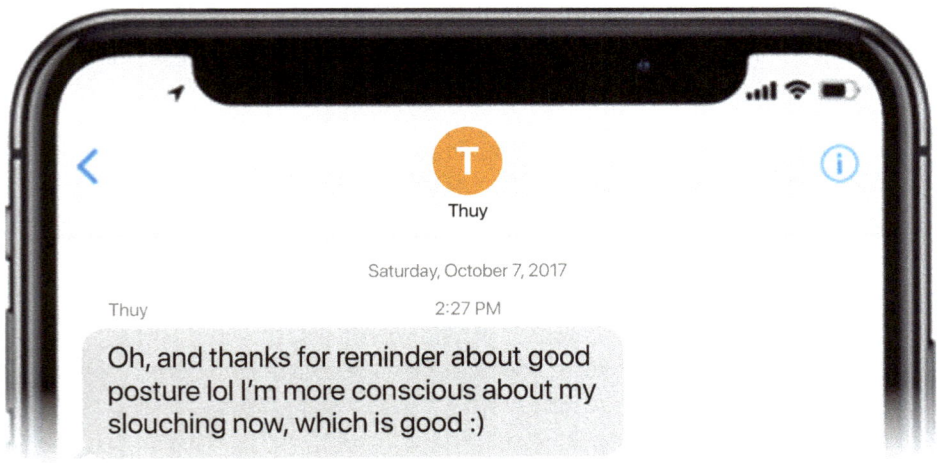

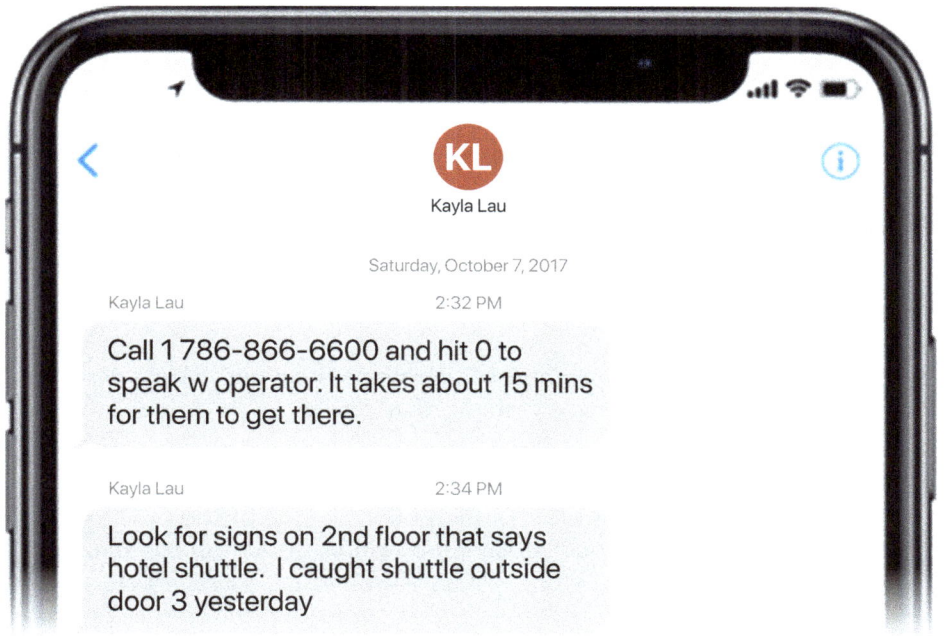

Nah, Reggie thought, *I ain't takin' the shuttle. I'mma take the bus down to Collins.*

Shortly thereafter, Raulin and Reggie began walking through the airport in search of the exit.

"So, what's the plan, doo?" Raulin asked.

"Keep your eye open for a sign that says 'Miami Mover'," Reggie instructed. "That's the bus line that's going to take us to Miami Beach. Once we reach Collins Avenue, we're going to hop off and meet Kayla at the Marriott—"

"Man, doo, I starving."

Reggie briefly chuckled at Raulin's usage of *doo*—his attempt at pronouncing *dude*. More than likely, he'd learned that pronunciation from hood people who ended their words with vowels.

"I was getting to that piece if you let me finish, Raulin. There's a restaurant across the street from her hotel. We can eat there."

"Right on. How long take us get there?"

"Probably 20 minutes. Hey, look over there. Let's walk down that hallway. I remember the bus was in that direction." Reggie pointed at the pink flamingos decorating the airport, a testament to Miami's tropical climate.

Upon turning the corner, Reggie and Raulin saw the signs for the Miami Mover bus. Once they reached the ticketing machine, and Raulin took out his wallet.

"No need, I got this one. The fare to Miami Beach is pretty cheap," Reggie said, putting in a five-dollar bill and getting two tickets and fifty cents back.

He and Raulin then made their way down the long stairway and to the 150 bus that would take them to Miami Beach.

During the bus ride, Raulin updated his Facebook status again and took pictures of the scenery. Bright, pastel-colored buildings, 80s art deco, and palm trees seemed to wave at them, welcoming them to town, particularly as they crossed Alton Road Bridge, where the bus ran the gauntlet of symmetrically lined palm trees on either side of the road.

* * *

"This is the place. Let's go in. I'll text Kayla to see what she's up to," Reggie said as he and Raulin approached the front of the Marriott on Collins Avenue.

They walked in and sat on the plush sofas, and Reggie opened up his phone.

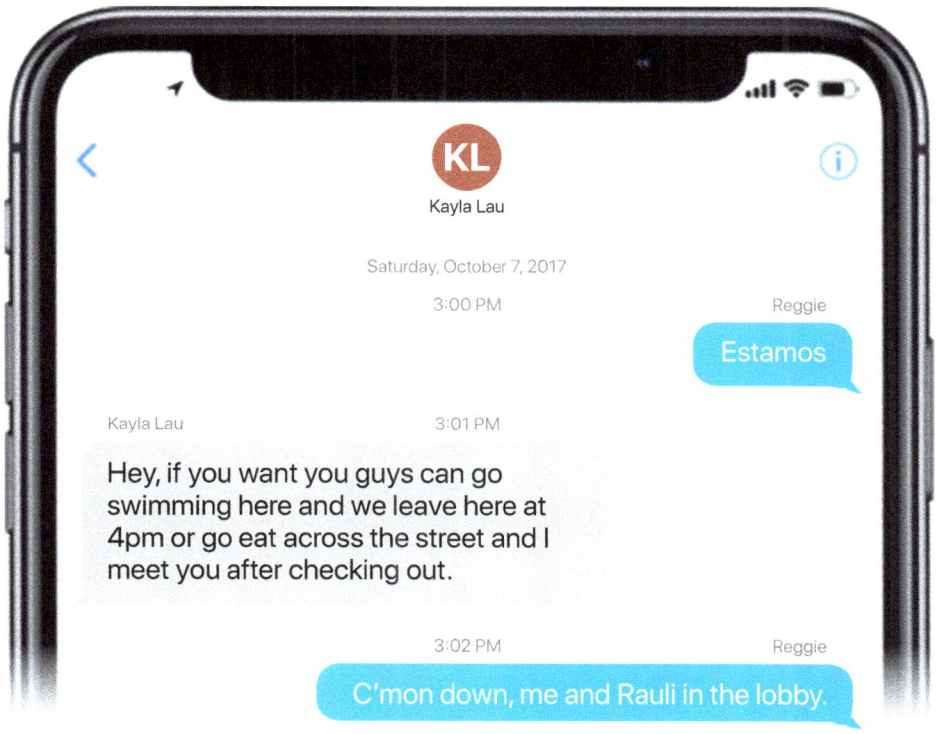

A few minutes later, Kayla appeared in the lobby. "Hey guys, you finally made it."

"Hey, Kayla," Raulin and Reggie said in unison as they shared a group hug.

"You're the lucky one who gets to travel for work and get a per diem that can feed a family everywhere you go," Reggie said.

"Yo, she's indapendan, doo," Raulin said.

"Yeah. Strong, independent, and don't need a muthafuckin' man," Reggie complimented.

They laughed.

"So, what did you decide to do? I gotta finish up some work before I check out," Kayla said.

"Raulin's belly is burning, so I think we're going to hit up that Peruvian restaurant across the street," Reggie said.

"Oh—eets a Perubiyaa restaurant, doo?"

"Make you feel like you're back home, eh Raulin? Unfortunately, serving fried guinea pigs is not something the people of the great city of Miami condone," Reggie teased.

"They eat fried guinea pigs in Peru?" Kayla crinkled her nose.

"Eets called *cuyi*. Ju just poot a little hot sauce an—"

"Raulin, a rodent is a rodent. I don't care if there's hot sauce on it or not. Stop trying to appeal to niggas by using hot sauce as an excuse like Hilary Clinton," Reggie said, taking another stab at Raulin. After the jokes and salutations, there was a brief, awkward silence.

"Hey, I'll walk you guys over and then come back and handle my business. This was a much-needed break anyhow," Kayla said a few moments later.

The three homies walked out of the lobby and into the streets of Miami Beach.

As they faded from the view of onlookers in the hotel lobby, Reggie patted Raulin on the back. "Well, they eat squirrel and possum in America, so I guess cuyi ain't that bad."

* * *

California and Florida are over 2,000 miles apart but share a common history with colonial Spain's influence. The phenomena by which cultures remain encapsulated in one time and place separate from the original culture is noted by Thomas Sowell's many works on cultures and migrations. This is the same phenomena that allows the cobblestone streets, high archways, and smooth clay roofs to be in both Old Pasadena, California, and on Espanola Way in Miami Beach. Espanola Way runs east and west perpendicular to Collins Avenue, the westside of Espanola Way is the promenade of Miami Beach. The buildings retain the old colonial Spanish styles. The anchor and boutique hotel of this promenade is called El Paseo.

Numerous times before, Kayla, Raulin, and Reggie had traveled the world together, like Three Musketeers or Three Stooges—depending on your point of view. People, including Raulin, who knew that Kayla and Reggie used to be involved ten years ago were often baffled that they still traveled together as friends. Their lifestyle directly challenged theory that men and women can't be just friends.

"Welcome back, Mr. Jenkins. I see you've brought a new friend." Luis, the hotel manager, looked in Raulin's direction.

"Yep. That's Raulin, my longtime friend who used to buy me beer in high school."

Luis chuckled and batted his eyelashes, his sexual orientation obvious at this point.

"Luis, darling, were you able get the room facing the inside for me?" Reggie asked. "Although the festivities are quite grand, I like my peace and quiet when it's time to sleep."

"Of course, Reggie. I remembered your preferences." Luis tapped on the computer keys in front of him with the urgency of a reporter. He then picked out the electronic room keys, ran them through the magnetizer, and handed them to Kayla, Raulin, and Reggie. "Enjoy your stay."

"Thanks, Luis!" Reggie said as the group walked off and headed upstairs with their luggage.

"Yoh, I think that doo's gay," Raulin said once out of Luis's earshot.

"He's the one who gives us such great deals on the rooms, and he manages this facility very well. If that's what gay hotel managers do, then they can all be gay for all I care," Reggie said.

* * *

RM

Raulin Mota

Saturday, October 7, 2017

6:17 PM   Reggie

Yo Rauli meet us in the lobby in 20 min

Raulin Mota   3:01 PM

Ok

Tst-tst-tst, Tst-tst-tst, Tst-tst-tst. The sounds of the guiro over cumbia and other Latin music reverberated throughout the restaurant area. People moved up and down the cobblestone road in groups, trying to decide where to eat while being hustled by Italian, Brazilian, Cuban, or other Latin offshoot restaurant workers who looked like international students.

Guys like Sergio, who looked like Calvin Klein models, or women like his girlfriend Armanda, who looked like Playboy bunnies, coaxed tourists to eat at Numero 28 pizza; the beautiful people of Miami were quick to seduce the average, corn-fed, American tourists into spending large portions of their disposable income.

"No, Rauli. You still don't get it, do you? The way the people move tells you a lot about what they're getting into. For example, look at them over there." Reggie pointed out a group of young, attractive women. "They're moving in a flock, like birds. Now look at those guys not far behind, scoping them out. You see that?"

Raulin looked at the mostly young black men, wearing pants sagging off their asses and more cornrows in their hair than the state of Iowa.

"Those dudes are a pack," Reggie stated.

"He-he-he," Raulin chuckled. "Apaca neegohrs."

"Raulin! How many times do I have to tell you, you gotta put an 'ah' sound at the end of the word so you don't sound racist!"

Raulin, Kayla, and Reggie laughed.

"Cheers to another vacation with family!" Reggie said as the three of them clinked their glasses together.

"Wanna play?" Reggie asked Kayla.

"Okay."

"You see them, coming into your field of view in five, four, three, two..."

Kayla turned and spotted a group of obese women.

"What do you call that?" Reggie asked.

"I dunno. A *herd?* "

"See, you're a fast learner!"

The group toasted once more, just as their napolitana pizza reached the table. Additionally, the server brought them mussels in champagne garlic sauce. The fact that Numero 28 pizza was also accompanied by a seafood restaurant and raw bar made Reggie's creativity come to life.

He and his friends each grabbed a piece of the margherita pizza at will and eyed the mussels.

"Good call on the mussels, Reggie." Kayla opened one of the little, black-shelled critters.

"Thanks, but you know why I got the mussels right? Because after you eat your pizza down to the crust, you can dip it in the sauce that the mussels are in. It tastes much better than the free bread."

After an evening of drinking wine, eating pizza and mussels, and washing the pizza crust and bread in champagne garlic sauce, Reggie joyfully paid the $84.59 bill, thinking to himself how great it was to still have loyal friends.

* * *

Ahh, they've got the best smelling toiletries. Reggie lathered himself with El Paseo's organic brand "Damana" body wash, with balancing Juniper extracts. After last night's revelry, he and Raulin had a night cap, and Raulin insisted on smoking a cigar, having an affinity for playing the "high roller" character.

Though slightly drowsy, Reggie didn't have a hangover, butstill felt a little out of it. Standing in the shower, he watched the water splashing off of the tiles, and then looked over at the painting on the wall, which read: Viajar Es La Unica Cosa Que Pagas Y Te Hace Mas Rico.

Ain't that the truth, Reggie thought as he finished lathering and braced himself for what he was about to do.

Okay, here goes. Eat your heart out, Wim Hoff!

Reggie turned his low-grade hot water knob all the way to the cold-water section. The faucet took a little time to convert, so Reggie washed the soap off his back and shoulders, but left on the conditioner, which he liked to wash with cold water while leaving a little extra in—advise given to him by an ex-girlfriend.

The water converted to cold, giving Reggie a shock that quickened his breathing.

Just got to hold out... Just hold out...

Gradually, the bottom of Reggie's feet began to tingle and get warm. Soon, internal warmth shot through him as his body self-heated, giving him a sort of high. He'd been practicing with cold showers back home, where they were much more brutal given the climactic conditions. But in the forever summer of Miami Beach, Reggie was lulled by the warm climate and wanted to hold that feeling. Yet, he tempered his comfort with discipline.

After drying off, Reggie put on American Eagle brand's Extreme Flex grey khaki shorts, and a Coupe Standard blue pastel sleeveless collared shirt purchased from H&M. He fastened the middle two buttons of the seven-buttoned shirt, wanting to allow the coastal breeze to caress his skin.

Knowing his friends were still asleep, he made his way to the lobby, exchanging greetings with the morning staff along the way.

Reggie stepped outside and took in a warm, gentle breeze.

Miami Beach mornings set the stage for the nights to come. The sounds of road improvement projects, drills and power tools, and rushing water washing the streets gave Reggie an appreciation for the people nobody saw by the time evening set in—the construction workers who made enjoyment for tourists possible.

Turning left and walking towards the ocean, Reggie passed Havana 1957, a Cuban restaurant boasting some of the best hangover breakfasts and hair-of-the-dog mimosas to get the partygoers back on track. The outside dark wood grain of the building and the bar inside--also with wood grain and encompassing glass shelves, mirrors, and lighting—accentuated the bottles on the shelves.

It's still poison, Reggie lamented, knowing he still enjoyed the feeling alcohol gave him. He just didn't like to bear the costs of those good feelings.

He walked down to Ocean Drive and gazed at the great Atlantic Ocean, marveling at its vastness and the way the sun shimmered off it. He listened to the rolling roar of the waves for a moment, then turned and headed back, his flip-flops scratching the grains of sand against the concrete as if walking over thousands of microscopic Rice Crispies.

I BEEN **READY**

U p early and ready to get cracking, Reggie started his morning by sending out texts, one to Thuy and the other to Raulin.

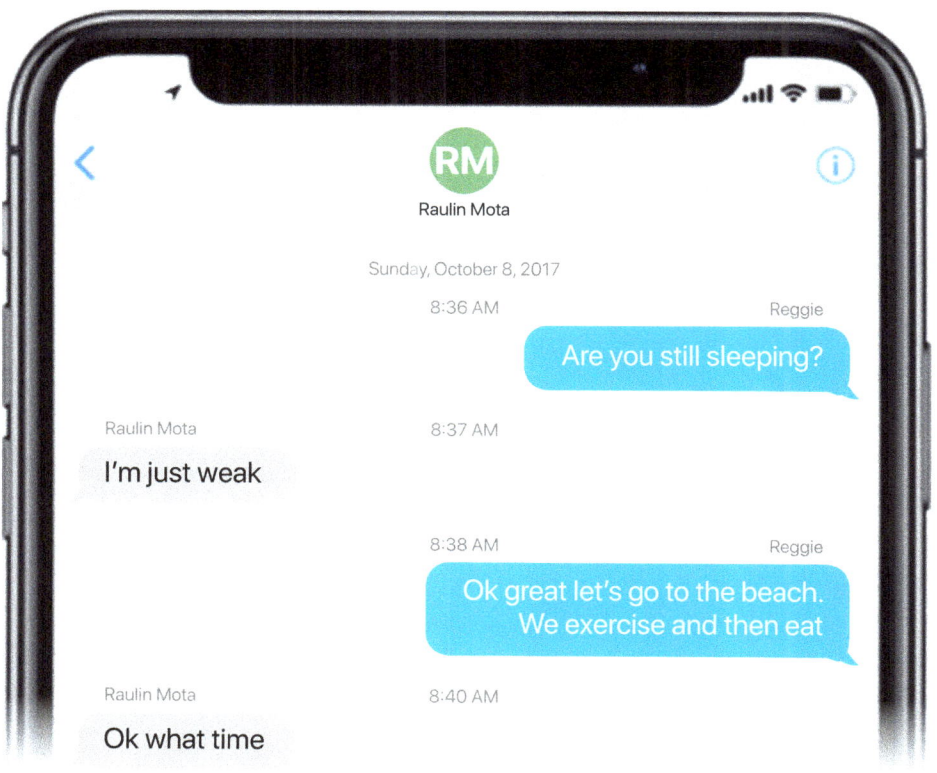

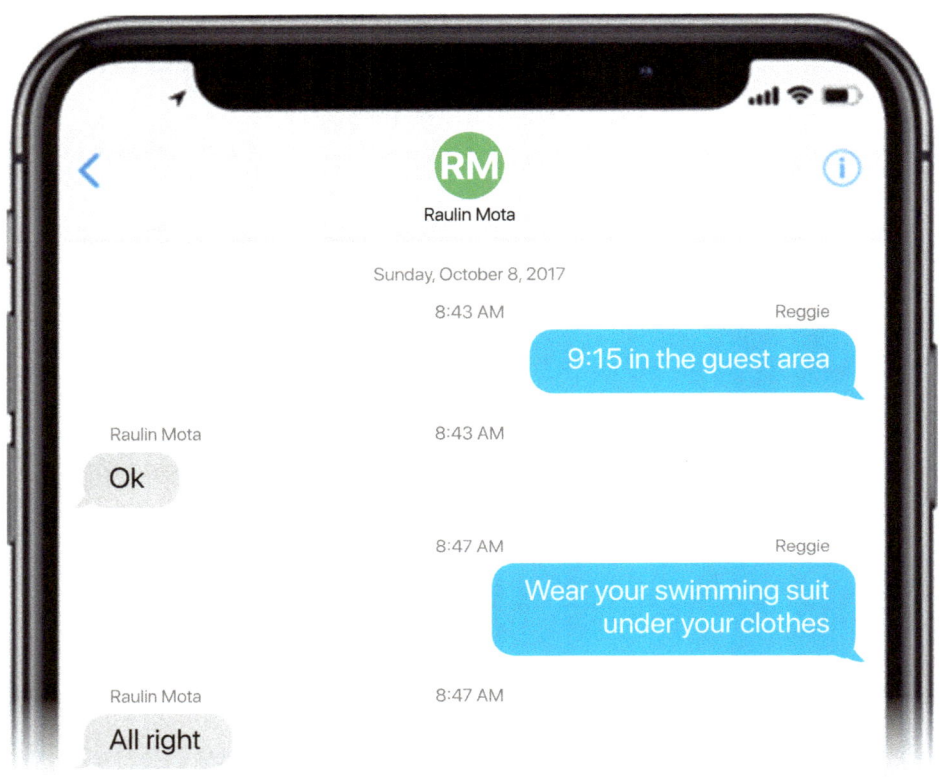

Raulin had meant to type that he'd just woke, not that he was weak. But the text had been sent anyway, coming out as a criticism of his strength and energy level.

The nine o'clock hour rolled around, and soon, Reggie and Raulin were reconvening in the guest area.

The guest area of El Paseo was on the second floor and resembled a small living room/study. It contained an Apple flat-screened computer, a flat-screened PC, a coffee machine with a hot water spigot for tea, and a countertop where free happy-hour wine was served in the afternoon. Running parallel to the guest area was a balcony with an old colonial appearance, providing a view of the restaurants along Espanola Way. If it wasn't for the tall buildings on Collins Avenue, the ocean might have been visible from the balcony too.

Raulin wasn't a morning person. But on vacation, he did his best to keep the good times rolling—engaging in morning coffee, fatty foods, sweet pastries, and long nights of alcohol and cigar smoking. In return, his mood and blood sugar waxed and waned like a diabetic on a roller coaster.

"C'mon man, I'm trying to hit the beach before it gets too crowded and the sun gets too high in the sky," Reggie said, attempting to hurry his friend along.

"I'm haft get my coffee," Raulin said, waddling toward the coffee machine like a duck searching for water in the middle of the Sahara. He fixed his morning beverage and then gulped it down like a bullfrog swallowing air, taking breaths in between.

To an outsider, Raulin and Reggie could be on the same team, the two of them being dressed similarly. Reggie had changed into his beach attire—a white button-down, short-sleeved, collared shirt with orange swimming trunks. Meanwhile, Raulin sported practically the same thing, the only difference being the fedora on his head, making him look like the love child of the Stay Puff Marshmallow Man and Bruno Mars.

"Yoh ready, doo?" Raulin said after tossing his empty paper cup into the trash.

"I been ready."

* * *

Imagine an unskinned potato with two beady eyes, a tuft of hair, feet, and a pair of orange shorts with a gash on the side. And next to it, a human-sized black ant with a peanut-shaped head and orange shorts.

This was Reggie and Raulin, looking like a couple of Baywatch rejects as they ran down Miami Beach amongst the beautiful MILFs in the morning sun.

In the midst of running, Raulin released several burps like a Similac-drinking infant.

"You okay, man?" Reggie slowed down from a stride to a Zulu trot.

Raulin nodded, although Reggie had meant it as a rhetorical question. His eating and drinking habits, not to mention coffee consumption on an empty stomach, had given him heartburn.

"We're almost to the pier! Keep pushing!" Reggie said, spotting the Miami Beach pier on the horizon.

They finally reached the pier, and the wind rewarded them with breezes that dried the sweat off their skin.

"We'll walk back. By then, Kayla will likely be up and ready to get something to eat," Reggie said.

Raulin, out of breath but still standing, nodded again. As they stood on the pier, Reggie looked in the directions of the luxurious condos littering the skyline on the southern tip of Miami Beach. *That's where I wanna be,* he thought, and then turned to Raulin. "Good work."

They gave each other dap and headed back to the hotel.

* * *

When Reggie reached the room, he noticed the blue light of anticipation on his phone blinking.

Aww, that's what's up. Butterflies fluttered through Reggie's stomach. But just as he was about to reply, the voice in his head brought him to a halt.

Reggie, you're in Miami with friends you don't get to see often—and other girls as well. Remember, Thuy said she didn't want to be exclusive. Let things flow as they flow. Don't sweat her. Call her back after you've spent ample time with your friends.

* * *

The afternoon arrived, and Raulin, Kayla, and Reggie picked up the hotel's complementary towels before heading to the beach.

Along the way, they discussed evening plans. Kayla wanted to go to the Lincoln Road shopping district to pick up some clothes from Zara in the event they went clubbing that night. Raulin, however, decided he would hang back.

An hour or so later, after fun in the sun and a few drinks, the three amigos returned to their respective quarters to rest and shower before tackling the rest of the day.

Back in his hotel, jubilant and buzzed, Reggie pulled out his phone and open Thuy's text thread. His fingers darted over the keyboard, guided by his unguarded emotions rather than his logical mind.

Reggie clutched the phone in his hand, waiting for a reply that didn't come right away.

Shit, I spoke my feelings too soon, he realized.

Had he scared Thuy off?

Before the self-deprecating thoughts could go any further, there was a knock on his door. He went to open it, and there stood Kayla, greasy faced with sun block as if she'd just finished grappling with Georges Saint Pierre.

"You ready to go?" she asked.

"Let's bounce." Reggie put his phone on silent and stuffed it in his pocket.

Outta sight, outta mind, he said to himself as they made their exit.

* * *

Reggie and Kayla went shopping and ate a light lunch, and the whole time, Reggie succeeded in disciplining himself enough to resist checking his phone. Upon returning to the hotel though, his resistance waned. He took out his phone and saw Thuy's reply.

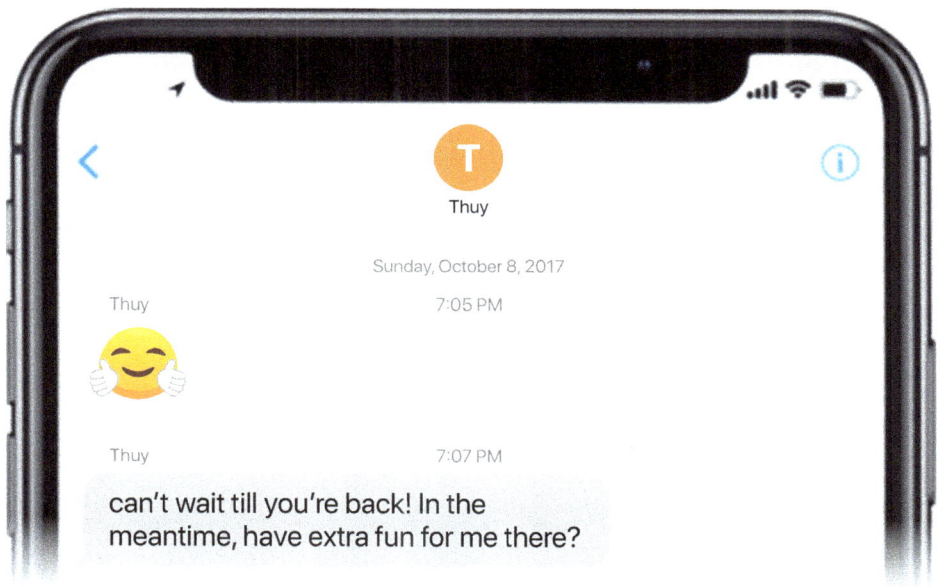

Grinning ear-to-ear, a pleasantly surprised Reggie replied.

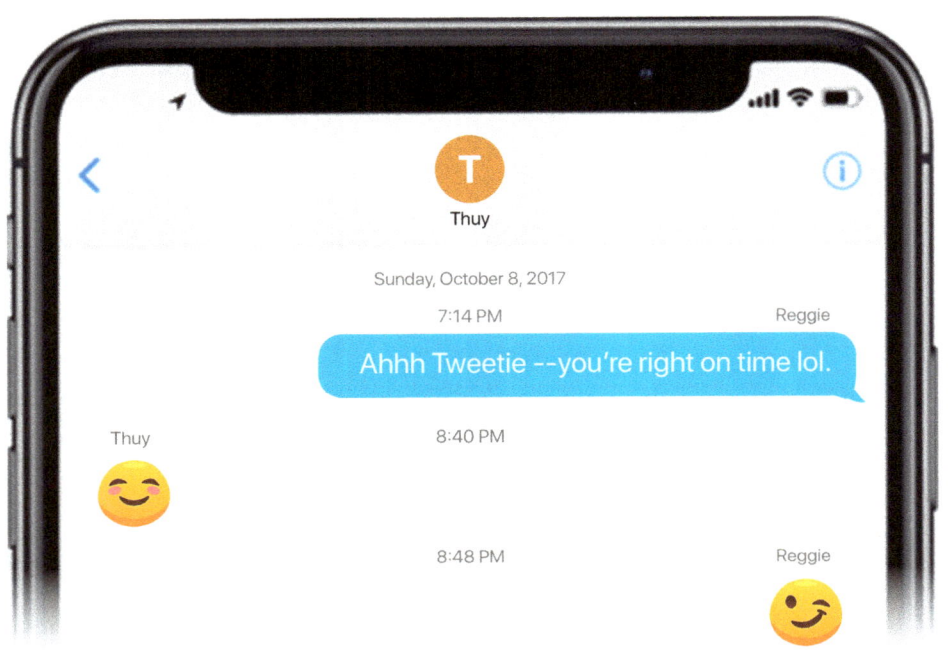

The exchange of smiley faces and texts was interrupted by an incoming message from Khalil. Taking a brief respite from Thuy, Reggie updated Khalil on his adventures.

Khalil was briefly hit with nostalgia at Reggie's mentioning of the popular 90s R&B song, featuring a double entendre both for being invited to a woman's place and ejaculating inside of a woman—an act that resulted in a visual that brought to mind cream-pie. Not to be mistaken for the literal cream pie, a cake filled with pastry cream comprised of egg yoks, sugar, and flavored with vanilla.

Did my man give that shorty a creampie? Oh shit! Khalil said to himself. He thought about the ecstasy he and his Indonesian wife shared—a treasure that both of them, being Muslim, enjoyed within the privilege of their marital union, from which his children had been born.

Not wanting to pry, but wanting Reggie to elaborate, Khalil reiterated:

   Now that I think about it, shorty did say she might be waiting on her prescription for birth control—I should check to see if she took her morning after pill, Reggie thought. He closed Khalil's text thread and reopened Thuy's.

Whew. Reggie enjoyed the pleasure of sex, but didn't want the costs of offspring.

He stared at Thuy's last message. Knowing his seed was safe with her, he debated whether to turn the conversation in a more lighthearted direction.

He sent a few more messages, and then went to shower and prepared for a night out.

A little while later, knocking sounded at his door. When he answered, Raulin and Kayla stood in his doorway, dressed to the nines.

"Yoh doo, you ready to begin?" Raulin asked.

"I been ready," Reggie said.

HAIR OF **THE DOG**

"Do Not Sit On The Furniture" is the epitome of the saying, "The smaller the club, the bigger the party."

The dwelling had all the feels of a warehouse club, but only a quarter of the size. Upon walking in, the immediate left side had a DJ's booth the size of a tiki bar. The booth housed the DJ, his compatriots, and his electronic gear. Additionally, there were brackets on an awning above the DJ so that he could hang various items relating to his particular brand—like dream catchers, for instance, signifying his South American heritage.

On the right, no more than fifteen feet in front and caddy corner to the DJ booth, was the fully stocked bar populated by awesome bartenders. The bottles in the background sat on transparent glass steps, dimly lit to give the bar an eerie glow. If color could talk, the light seemed to hum.

The left-hand side contained a continuous couch seemingly built into the wall, spanning from the front to the back of the club. Tables were peppered in front of this couch in various intervals, plastered with the "Do Not Sit On The Furniture" signs.

Reggie looked at the tables, seating, and the people occupying them—ranging from lovebirds making out, to groups of friends chatting.

They probably post "Do Not Sit On The Furniture" signs because they want people up dancing, not sitting around, he thought.

Reggie peered toward the back of the club, where the lighting was brightest and there was a hallway leading to the bathrooms. The hallway also had a door leading to a socializing and smoking area outside.

Reggie then looked upward and saw the jewel of the club—a deluxe disco ball strobe light chandelier shaped like a flying saucer surrounded by crystal beads. Shark-shaped ornaments revolved around the disco ball within the bounds of the crystal beads, creating the illusion of sharks swimming around the shimmering centerpiece.

The walls of the club reverberated with a *Dum-Ba-dum-dum...dum-ba-dum-dum, dum-ba-dum-dum,* the sequence repeating like the party in Zion after Morpheus gave his rallying speech in *The Matrix Reloaded.*

Raulin, Kayla, and Reggie found a spot on the dance floor, joining other partygoers and dancing in formation to the songs that played. One woman hit it off with Raulin, and they took their conversation to the bar.

"Hey Kay, let's go outside. I wanna smoke a *jack,*" Reggie said.

"But you don't buy cigarettes," she replied.

"I know. I'm going to *bum* one."

Kayla walked with Reggie to the back of the club and out into the courtyard, where Reggie bummed a cigarette from a festive clubgoer and thanked him graciously.

If I'm going to smoke, Marlboro Light is the way, he thought as he and Kayla took seats in a couple of the chairs outside, then proceeded to people-watch.

After taking a couple drags, Reggie offered Kayla one, but she waved him down.

"Remember the time you took me to Mexico for my birthday?" Reggie asked.

"Yeah, that was fun."

"Yeah, the club was like this, except it reminded me of a stadium. And there were the two platforms where the dancers were doing all kinds of tricks, like a low-budget Cirque Du Soleil."

"Like when the guy had fire at the end of a chain and was swinging it around," Kayla recalled.

"Right. That took talent." Reggie paused to smoke. "You remember when I drank that tray with all of the flaming shots of liquor?"

Kayla nodded and chuckled. "Yep. And it didn't even get you drunk."

"I know. I had such a super high tolerance. You know, I've cut back a lot."

"Yeah."

"After all I've done, I gotta pace myself. I'm getting up there, you know."

"We're all getting older."

"Yeah. I guess I've been feeling it a lot more lately. Been kind of, you know, thinking about my own mortality. I've also been thinking about whether or not I'm fulfilling my purpose in this life."

"You think too much, Reggie."

"I know."

Reggie took another pull of the cigarette he'd bummed, inhaling the smoke and holding it in. The nicotine permeated his alveoli and rushed to his head. He wished he could hold in the smoke for an eternity.

Leaning back in his chair, he gazed up to the sky, taking in the whisps of clouds carrying moisture from the tropical fronts. He then looked around at the people nearby. They were all different ages, but mostly younger.

Was he the only one who felt out of place?

His lungs gripped him, and he finally exhaled the smoke. His head started to waver, the nicotine, alcohol, hum of the crowd, and thumping base inside the club all working together to take him far off in his mind. Thoughts and memories mixed and mingled, and for a moment, he didn't know where he was.

"I'll be ready to go soon," Kayla yawned, breaking Reggie from his reverie.

Reggie glanced toward her. Kayla was never afraid to express her desire to sleep. Reggie was honestly surprised she'd stayed up this late to begin with. She was the kind of person who could fall asleep at a rock concert.

Reggie put out his cigarette. "I'm ready too. Let's bounce. I'll grab Raulin."

* * *

The South Florida sun beamed down on the good and bad alike. From the tip-top rich Miami playboy with a swimming pool in his courtyard, to the bag lady who carried all of her possessions on a shopping cart— everybody slept. And when the day started anew, all the actors in the play of life, regardless of their background, got up for another day of the same game.

A seagull landed right outside of the bathroom windowsill and stared Reggie dead in his eye while he took a piss.

Afterwards, Reggie started to contact Kayla, but stayed his hand.

Naw, I'll let them get at me when they're ready. I hope Raulin scored. He stayed at the club extra late. I'll go hit the beach and see what's poppin'.

Reggie changed into his swimming trunks and then looked in the mirror.

Shit! he thought, observing the bags under his eyes. He grabbed his mirrored sunglasses, and made his way to the lobby, encountering heavier traffic than usual. Friendly people nodded hello to him, and hotel staff asked his wellbeing. Reggie powered through the interactions with a forced smile on his face, knowing they were all just trying to be nice even though he wanted to be left alone. His primary goal was to get to the ocean and let the water and breezes energize him.

Along the way, he realized his problem.

Fuck! I've got hair of the dog!

Fortunately, Reggie knew how to solve the matter. As soon as he crossed Collins Avenue, he headed into Andrix, a pastry and pizza shop populated by pretty-faced, wide-hipped Latin babes.

Making his way to the counter, a sight stopped him in his tracks.

Prosecco! Yes!

The woman behind the counter seemed to read his mind, a bright smile lighting her face just before he approached. "Good morning, sir. Can I—"

"One prosecco mimosa!" Reggie shouted, interrupting her mid-sentence.

"Right away!" She exchanged smiles with him before turning to prepare his drink.

Reggie watched her pop open a bottle and let the orange juice and champagne make sweet love, becoming one.

"Breakfast of champions," a male voice sounded behind Reggie.

He turned and spotted an older white gentleman wearing a tropical shirt and flip-flops that slapped the ground like the lips on Mushmouth from *Fat Albert*. "No doubt, I've got hair of the dog," Reggie replied.

"Hair of the dog? Oh no, bro! You gotta keep the party going!" the white man said, then briefly sniffed and wiped his nose.

I'm sure he has a little more help than I do keeping the party going, Reggie thought. *Maybe I should buy him a dr—*

"Here you go, sir." The young woman behind the counter handed Reggie his mimosa on a tray with a chocolate éclair. A *C-c-c-c-combo breaker* to his mental thought pattern of looking to ski in the summertime.

"Thank you, miss, but I didn't order the pastry," Reggie said.

"It's on the house," she said with a pearly white smile. She looked like the lovechild of the Noxzcema and Clerasil girls from the 80s. She proceeded to place a card with the name of the business and the website on Reggie's tray. "If you don't mind, could you please give us a good rating on Google?"

"Not at all. Not at all..." Reggie met her gaze and found himself mesmerized by her charm, and anticipating the temporary boost he'd receive from eating sugar and drinking more alcohol.

Just as he suspected, he started feeling better as he sat to eat and drink.

Ahh, Miami, Sin City of the east.

* * *

"Reggie! Reggie!" Kayla called, knocking on his door. "Me and Raulin are going for lunch. You want to go? Reggie?" She knocked on the door again.

Inside, a napping Reggie stirred awake.

Fuck, what time is it? He squinted at the clock. *2:22? Shit, I must've slept a good couple hours.*

The knocks on the door drifted through his hotel room again.

"Okay, Kay. Hold on a sec!"

Reggie got up and threw water on his face to make sure he was decent, then opened the door.

"Dang, you okay?" Kayla looked him up and down. "I was worried about you when you didn't answer the door. You usually get up early. I thought you'd be the one waking me up."

"Well, this time, I got up, had a mimosa, ate a pastry, then went to the ocean. I initially wanted to get into the water, but this cool ass dude I met in the pastry shop treated me to more mimosas. We shot the shit, then I headed back and took a nap. Now, here we are."

"Wow. Even when you're hung over, you're always meeting people."

"You talked to Raulin?"

"Yeah. I ran into him in the guest area getting coffee. He hung out with that girl last night, then came back super early."

"Oh, okay. You know what inquiring minds want to know?"

"What?"

"Whether or not Raulin got laid. I know you didn't ask him, so let's go find out. Gimmie 20 minutes, and I'll meet y'all in the guest area."

"Psst. Okay." Kayla made her exit, and Reggie, now fully awake, was ready to start the process all over again.

* * *

Ever wanted to take a bath in guacamole? Then, *Oh Mexico!* is the spot. The place specialized in different kinds of guacamole dips in bowls so large, you'll swear your whole body can fit.

The crew chased their highs with freshly made margaritas and getting caught up on Raulin's excursions. They found out that although he didn't get any, he'd made out with the woman while walking near the ocean and then saw her off in a cab. Reggie was happy for Raulin, who didn't get the attention from women the way he used to in the 90s.

As they continued to chat, Reggie got his buzz going again, and Thuy popped into his head. He pulled out his phone, deciding to send her a text.

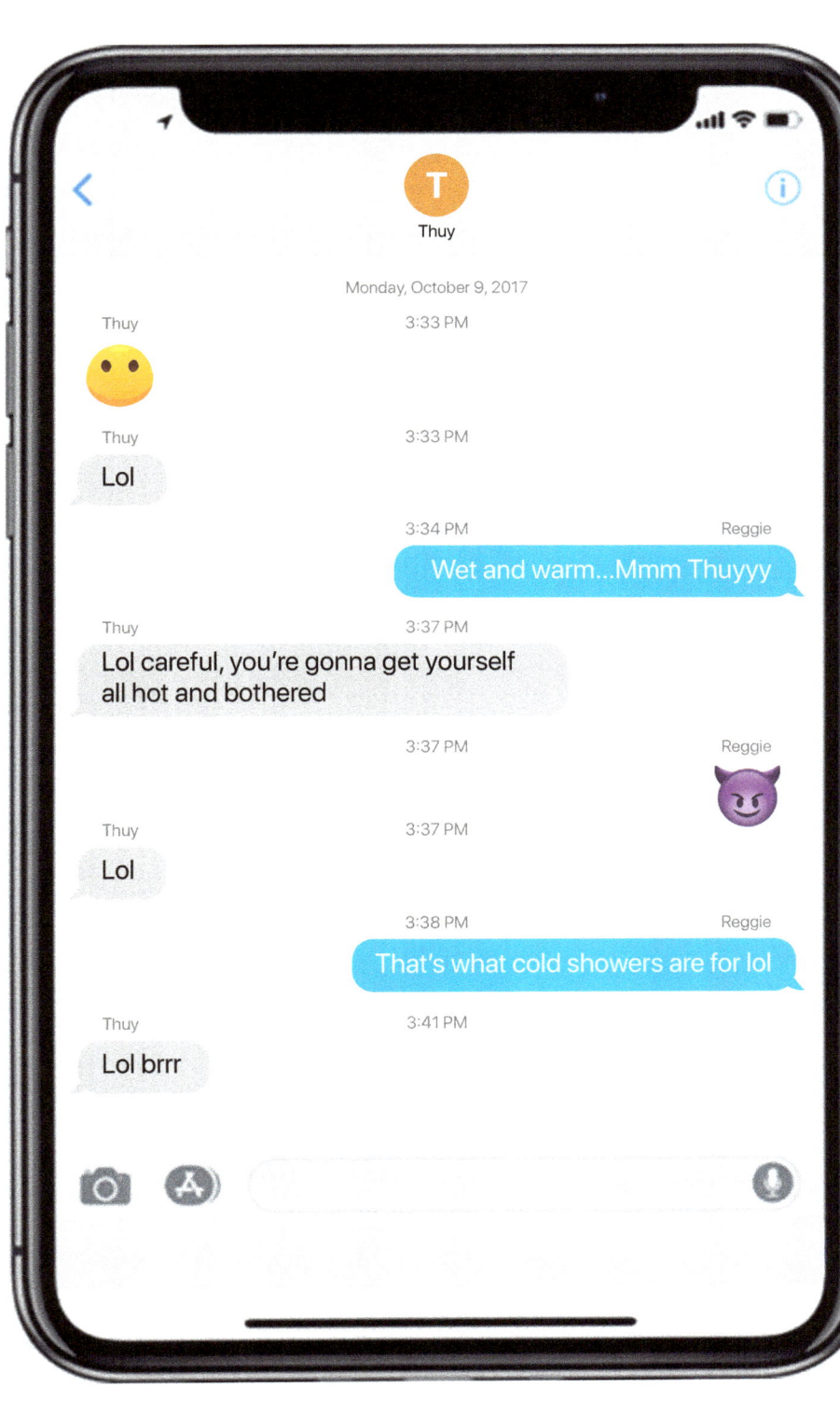

Reading Thuy's last text, Reggie decided to follow his policy of letting her have the last word so that he could take the lead when their conversation resumed. He finished eating with his friends, and afterwards, they returned to their own rooms to do their own thing. Clubbing the previous night had taken a lot out of them, leaving them feeling less adventurous this following day.

Back in his room, Reggie was watching *Animal Kingdom* when noticed the blue light on his smart phone blinking.

Oh shit! It's happy hour! Reggie realized, glimpsing the time on his phone after reading Thuy's last message.

Leaving his hotel room, he ventured down to the guest area, where a few free bottles of red and white wine had been set out, with five-ounce clear plastic cups stacked beside them. The bottles of wine and the cups sat on top of a wooden cabinet with a marble countertop.

El Paseo's guest area doubled as a business office and a lounge— a desk containing the PC and the Mac on one side, and the wine station adjacent to couches, lounge chairs, and a coffee table on the other. The wine was offered through an honor system as guests mingled about and lined up for happy hour.

Eyeing the equally long cabinet where the coffee machine was stationed, Reggie suspected the supplies for both coffee and wine were underneath. He lined up with other patrons at the happy hour bar, and when it was his turn to pour his wine, he opened the woodgrain cabinet doors below eye level.

Ah-ha! I knew they kept the wine here!

Noticing Reggie's discovery, other patrons lined up behind him and exchanged joking glances.

"Why limit happy hour to five p.m. when it can be anytime you're thirsty?" Reggie said, glancing back at the people behind him. They laughed and nodded with why-didn't-I-think-of-that expressions on their faces.

Now with plenty of wine to spare, Reggie drank and chatted with a couple of the patrons for a while before realizing Kayla and Raulin hadn't come down. Pulling out his trusty smart phone, he typed to Kayla in botched *jyutping*.

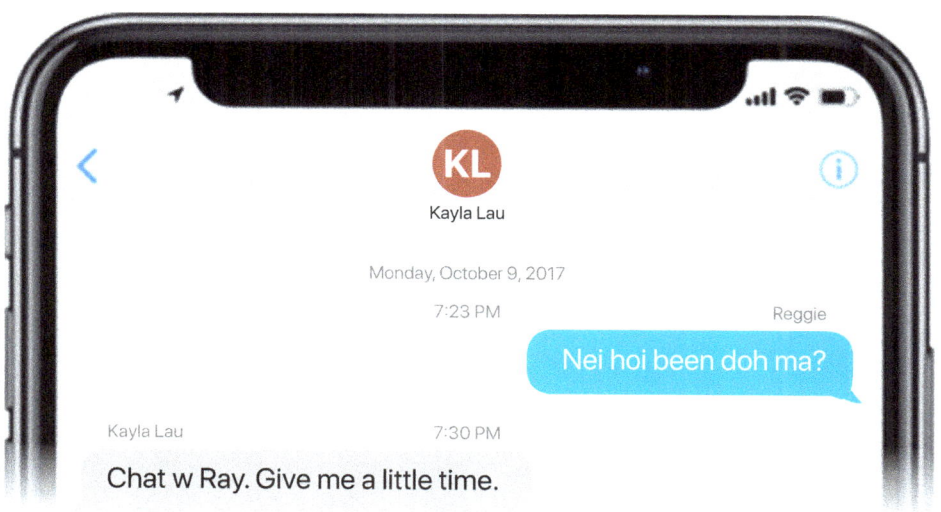

That's cool. She can marinate with her man. Reggie recognized the irony that both he and Kayla were chatting with their lovers during a brief respite from hanging out together.

Knowing Raulin, he's probably wandering the streets. He'll probably get at me later.

Satisfied with his happy hour consumption, Reggie headed back up to his room and then noticed the message indicator light blinking on his phone.

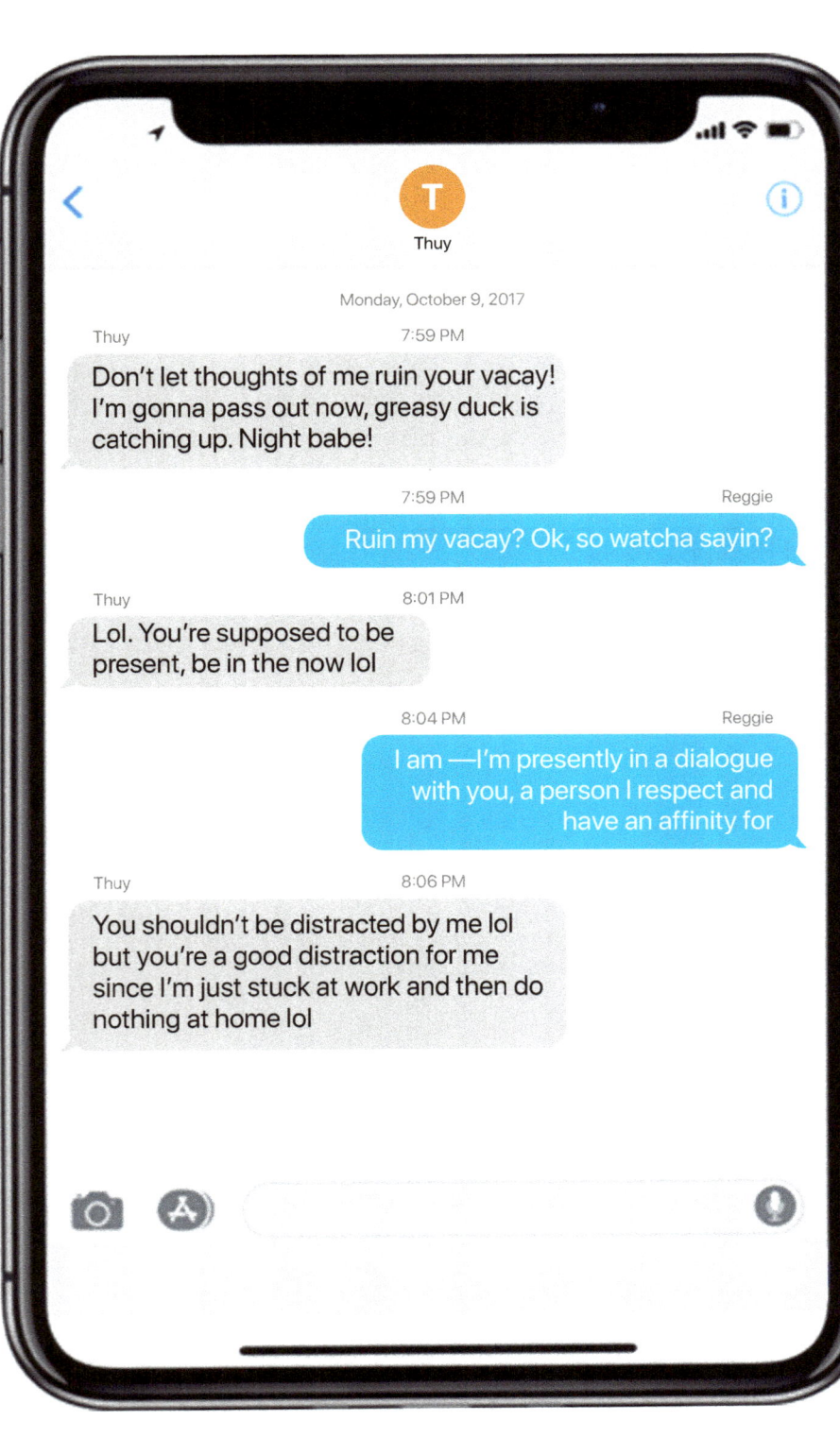

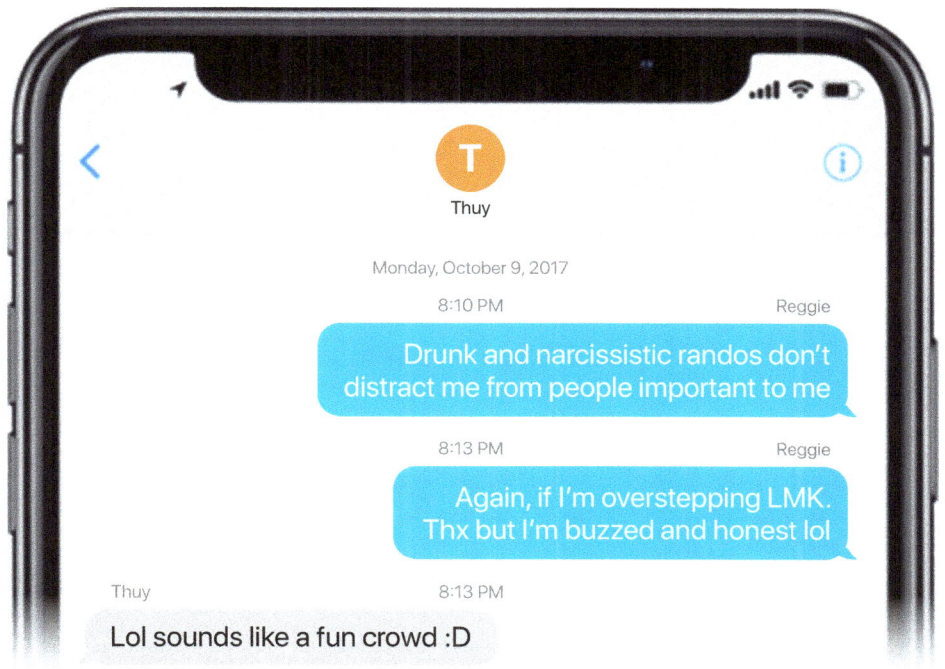

Reggie wanted to be a little sentimental, although he was partially lying. At the happy hour, most if not all of the hotel denizens were visiting from overseas and were actually quite nice. But in general, Miami Beach really was filled with drunk and narcissistic people. What caught Reggie though, was that Thuy considered it fun to hang around those kind of people—not to mention her choosing to comment on it rather than his statement about respect and affinity.

There's a lot of truth in jest, but I'm not ready to red-pill her just yet. Dating does have a fun side.

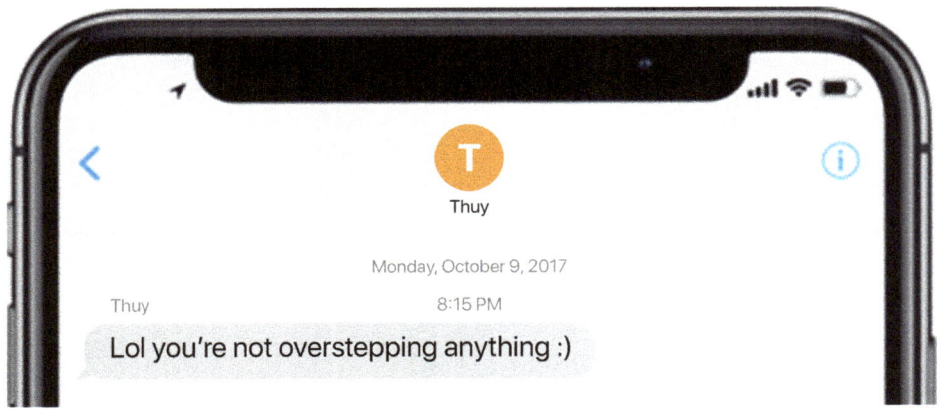

Okay, okay, so she likes chatting with me—that I'm giving her my time. How should I resp-

Before Reggie could finish the thought, his phone dinged with a message from Kayla.

Kayla Lau

Monday, October 9, 2017

Kayla Lau — 8:17 PM
R u at senior frog?

8:17 PM — Reggie
It's Señor Frog, Kay. I thought you grew up in East LA?

Kayla Lau — 8:18 PM
Whatever.

8:18 PM — Reggie
I'm just fuckin' witcha Kay, you tryinda go?

Remembering he hadn't responded to Thuy yet; Reggie quickly reopened her message thread and gave a touch-and-go reply.

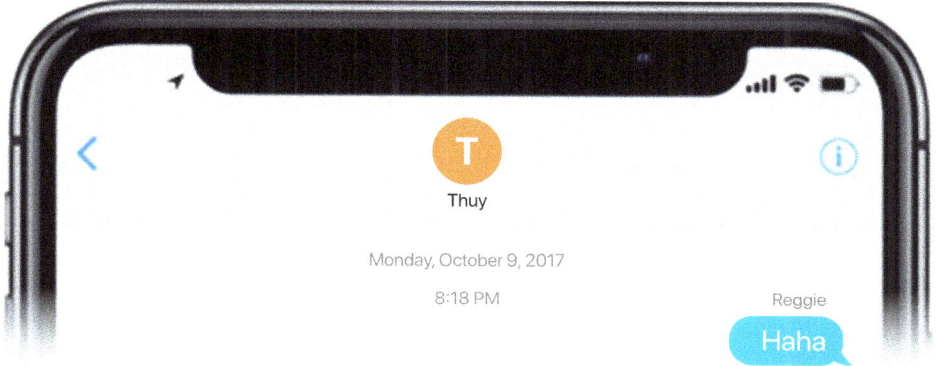

He then resumed his conversation with Kayla to figure out what the crew would be up to for the night.

Reggie threw on board shorts, a t-shirt, and versatile shoes, as he knew places like Señor Frog. As he came down the stairs to meet Kayla, he got another notification on his phone.

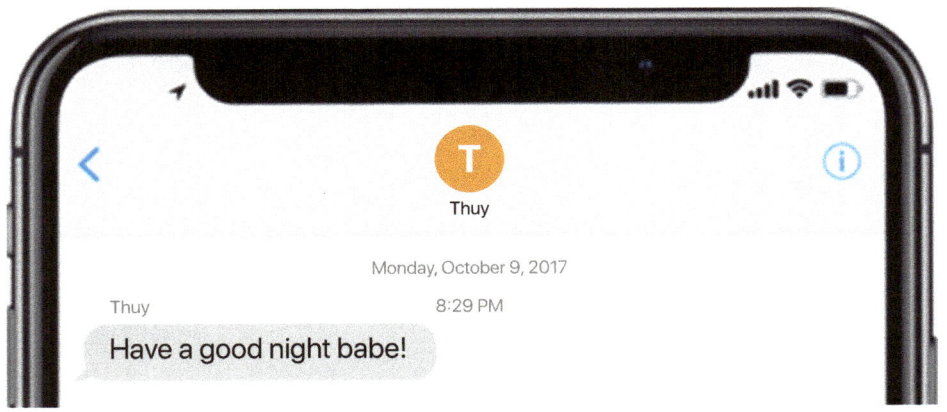

I'll save it for latersz, eh, Reggie said to himself in an East Los Angeles accent, mentally preparing for Señor Frog. As he approached the bottom of the stairs, Kayla awaited, wearing a t-shirt, blue jeans, and slip-on shoes—her traditional, Chinese American everyday garb that she wore to run errands; she wasn't trying to impress anyone.

"Whatup, Kay? You ready to rock out like we did back in the day in Cancun?" Reggie said.

"I'm ready," she replied.

* * *

Although Señor Frog had a Mexican theme, it was essentially a dive bar lined with frogs wearing sombreros, maracas, and other red, white, and green items. Like every other American culturally appropriated chain franchise, Señor Frog was geared towards drunk college students and tourists who liked being exotic when convenient—kind of like African American women who cruise to Caribbean countries while eating fried catfish and drinking white zinfandel box wine.

Unlike Oh Mexico!, where the crew had enjoyed kiln-deep guacamole, Señor Frog's specialty was dishes like enchiladas and nacho supreme—essentially corn chips, meat, and cheese. The food was indistinguishable from puddles of barf just beside the urinal, where some unfortunate Josh got *sloshed* and didn't make it within field goal range of the toilet.

"Laa-laa-laa-laa, la-da-da-ta-da-tadaa…" The crowd in Señor Frog sang along to LMFAO's song, "Shots" while Kayla and Reggie sat at the bar side.

"Oh my God, Reggie, I didn't think they could pour a whole bottle of corona into my margarita. I mean, the glass looked so shallow."

"Yeah, I know. It's like a trick glass."

Reggie and Kayla finished their CoronaRitas and took a couple shots with some festive tourists. Eventually the song, "Feeling Hot Hot Hot" by the Merrymen started playing and a conga line formed.

"Hey Kayla, c'mon! This is just like the Buster Poindexter dance!"

"Naw, that's okay, Reggie."

"It's your last night in town! Cut loose."

"Naw, that's okay. You go enjoy yourself."

Once the conga line neared them, Reggie grabbed Kayla's hand, yanked her off the bar stool, and pushed her into the last person on the conga line. Then he got behind her.

Initially reluctant, Kayla soon realized more people were joining behind Reggie. Not wanting to break the line, Kayla stayed, and eventually started enjoying herself. A smile slipped onto her face, and not before long, she was singing "hot, hot, hot" along with the people at the bar.

Kayla was one of the most introverted people Reggie knew and seeing her laughing and singing made him believe that perhaps life wasn't so hard after all.

* * *

Reggie sat up in bed with the TV hooked up to Netfilx, watching *Travelers*. He shot Thuy a quick message.

Damn, I had a good buzz going. I was hoping we could get a little dirty talk in. Oh well, it'll be a couple days until we meet again, so I'll save it for latersz.

Letting Thuy have the last word as usual, Reggie powered down his phone and nodded off.

VERBAL **THAI CHI**

Reggie stifled a yawn and rubbed his eyes as he made his way out of the hotel, trailing alongside Kayla. It was the wee hours of the morning, and Kayla had ordered an Uber to take her to the airport.

"Should be here soon," Kayla said, checking the Uber app on her phone to see how far away her driver was.

"Okay," Reggie said, noticing two other girls nearby, also appearing to be waiting for a ride. They exchanged glances with Reggie and Kayla, and then resumed their chatter, their youthful voices humming through the quiet, early-morning air.

"Ahh, here it is," Kayla said, looking at an approaching car. Yet, as she moved forward toward the car, so did the two girls.

"Umm, actually, I think that's *our* Uber," one of the girls said.

Kayla stared back at her in confusion and shook her head. "No, I'm pretty sure it's mine."

The vehicle pulled over and parked, the driver peering through the window to eye all four of them.

"Well, where are you two going?" Reggie asked the girls, intervening.

"To the airport," one answered.

Reggie looked at Kayla and shrugged. "The car looks big enough to fit you all."

"We'll see..." Kayla said skeptically. Not before long, they were all piling their luggage inside. Then, seeing that they all could comfortably fit, they agreed to share the ride.

Glad the minor crisis had been resolved, Reggie said his goodbyes to Kayla, and returned to his hotel room. On his bed, he noted his phone's message indicator light blinking.

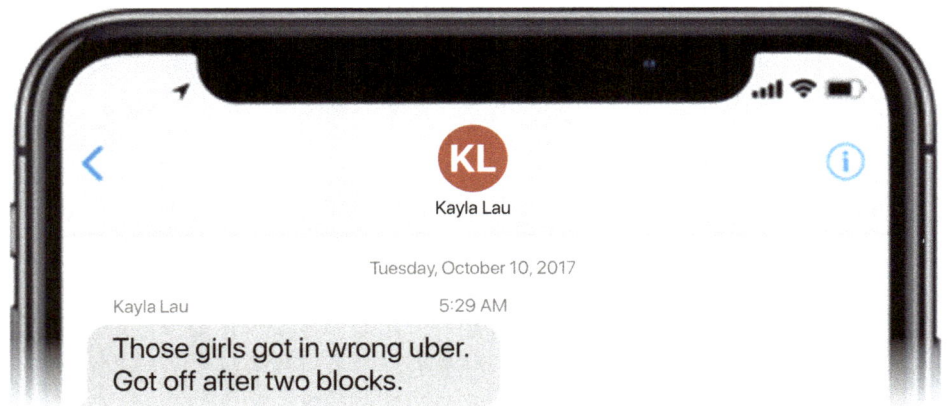

Reggie chuckled. *Ha, I knew everything would work itself out. Now, lemme holler back at Thuy's message from last night real quick.*

Before Reggie could respond to Thuy though, Kayla sent photos of him and Raulin on the beach, running in and out of the water. Raulin looked like a tequila worm with arms. Reggie laughed and responded to the group message.

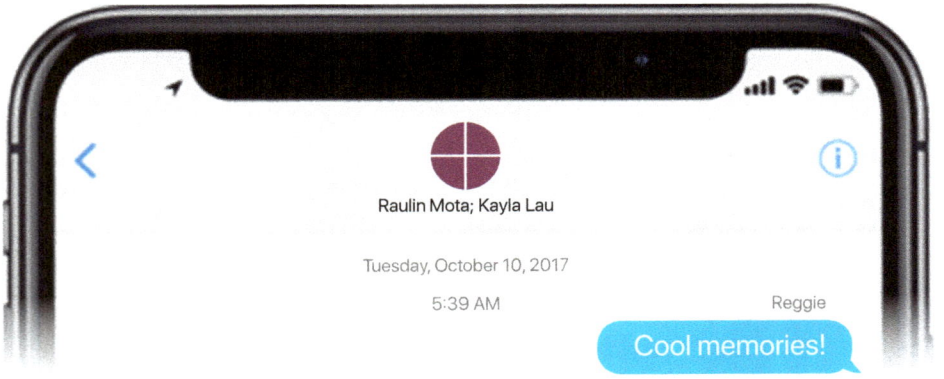

Closing the group thread, he reopened Thuy's text thread to respond to her message about her roommates kicking her off the couch. He then cut on the TV, hoping it would help him stay awake for a while. With Kayla still in transit, he figured she would eventually holler back at him, and he didn't want to miss her text. He wanted to be sure she was good and had boarded the plane home.

As expected, he was soon receiving play-by-play updates from his bestie as she made her way through the airport and evacuated her bowels.

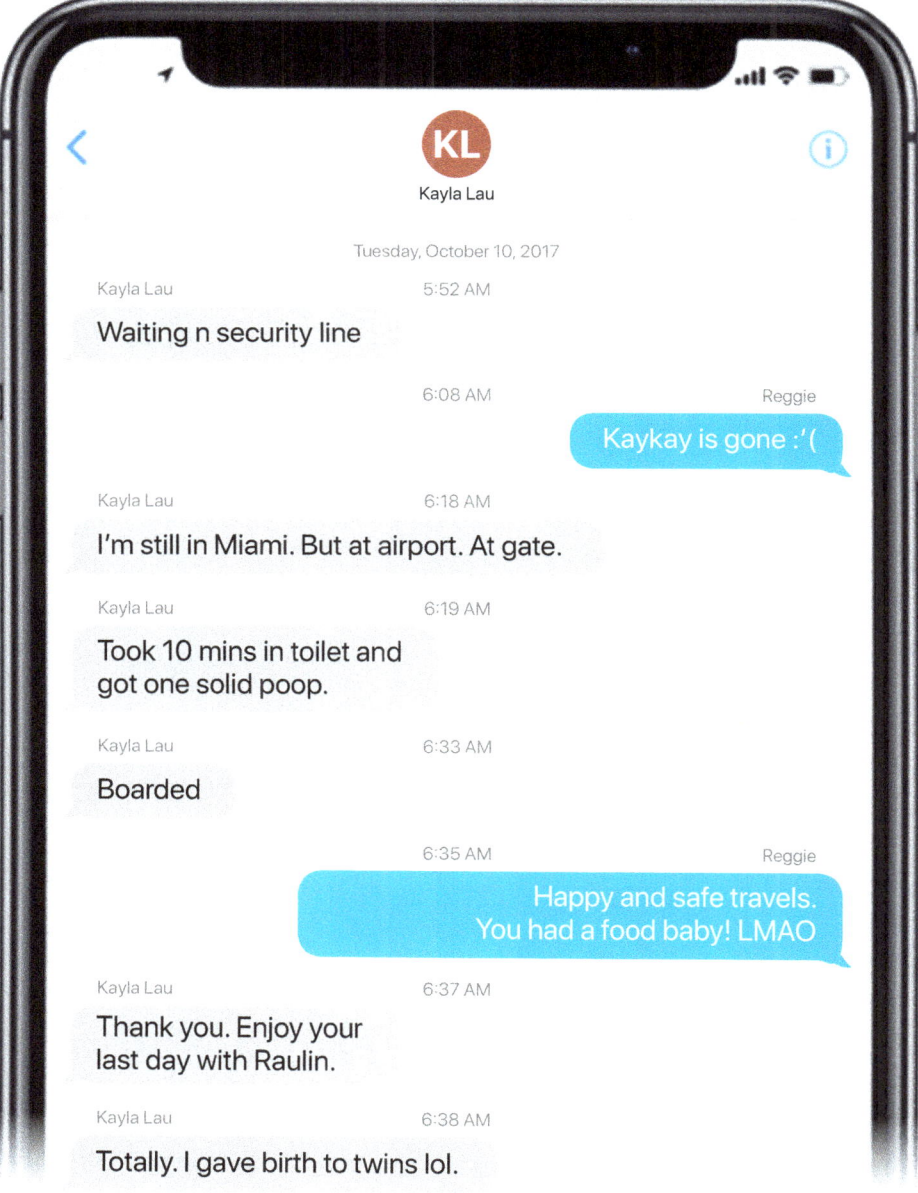

Content that Kayla had boarded the flight, Reggie watched the blue whales on TV in the deep blue ocean as they swam like live submarines. It was surreal to see the sun poking through the water while groups of whales, including a mother and her calf, swam. Watching their majestic tails, the serenity of it all lulled Reggie to la-la-land.

* * *

The sun peered through the blinds and the sound of street washers, jackhammers, and construction crews permeated the air amidst salsa music playing in the background.

Shit. I must've dozed off.

Reggie looked at the TV, which now showed scenes of the artic wilderness—white foxes, polar bears, and seals of all sorts roamed the frozen tundra. After giving thanks that D.C. wasn't as cold as the artic, Reggie turned his attention to making the most of his last day.

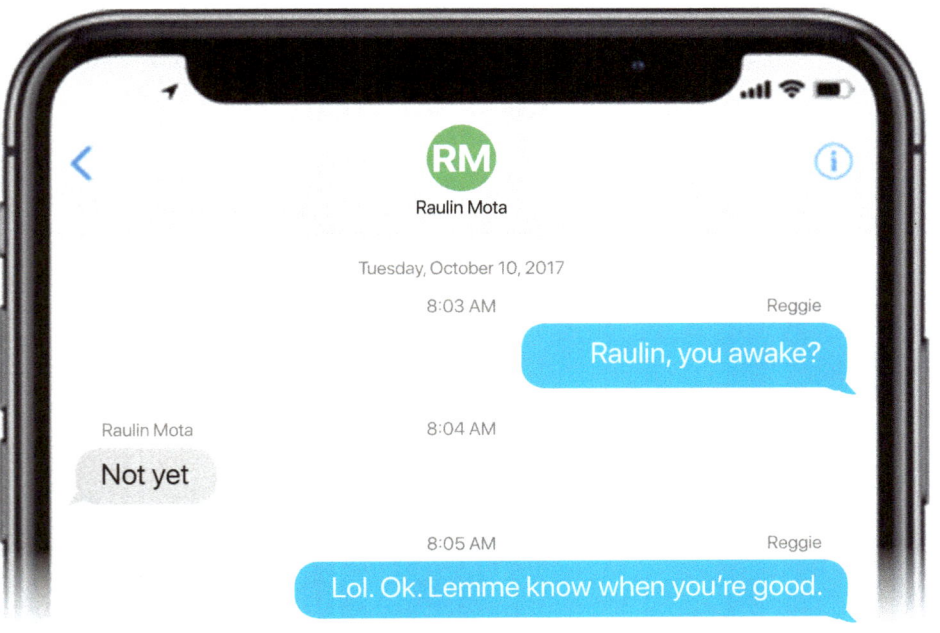

Raulin—my nigga is a funny dude. If you're not awake, you're not going to respond to a text, moron. You don't respond to the text, obviously awake, and then say you're not awake. This dude needs more training.

Mentally berating Raulin, Reggie pre-packed he clothes he wouldn't need, then decided to get some fresh air. Leaving his phone in the room, he moved through the hotel, where he was once again greeted by the friendly hotel staff. Once outside, he took a deep breath as he peered up at the sun peeking through the palm fronds.

He patrolled Espanola Way for a while, watching the various businesses setting up and people preparing for the day. Then he headed back up to his room. Again, upon his return, his phone's indicator light was blinking. He had a missed call from Raulin, and a text message from—you guessed it—Thuy.

She got me on the acid reflux message. Touché. I know shorty's missing me, Reggie thought before returning Raulin's call and learning that his friend was ready for their morning run on the beach. After establishing his meet-up with Raulin in the lobby, Reggie messaged Thuy back.

Raulin and Reggie headed to the beach for their ritual run. And by the time they returned, Reggie had received multiple messages.

Thuy

Tuesday, October 10, 2017

Thuy   10:50 AM

It's all gloomy :/ how's weather at your place?

10:52 AM   Reggie

Sunny about 85 with a little breeze

Thuy   10:52 AM

Oh shuddup lol

10:53 AM   Reggie

You know the funny thing is that I am trying not to overwhelm u, but at the same time I enjoy messaging you — I guess that would make me bipolar? Lol

Umm, okay, Reggie thought. *I'll take that, but I intended on it being a joke.*

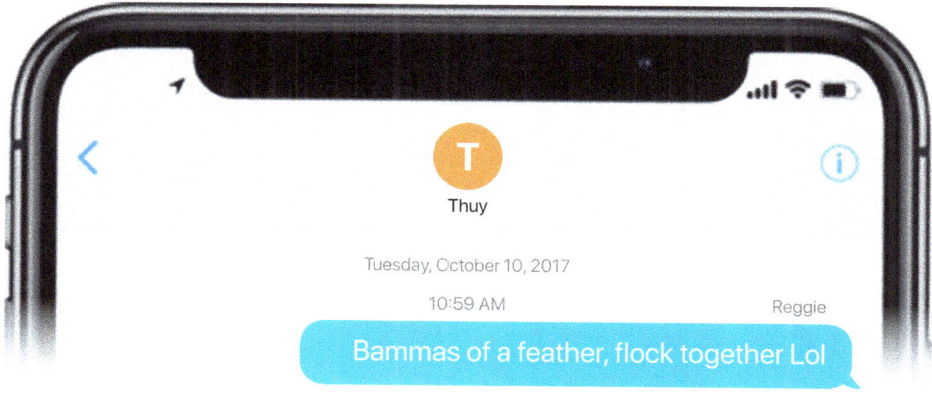

Thuy

Tuesday, October 10, 2017

10:59 AM   Reggie

Bammas of a feather, flock together Lol

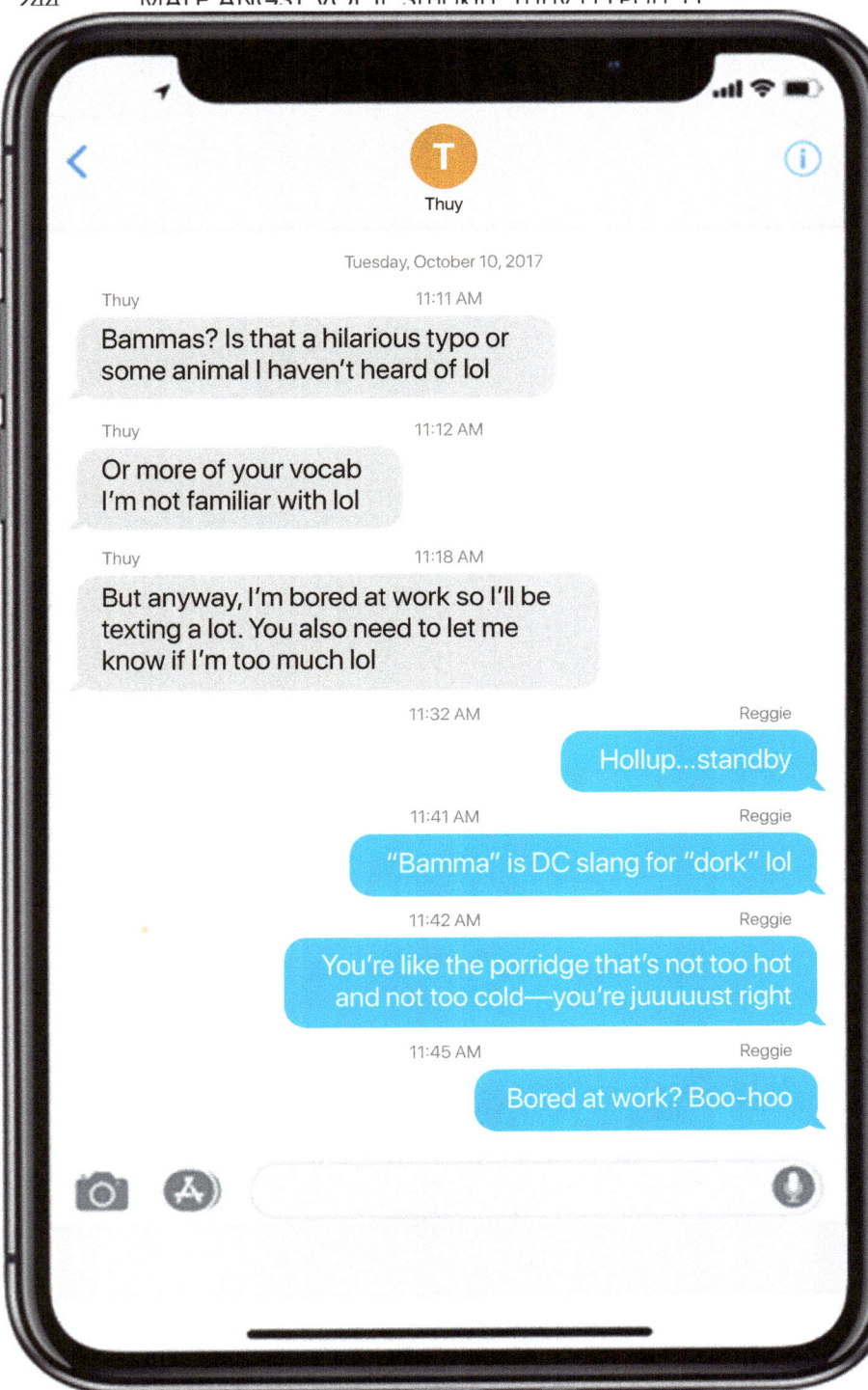

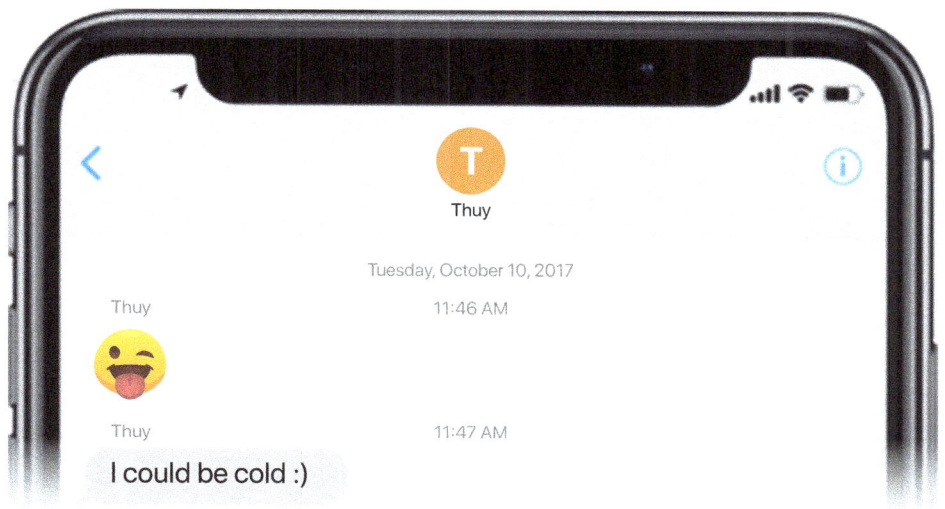

In response to Reggie's message about being just right, Thuy had thrown out a micro shit-test, slightly disagreeing with him.

Although I'd be lying, how do I say, 'I don't give a fuck' without saying 'I don't give a fuck?' Reggie pondered. Suddenly, thoughts from *Sons of Anarchy* came to mind, particularly a quote from Clay Morrow.

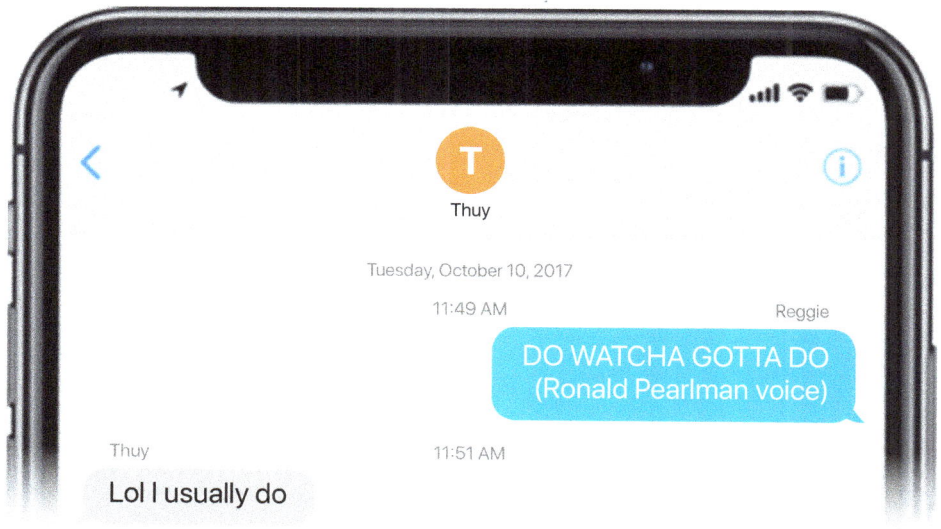

Ouch. Quick counter. Okay, so I'll just leave this for later.

Declining to respond for the time being, Reggie went to get lunch with Raulin. After eating, they sipped beer while deciding how to spend the rest of the day. By his third beer, Reggie had worked up a buzz. And as they sat in the restaurant, Charlie Puth's song started playing.

"You just want attention..." Puth's voice sounded through the dwelling, singing the opening line.

Oh my God, not this song again. This must be super popular now. It's everywhere, it's—Reggie's thought halted as he noticed his phone's indicator light blinking.

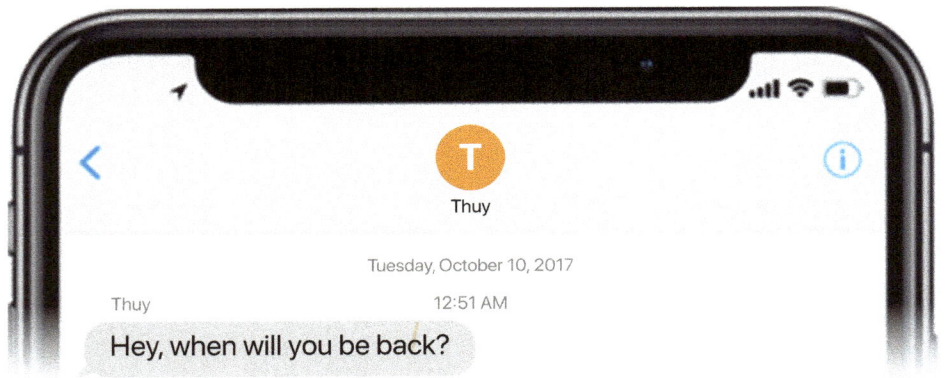

"Whoo hoo!" Reggie exclaimed out loud. *Gotcha, bitch!*

Reggie grinned, proud of himself for successfully averting Thuy's verbal microaggressions with verbal Thai Chi of his own, and getting her to message him twice in a row.

"What's goin' on, doo?" Raulin asked, startled by Reggie's abrupt cheering.

"Nothing, man. You wouldn't understand," Reggie replied, still staring at his phone. *Okay, she's conceded. Let's bring the rhythm back with a little humor.*

* * *

The day went on, and Thuy and Reggie texted intermittently. Through their message exchanges, Reggie learned that Thuy had time away from major projects during the day, and that she was clearly pretty stoked about reuniting with Reggie. They also talked about how she was reacting to the birth control, and if she'd been getting plastered lately.

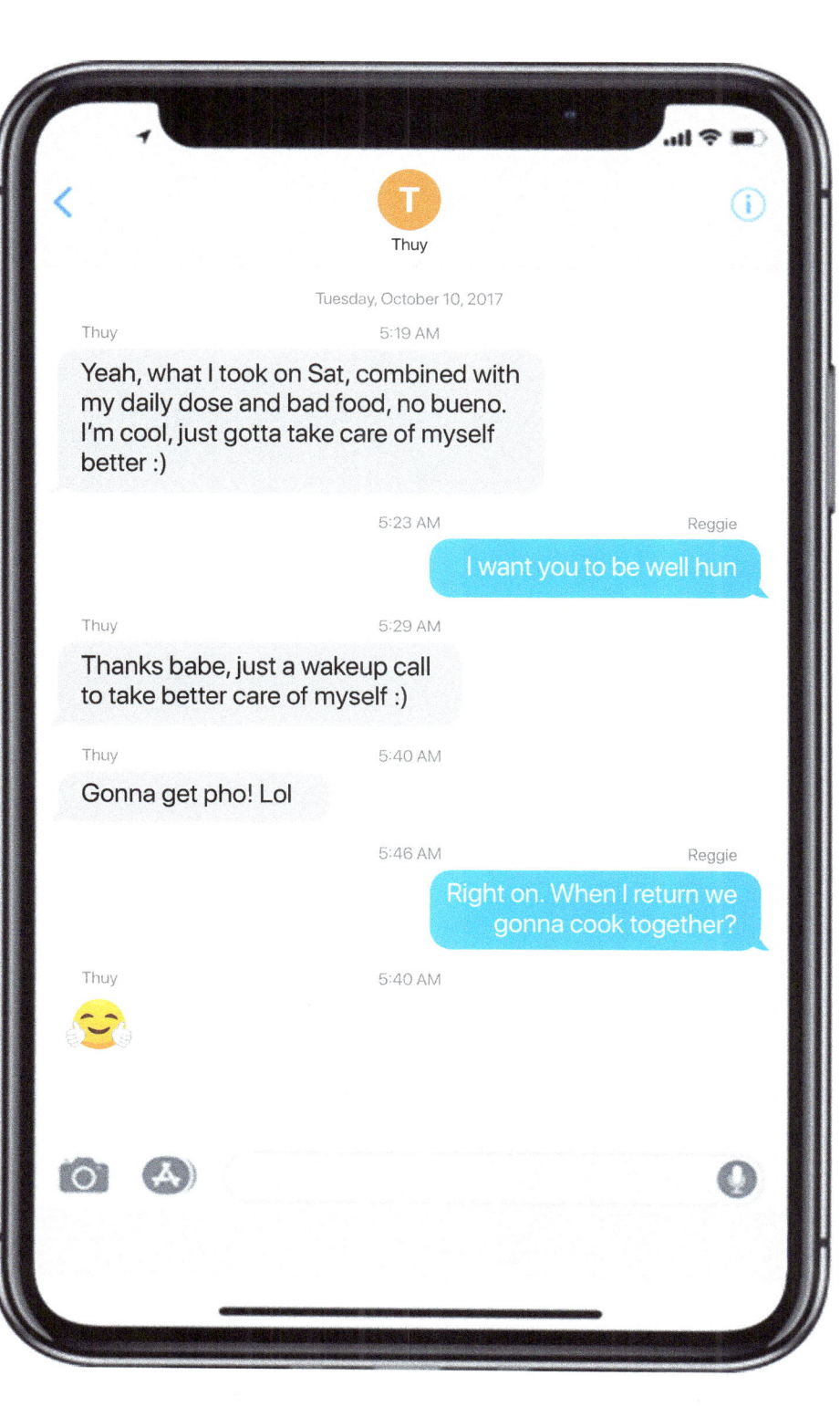

All the while, Reggie kept thinking about how his intention was to slow his roll as he returned to normal life. He found himself growing convinced that Thuy's personality was very mercurial, and was unsure about her propensity for partying.

BOOTY **MOUF**

Ocean Drive was bustling under the afternoon sun. More people had come in from the beach to play about in the bars and restaurants that lined the street. Raulin and Reggie had a table on the patio that lined the sidewalk, allowing them to people-watch against the background of the ocean and palm trees waving in the breeze.

"Ahh, this is the life, my dude," Reggie said, kicking back in his chair. "What do you want to order?"

"I'm get drunk, Reggie."

"Right on, Rauli. Check it out." Reggie pointed to the drink menu. "The King Koronita. Sixty ounces of pure pleasure. Choose your tequila."

Raulin moved his big bulldog-shaped head in to view the menu more closely. "Looks good, doo."

Reggie waved over a cute waitress with dimples boring holes into the side of her face.

"Hi, guys! Welcome to Corona Café! Do you know what you'll have to drink?" she said with a smile.

"Yeah, give us two of these." Reggie pointed to the selected drinks on the menu.

"Ah, the King Koronita. Good choice! I'll be right back with your order."

"Thanks," Reggie said as the waitress walked off. He then noticed Raulin eyeing the young woman as if she was fresh off a meat hook. His eyes followed her like Google maps.

"I'm think that girl is Benasolana," Raulin said.

"She could be. But she got a Colombian vibe as well. You know, dark hair, tan, dark eyes."

"It's called *morocha*."

"She can be a *morocha, colocha, mi loca*... She's fine in my book."

Shortly thereafter, the waitress returned with two huge margarita-filled glasses, the tops looking like the bottom half of flying saucers. Two Corona beers were stuck headfirst into the glasses, still not completely emptied into the sour alcohol mix. Squiggly, loopy straws, like the kind kids drank from at state fairs, protruded from the drinks.

"On the count of three," Reggie said after seizing one of the glasses.

"Whaddya mean, doo?"

"You said you want to get drunk, so we're gonna guzzle this drink like it's an overrated slurpee. We don't have to finish it all in one shot, but we should make the most of each guzzle."

Raulin nodded in agreement, Reggie proceeded to count down from three to one, and then they were off to the races. Taking a few breaks in between for the sake of brain freeze and burping, Reggie and Raulin sipped their way to the bottom of their glasses and grew heavily buzzed.

"Yo, Rauli, I just noticed these drinks were thirty bucks each!"

"Yo, doo, how much liquor they put?"

"I think they put like sixty ounces, plus two coronas."

"No way, doo. A corona is twelve ounces. The glass is too small for five coronas to fit. They lying, doo."

"I don't know, but I'm lit!"

The waitress came back to the table, noting the visibly jubilant Reggie and Rauli. "Damn! You guys finished the drinks that quick?"

"My man Rauli said he wanted to get tipsy, so I told him, let's hop to it."

Raulin nodded to the woman. "Ju es Benezolana, o ju from Colombia?"

"Neither, mi amor. I'm mixed Panamanian and Cuban," she replied.

"Wow, that's a nice mix. Fifty percent Panamanian, fifty percent Cuban, but one-hundred percent Caribbean," Reggie interjected.

"Yep," the woman said confidently. "Can I get you guys anything else?"

"Yeah. When were you going to tell us the drinks were thirty dollars a piece? You said it was a special. I had to turn the menu over to see the prices."

"I hooked you up with Patron, and the glasses are sixty ounces."

"No way," Raulin said. "I bet you five dollars that you can't put five coronas in there."

"Hold on, I'll be right back." The woman retreated into the establishment, then returned with a bucket of six coronas.

Raulin dumped the ice out of his margarita glass.

"You ready?" the woman asked.

Raulin and Reggie nodded in unison.

"Here goes." The woman opened beer after beer, and poured them into the glass. The glass looked like it would fill to the max by the third beer, but it was a trick glass, constructed like a funhouse mirror. The diameter gradually increased, permitting more fluid to accumulate. It was akin to comparing a short wide cup to a long tall cup; the two could have equal volumes despite having different surface areas.

By the time the waitress started pouring in the fifth beer, the fluid accumulated until it sat perfectly at the top edge of the glass without spilling over.

Reggie and Raulin paid the waitress extra, including her bet winnings, and stumbled out into the strip. It was then that Raulin began to take character, his alcohol consumption transporting him to a world where he thought he was Bruno Mars. He purchased a fedora and harassed the street vendor girls selling cigars and chewing gum, whom tolerated him for the sake of tips. Long gone were the days of Raulin wearing French Connection United Kingdom (FCUK) shirts, and Diesel pants with multiple zippers. Whenever he got drunk, he found himself in a money-spending mood.

Waiting on Raulin to finish making purchases, Reggie picked up his phone to text Thuy.

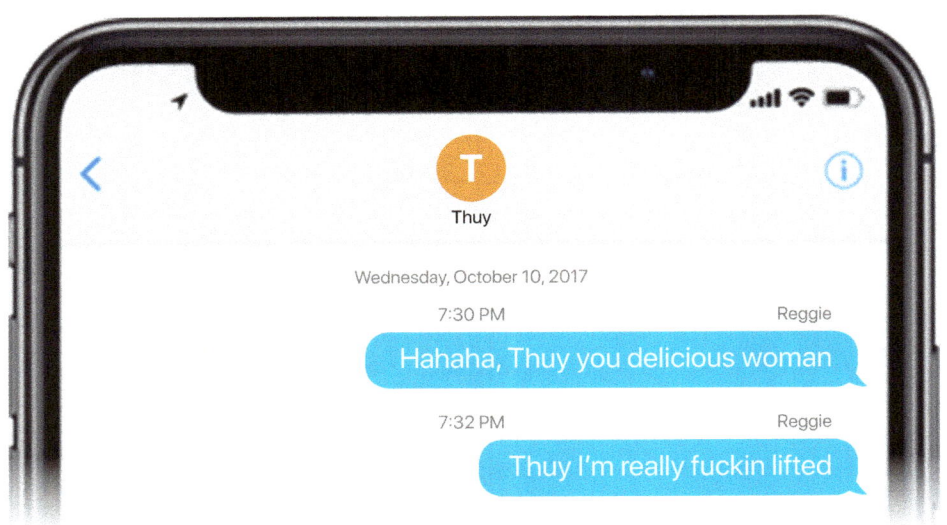

Raulin bagged his purchases, and Reggie puts his phone back in his pocket. He then joined Raulin along the strip, where they encountered people passing marijuana around.

"I got five on it!" Reggie emphatically opened his hands like Ronald McDonald about to make an 'M', the gesture meant to low-key ask if the two Miami partygoers—an African American couple—would welcome Reggie and Raulin into their cipher.

The man nodded, and Reggie and Rauli walked over. Reggie took out a five-dollar bill and handed it to the man.

"Nawl, y'all good," the man said, turning down Reggie's money.

"Well, at least let me buy you guys a drink or somethin'."

"Nawl, we fixin' ta head back eeun after this." The man handed Reggie a nicely rolled blunt, save for the end, where the *pull hole* appeared collapsed from saliva.

Aww shit, this nigga got a booty mouf, Reggie thought, although a little hesitant to offend. He looked at the man. "Can I borrow your lighter, fam?"

He handed over the lighter, and Reggie used it to "toast" the end of the blunt where he would smoke, disinfecting it and burning off the extra saliva as well. As Reggie passed the pull end of the blunt through the flame, the spit sizzled.

Nasty-ass nigga... I don't know what y'all be doin' with each other, but I don't want no part in it, Reggie thought bitterly, as if entitled to smoke behind others and judge them for the way they smoked. Finished sanitizing the blunt, Reggie avoided eye contact with the host and hostess as he started smoking. After a couple drags, he finally looked at the couple. "Where y'all from?" he asked in a matter-of-fact tone with smoke floating out his mouth.

"Aluhbummuh."

"Right on." Reggie took another puff. "I got family from Alabama, in Aniston."

"Aniston, aukay. We from Bumminhayum."

"Ah, Birmingham. That's where all of the parties were happening in the 90s. I remember because my bigger cousins used to go there during our family reunions. Now Birmingham has only one strip."

"That's about right."

After passing the weed around and making small talk, Reggie found himself in for more than he bargained for. The weed was stronger than he had anticipated. Initially, his thoughts started to soar. But then they descended as negative, paranoid, self-deprecating thoughts crept in. Reggie felt like evil was preying on his insecurities, antagonizing him.

"Raulin, I need to get a drink," Reggie said. The only way he knew how to quell the thoughts was with more liquor, to which Raulin obliged.

Finally, after he and Raulin were significantly wasted, they made their way back to the hotel.

"Yo, Rauli, I'll see you later, man... I gotta chill a lil' bit."

"Right on, doo."

Reggie got back to his room and checked at his phone, but there was no blinking indicator light. That was no deterrent from his drunk texting though. Drunkenness was a plausible deniability that kept on giving.

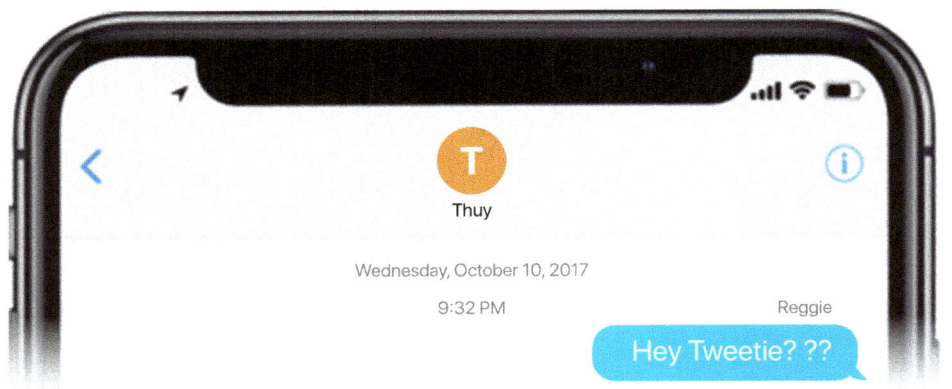

Fuck, I wonder what she doin'. I know it ain't cool to call twice, but fuck it, I'ma call her and deal with the repercussions tomorrow.

Rationalizing that liking her and wanting to talk was a good enough reason to call again, he picked up the phone and dialed Thuy.

Fuck! Voicemail!

He swallowed his spit and left a message.

"I know you probably out—out and about—livin' yo' best life. I don't know what to tell you, Thuy... I'm just here in my hotel room, overlooking the palm trees, watching the people move about the street. The music's blastin'. I'm kinda trippin' cause I'm kinda high. And I just can't help but think how much fun it would be to have you here with me. They say don't bring sand to the beach, but I say fuck that. I would rather squeeze your little *banh mi* buns in the palm of my hand. Babe, I'm blizzted. Hope I don't play on yo' phone. Don't leave a nigga hangin'. Peace."

Ending his message, Reggie put his phone down, crashed onto his bed, and passed out.

* * *

Choking on his spit, Reggie awoke coughing profusely.

Fuck, I got acid reflux again. When I get back, I gotta slow down.

Reggie looked at the clock. It was 1:40 a.m. The city lights beamed through cracks in the blinds. He looked at the many shapes the shadows created in his room, and the silhouette the snack bar made on top of the refrigerator. Then, out of the corner of his eye, he noticed the blue indicator light!

He eagerly picked up his phone.

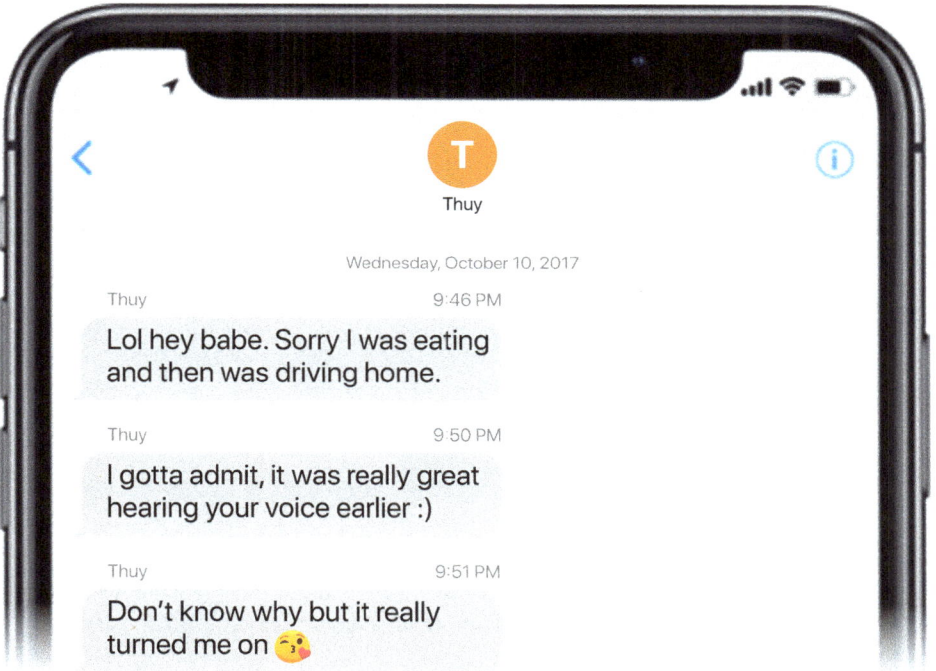

Reggie smiled, then crafted a message of his own.

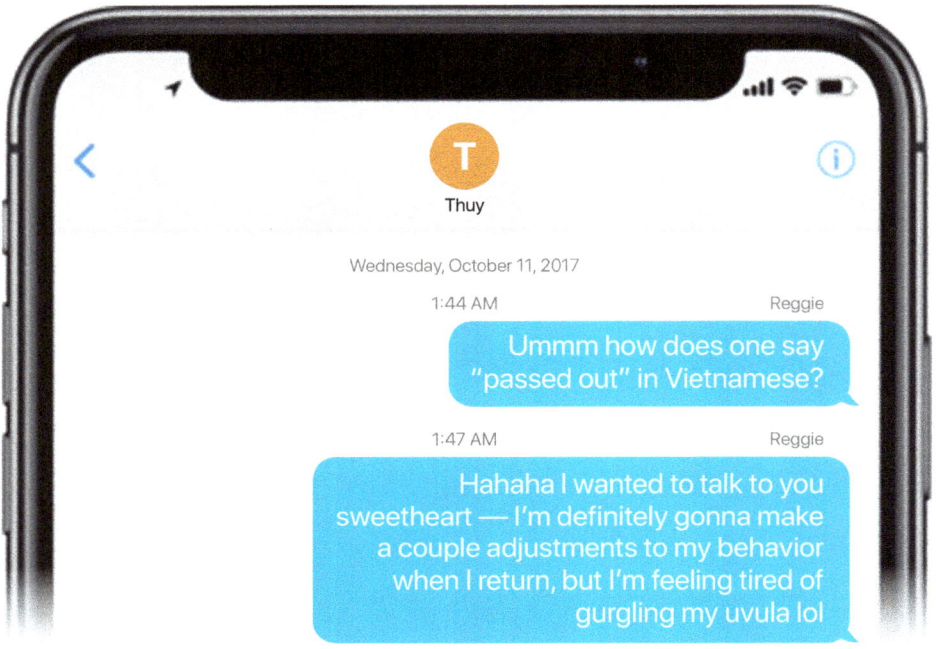

After sending this last message to Thuy, Reggie noticed he'd missed a text from his good friend, Jeffrey. It was a picture of Walt Whitman poetry—notable because Jeffery was the one to get Reggie into the *Breaking Bad* series, whereby the poet first made his way into Reggie's awareness.

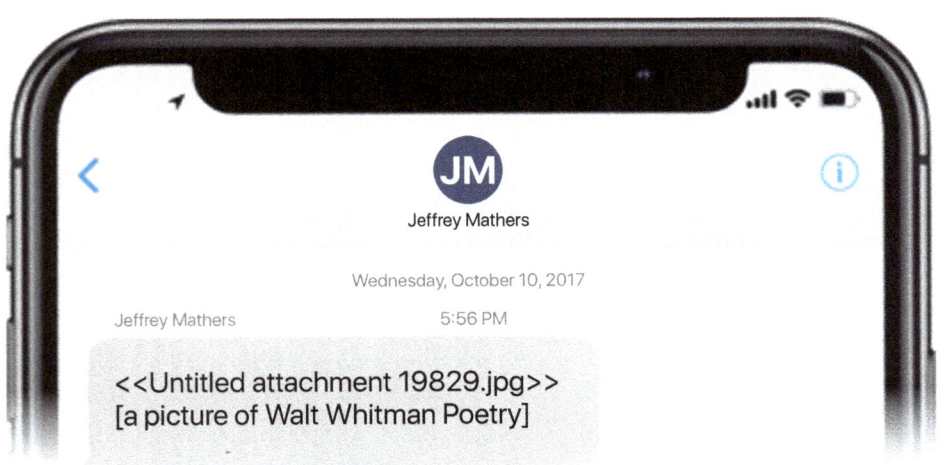

I wonder if Jeffrey's still awake.

Convinced Jeffrey was the one friend he could contact at any time, Reggie went ahead and texted him.

Jeffrey Mathers

2:17 AM   Reggie

> I got indigestion from eating late and drinking — in Miami beach now

Jeffrey Mathers   2:21 AM

Always know that you're a strong dude and your investment in another won't crush you.

Jeffrey Mathers   2:23 AM

But the feeling when you get when you're with another can't be substituted, that shit is genuine

2:23 AM   Reggie

> Can't think of anything that can make you feel the same

Jeffrey Mathers   2:24 AM

You gotta risk it

2:26 AM   Reggie

> I know my dude --I'm tripping balls because I'm "back in the saddle " LMMFAO. But I'm digging this chick like an undertaker lol

As Reggie began feeling more assured in his decision and made up rap lyrics in his texts, his acid reflux faded.

Giving his phone a rest, he went back to sleep.

* * *

Ugh, my head. I had one too many last night. Reggie stirred, his face partially buried in his pillow. The room was dark thanks to the thick curtains, but little spots of light still made it through the cracks. And in addition to the small flecks on sunlight coming through the curtains, another light pierced through the darkness—Reggie's flashing phone.

Reggie reread the last message he'd sent to Thuy before reading her reply.

Although Reggie was glad Thuy accepted him as he was, he presumed their dialogue yesterday indicated their mutual agreement to take better care of themselves.

She's probably the type to get all fucked up and want to change her ways once things get uncomfortable. But after recovering, she goes right back to her old ways and gets fucked up again. I guess we were all like that once.

Reggie quaintly reminisced on DJ Quik's song "Tonite", whereby he was on his knees praying to the porcelain God, saying, *"I'll never drink again if you let me live."* Yet, later in the verse, he says, *"We're doing the same ol' shit tonight."*

Not before long, Thuy and Reggie were exchanging texts while Reggie and Raulin were waiting for the 150 bus to take them to the airport. Though Reggie was still physically in Miami Beach, his mind was already wandering on what he wanted to do to Thuy. He recalled how good she'd felt between the sheets—the softness of her skin, the warmness of her love, the scent of her hair, and the sound of her moans.

Reggie was also excited to see Thuy's reaction to the gifts he'd picked up for her—a beach tank-top and a towel from one of Miami's "Surf Style" shops.

On the way back to the airport, Reggie and Raulin observed the scenery, taking in the pastel buildings, the plentiful palm trees lining Alton Road, the many convertible luxury cars cruising the streets with their tops down.

Goodbye, Miami Beach. I'll be back again soon, Reggie lamented.

* * *

The airport terminal was full of Washingtonians headed back to the D.C. area from Miami. Reggie recognized his own—the rows of buzzard-necked, brainy, less-attractive people tapping away on their laptops and sipping frappes, taking up extra space and empty seats.

"It's good to see their metro etiquette has followed them to the airport," Reggie said, leaning back in his seat and pulling out his phone.

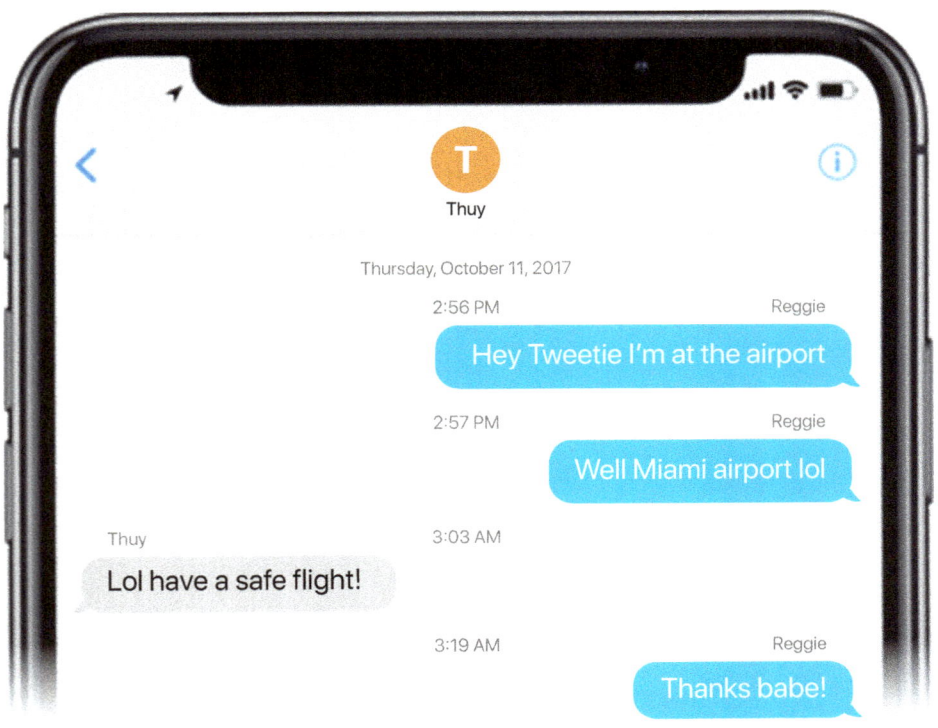

With nothing more to say, Reggie put away his phone and prepared to take a short nap.

After a little over two hours in the air, the lush pastel and green background with blue water and white-crested waves transformed into a brown and grey wasteland with cold lake water and grey buildings that were as square as the personalities of the bureaucrats inhabiting them.

As the plane landed, the pilot gave his well-wishes to the passengers at their final destination, spouted some gibberish about American Airlines credit card promotions, said the word *crosscheck*, and then let the plane release beeping sounds, to which people started unbuckling their seatbelts.

Arriving inside of the airport, Reggie turned on his smartphone to text Thuy.

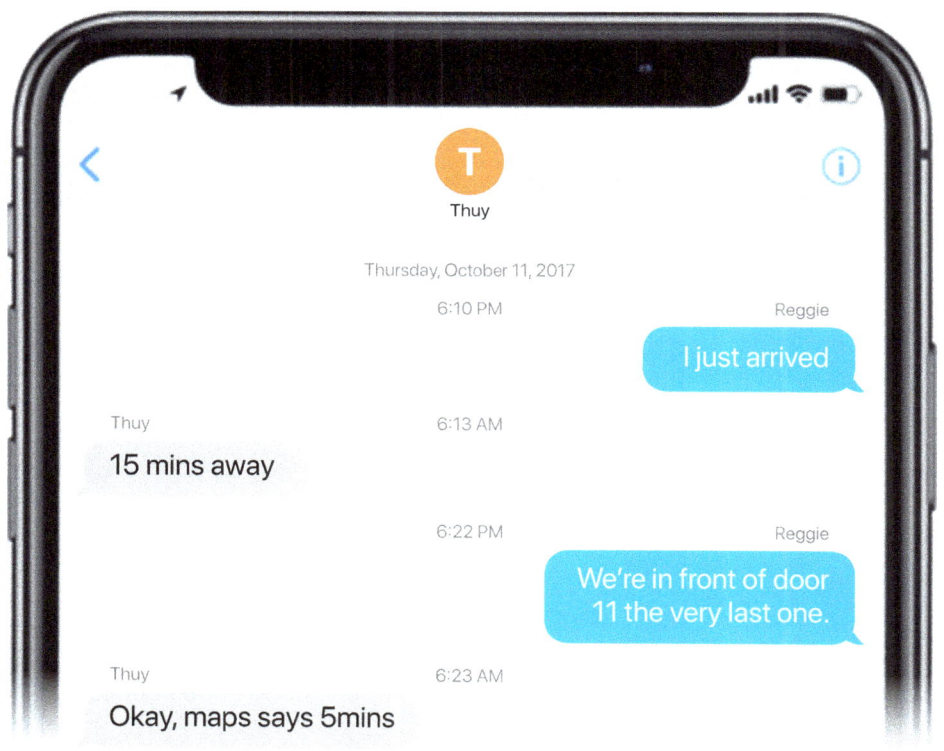

"Hey Rauli, Thuy should be picking us up in about five minutes," Reggie relayed.

"Okay, that's what's up."

"What you gonna do when you get home?" Reggie asked.

"Just chill. Get ready for work. Maybe drink wine."

"I can dig it."

"Ju and Tweed gonna hang out?"

"I hope so. She and I had been talking a good game all the time while I was in Miami, so we'll see what happens. I'm looking forward to having a good time with her. Maybe we'll get dinner. Who knows. I still have to work tomorrow."

"That's what's up, joh."

Just then, Reggie saw a blue Kia approaching where they stood. The car passed quickly though, preventing him from getting a clear view of the driver.

"Yo, Rauli, I wonder if that's her? Maybe she didn't recognize us. Lemme check."

Knowing Thuy was close, Reggie's anticipation and excitement skyrocketed. He imagined her getting out of the car and embracing him—maybe placing a quick peck on his lips.

His legs trembled slightly as Thuy's car pulled up.

Ahh, it's that model. He looked at her blue Kia, which was a slightly different style from the one that had previously passed. As the car slowed to a stop, butterflies sprouted in Reggie's stomach. In addition to his eagerness to see Thuy, the boastful side of his personality also wanted to show off their "love" in public.

Reggie walked up to the car, expecting Thuy to get out and at least hug him. But she stayed inside.

Reggie walked up to the driver's side as airport traffic zoomed by. Yet, instead of getting out of the car, Thuy rolled down her window as if Reggie was a cop making a traffic stop.

"Hey," she said a-matter-of-factly.

"Hey…" Reggie paused, waiting on Thuy's response—wanting her to show just an inkling that she missed him. But there was nothing. Reggie cleared his throat. "Hey, Thuy, can you open the trunk please? We have only one bag each. I'm sure it'll fit."

Thuy nodded, popped the latch that opened the trunk of her car, then rolled her window back up.

Reggie stood there for a moment, dumbfounded.

After all of the shit we were talking to each other, now she's acting colder than the tundra. I hope Raulin isn't getting this whole interaction… Reggie glanced at Raulin, who thankfully wasn't paying much attention.

Good. He didn't see me just get rejected in public, Reggie thought. *I wonder what all of the other people passing by are thinking. That she's some glorified Uber driver or something? Do they actually believe we're together, or do they think I'm harassing her?*

Reggie noted the people watching a Black man and a Hispanic man loading their luggage into the back of an Asian woman's car. Where they're from, Asian women usually took Ubers driven by other "non-model" minorities rather than drove Ubers themselves.

After receiving what he interpreted as the cold shoulder from Thuy, Reggie hopped in the front seat while Raulin hopped in behind Thuy. Reggie pulled down the visor mirror, pretending to check himself but was actually spying Raulin's reaction.

Seeing that Raulin was just texting on his phone, Reggie put the visor back up and turned his attention to Thuy. "So, was traffic extra thick today?" he asked, trying to salvage the mood.

"Coming down, it wasn't bad. But looking at the traffic on the other side, it looks like it's gonna be a parking lot going back," Thuy replied.

"I see. Well, it shouldn't bother you too much, since you're used to the LA area traffic."

Thuy rolled her eyes. "I haven't been back to the LA area in a few years. D.C.'s getting congested like LA though."

"Maybe it's because all of y'all are migrating over here."

"Whaddya mean 'migrating'?" Thuy snapped.

"Uh, I meant umm… I meant that because the D.C. area has a lot of jobs, it attracts people from other parts of the country, but—" His words coming to an abrupt halt, Reggie glanced at Thuy's face. She was looking forward, intently focusing on the traffic. "You know what? I'm just gonna shut up." Reggie looked out the passenger's side window. He gave it a minute, then he pulled the visor down to "check himself" again. This time, when he peered at Raulin through the mirror, Raulin shook his head in disapproval.

* * *

"Welp, we're here. Thanks for the ride, babe." Reggie briefly looked at Thuy before getting out of the car, wondering if she would move in closer to show him some kind of affection. But still, she gave no reaction and showed no emotion. Reggie, feeling the pause was long enough, resolved to disembarking the vehicle.

"Hey, I hope I didn't come off the wrong way. We'll holla later?" Reggie asked tentatively.

"Mm-hmm." Thuy nodded in a harried manner.

Reggie looked up to Raulin. *"Vamonos de este lugar."*

Raulin nodded and collected his luggage from Thuy's trunk before rounding to her side of the car. "Thank you for the rye, Tweed."

"You're welcome." Thuy offered a half smile, appearing a little annoyed by Raulin adding a "d" to the end of her name. Then, once Reggie got his luggage, she sped off.

"I don't know why you like that Asian. She's kind of mean," Raulin said, blinking his eyes as if he was a rabbit nibbling on a carrot.

"I don't know what got into her, but I'm gonna let her cool off for a bit. I'm gonna give her some space. C'mon, let's hit one more bar before we call it a day."

"Right on, doo."

www.ingramcontent.com/pod-product-compliance
Lightning Source LLC
Chambersburg PA
CBHW061057100726
47911CB00012B/278